The Hou

Born and raised in Sheffield, Joanne Clague lives in the coastal village of Laxey in the Isle of Man with her husband, children, dogs and other assorted wildlife. She has worked in print, radio and broadcast journalism in the north west for the past three decades and is now a full-time writer of historical fiction set in nineteenth century Sheffield.

Also by Joanne Clague

The Sheffield Sagas

The Ragged Valley
The Girl at Change Alley
The Watchman's Widow

The House of Help for Friendless Girls

The House of Hope

The House of Hope

Joanne CLAGUE

CANELO

First published in the United Kingdom in 2024 by

Canelo
Unit 9, 5th Floor
Cargo Works, 1–2 Hatfields
London SE1 9PG
United Kingdom

A CIP catalogue record for this book is available from the British Library.

Print ISBN 978 1 80436 797 1
Ebook ISBN 978 1 80436 798 8

Cover design by Rose Cooper

Cover images © Arcangel, Shutterstock

Look for more great books at www.canelo.co

Printed and bound in Great Britain by Clays Ltd, Elcograf S.p.A.

I

For my sisters

PART ONE

Winter 1887

Chapter 1

There it was again, the sound of the door knocker rattling in the wind like a nail being tapped into a coffin. Hetty Barlow shook her head, scolding herself for entertaining such a macabre thought, and bent to finish the sentence she had been writing. Still, the back of her neck prickled. The surrounding dark was a tangible thing, made blacker by the pool of yellow light cast by the oil lamp on her desk. She wiped her pen and laid it down beside the inkpot and blinked at the page of the ledger, where the words she had just written danced and blurred together. She'd got to the age where she required spectacles.

Or, more likely, her eyes were simply weary of the late hour. She closed them briefly but that only seemed to heighten her other senses – the musty smell of the shawl around her shoulders, the sound of the wind that needled the knocker, made it clack like the dry bones of the dead. There she went again. She rubbed her eyes and focused on the words on the page, where she had inscribed the newest entry.

Eliza Corbett, aged fourteen. This child's killing me, her mother had declared.

There was no call for the histrionics, as far as Hetty could see. It was plain from the surly demeanour of the girl, who was practically thrown over the threshold by her mother, that the end of a tether had been reached. That,

3

and the revelation she had been picked up for loitering outside the soldiers' barracks at Hillsborough, her lips and cheeks rouged. And not for the first time, either. Send her to the Shrewsbury convent, the mother pleaded. I can't afford the railway ticket.

It was a neat solution and would be done quickly, tomorrow or the day after, to avoid the taint of scandal infecting the house. Hetty narrowed her eyes to make out the hands of the clock hanging on the wall. Tomorrow had already arrived. The potential novitiate had long since been given a meal and a bed in the attic dormitory. She would now be either in the land of Nod or staring into the dark, contemplating her fate. It made no odds to Hetty Barlow. A decision had been reached and it was her job to ensure a smooth passage for the girl. She flexed her hands. When she retired for the night, she'd keep on these fingerless gloves that she'd found in the clothes basket, although the wool made the skin on the back of her hands itch. The embers in the grate had long since faded and died. She had left instruction for a warming pan for her bed, and that had duly been delivered, but she had stayed up far later than she'd anticipated.

There would be more residual warmth in the hearth tiles than between the sheets.

Hetty blotted the page and closed the book. She was careful not to disturb the scraps of paper on which notes had been jotted in pencil. These would be transcribed into the relevant page in the ledger when time allowed. A ruled page for every girl and woman, recording their arrival, their circumstances and demeanour, and their departure. She might send a woman on her way after only a night, or after weeks or even months spent under what Hetty's employers must come to consider her roof. Some promised to write, and a few did. A girl might return, as a visitor celebrating her new good fortune, or in need again and a bed would be found.

Or not. If a whiff of intoxication was detected, the door would be gently but firmly closed. There were standards to be maintained, and her own position to protect. She must conjure the absolute authority expected of a warden and weave herself into the fabric of the house. She had come with excellent references and Amelia had been found a job. They had been lucky. Now she could scuttle her past like an old ship, a ghost ship full of malignant spirits.

Why did the dead of night conjure such images? It did no good to tell herself that in the cold light of day she would be ashamed of these febrile thoughts. The hairs on her arms rose just the same.

Outside, the wind continued to roar like a trapped bear. The house creaked and whistled in reply. Her quarters were on the ground floor of the gable end building in the terrace of tall Georgian houses that fringed a large cobbled square. The elegant façade of the House of Help was the same as all the others, although most had been converted from grand residential dwellings to offices, shops, taverns and apartments. The square was a hidden gem, sandwiched between notorious slum housing and the large department stores and shops in the centre of the town. Hetty had spent some anxious minutes negotiating filthy alleyways when she set out to attend her interview, and had been pleasantly surprised – and relieved – to turn a corner and find herself suddenly on the edge of the lively square.

Paradise Square. A fine address for the beginning of a new chapter in her life, and Amelia's.

The original rooms in this house – the receiving room, games room, study, dining room and library and the spacious bedrooms above – had been altered to suit the requirements of the trustees. The quarters Hetty had been given had once been the main parlour and an anteroom, which meant she had the largest accommodation and was closest to the front door to the property, which she preferred, although not on a cold night such as this when the weather was knocking for entry.

Hetty carried the lamp from her desk in the anteroom to her bedside table, and was about to turn down the wick when another sound cut across the wailing wind – the unmistakeable rumble of carriage wheels over cobbles. *At this ungodly hour.* Curious, she went to the window, lifted the heavy curtain to one side and peered into the dark. It was absolute. There were no daggers of light coming from within the other buildings, no moon or stars pricking the sky. She strained her ears. Nothing. The square had not been the destination of whoever had ridden by. She remained at the window for a few seconds more, her skin prickling in the cold draught whistling through the frame, then turned away, towards her bed and a few blessed hours of sleep.

She had not even taken a step before three heavy raps on the door reverberated through the house. Her hand flew to her throat but she recovered herself quickly. She had been startled by the sudden noise but there was nothing untoward to worry about. It was not unknown for the constable to deliver a girl in the early hours of the morning. Hetty took a deep breath, picked up the lamp and hurried from her room.

The house was in darkness, the weight of all its sleeping occupants pressing down on her. She crossed the hall in a silence that seemed deeper than before, drew back the bolts, and straightened the lace collar of her dress. Then she cleared her throat and opened the door, prepared to greet a figure of authority.

The woman standing before her was slightly taller than Hetty. She had one hand flattened against the wall for support, arm outstretched, and a bare head that sagged between narrow shoulders. She wore no shoes. Her feet, planted on the stone step, were either dirty or bruised. She was alone. Hetty took all this in and drew a shaky breath. She raised the lamp.

'This is a fine time of night.'

It seemed to take an immense effort for the woman to lift her head. She looked young, a girl. Her hair was loose, tendrils pasted across her face. One of her eyes was swollen shut. Hetty winced at the sight of this. There was a darker patch, like dirt, on the side of her head. She wore a loose dress covered in flaps and pockets – the garment looked like a factory uniform. Could this be an escapee from the asylum? She glanced at the woman's hands. They were empty. She had nothing at all except the clothes she stood up in. A lack of possessions was not unusual for some of those who arrived at the house but injuries were less common. This one ought to have found her way to the infirmary.

Hetty lifted her lamp higher and looked to left and right before sweeping her gaze over the square. There was no movement, no shadowy bulks that should not be present. The woman or girl – she thought she might be eighteen or nineteen, around Amelia's age, and half Hetty's – was alone. This was unusual, although not unheard of. Females in need were generally delivered by police constables, station porters, or agents of the house.

A few came unaccompanied, and pleaded their case, but this was the first time Hetty had seen one in this state.

She recalled the sound she had heard earlier, of carriage wheels on cobbles.

'Where've you come from?'

No reply.

'Did somebody bring you here? Where did they go?'

The woman gasped and shook her head hard enough to make her sway and lose her grip on the wall. Hetty caught her elbow to prevent her tumbling down the steps. She wasn't sure she'd be able to lift her if she fell. She would have to fetch somebody from inside the house to help. As it was, she realised grimly, she was going to have to turf Amelia out of her bed.

'I've got you, love, come on. There's a bed I can put you in.' She was about to make herself unpopular with Amelia, again, but it couldn't be helped. 'Lucky for some, eh?'

Inside, and with the door safely bolted, all remained silent. 'Good job I'm here to let folk in,' she said. 'Nobody else seems bothered, do they? I'm Miss Barlow.' Self-consciously, she added: 'The warden.'

That word – *warden* – still felt foreign on her tongue after eight months in the job. In any event, the woman didn't respond. Instead, she raised a hand to the wall and ran slender fingertips over it, in seeming wonderment. The wallpaper was the original, striped thinly in gold and pink and blue, and now on just the respectable side of shabbiness. Did the girl have a muddled mind? Once she had wrenched her gaze from the wall, she allowed herself to be led along the ground floor hallway.

There were four beds in the back room across from the water closet, all presently occupied. Hetty stopped before entering and gently tapped her knuckles on the closet door. 'Do you need to…?' The girl shook her head, and fell heavily against the wall. Hetty grasped her upper arm to prevent her from falling and was surprised by the ample firmness of her flesh. One thing this girl was not suffering from was malnourishment.

'You need to stop shaking that head of thine until we've had it looked at.'

An unwelcome thought crossed Hetty's mind.

'Are you ill with a fever? Do you have a rash?'

A whispered *no*.

Hetty suppressed a shudder. Adding smallpox to a crowded house would be a recipe for disaster. As warden, she would be blamed for any outbreak that meant closing the door to needy women. She decided to take the girl at her word. Perhaps she had been knocked down by the carriage Hetty had heard passing, or was the victim of a robbery, had her shoes stolen, her possessions taken, and fetched up on the doorstep of the House of Help by chance. And all the commotion hidden by the wind that still howled around the square.

In the ground floor dormitory, which had in a past life been the back parlour, she guided the girl towards the blanketed hump in the bed furthest from the door. 'You can sleep here and we'll get the doctor out to you in the morning, and then we'll see what's what.'

She shook the occupant of the bed by the shoulder. 'Amelia. Wake up. Amelia!'

A muffled voice. 'Are you kiddin'?'

'Look sharp, would you?'

No further explanation was required. Amelia muttered and sighed but got up and padded, still half-asleep, out of the room. She would fall into Hetty's bed and be back in

9

the land of Nod in seconds. Amelia slept deeply, always. Hetty envied her this blameless slumber. She smiled wryly, knowing that in the morning, Amelia would complain to anybody prepared to listen – *Turfed out of bed in the middle of the night, as per, and then kept awake by my sister's snores.* Hetty returned her attention to the girl, ready to assist as she lay down and pulled the blanket up to her chin. She made a sound and Hetty bent towards her.

'What was that, love?'

Bed springs creaked from further down the room. 'Can tha keep it down? I'm on the eight o'clock to York tomorra.'

'Good for you,' said Hetty. The voice belonged to Ethel Jenkins – fresh out of the Gell Street servant training school and off to a York townhouse where she'd been found a live-in position. Hetty turned back to the girl. 'What did you say?'

'Thank you.' Her voice sounded hoarse and Hetty wondered whether further signs of abuse might be found around her throat.

'Ah, there's somebody in there after all. Where've you come from?' She waited, thinking of the ledger and the fresh page this new arrival would take. Not tonight, though. 'Do you have a name?'

The girl turned her head away from the lamp and mumbled indecipherable words.

Hetty touched her hair, her fingers coming away sticky. She grimaced. Yes, beaten and robbed. She'd have to report it to the police. She thought fleetingly of the health voucher that lay in the top of the donations box, enough for an examination by the doctor and one or two days' stay in hospital, if necessary. Let the doctor decide which course of action was best. The girl might not wake up at all.

The thought made Hetty shudder.

'You're safe here.'

'I don't know.'

'Oh no, my girl. Nobody's getting in to my house, I can tell you that for nothing.'

'My name.' She kept her face to the wall. 'I don't know it.'

Hetty frowned and leaned closer, although all she could see was the matted hair on the back of the girl's head and a ragged-looking earlobe.

'What do you mean?'

Her first assumption had been correct. This one was addled in the head.

The whispered words came in a rush, hissed almost angrily in a way that sent a chill down Hetty's spine.

'I don't know my name. I've lost my memory. I don't know who I am.'

Chapter 2

She had believed with all her heart that he was going to kill her.

When the enormity of her monstrous lie threatened to overwhelm her, she forced herself to relive the terror of the carriage ride through the black night. When shrewd eyes sought out hers and the truth was pulled towards the tip of her tongue, she clenched her teeth and recalled the wildness in her cousin's expression. She was certain the warden, Miss Barlow, had already sized her up and found her wanting. So be it. *Follow my instructions exactly*, he'd told her. *I've gone to a lot of trouble on your behalf. I must be sure you understand.*

All the women seated around the kitchen table were watching her, either covertly or brazenly staring. She nibbled at the crust of a slice of thickly buttered bread she'd been given, her gut churning like the water that gushed over the weir at home. *Home*. Panic rose in her throat. She gulped and reached for her tea. It was strong and heavily sugared – for the shock she'd suffered, Miss Barlow told her, as sugar wasn't cheap and the budget didn't stretch to luxuries. The chipped mug the tea came in was so large that, when she sipped from it, most of her face was hidden. It was a small mercy.

There were two people in the kitchen who were not paying any attention to the newcomer. These were two young girls kicking each other in a ferocious manner under the table. She couldn't comprehend how children might find themselves at a place like this. What must their home circumstances have been like? The sound of clog on shinbone made her wince. As she was taking in her surroundings – a large oak dresser, a wide sink with cupboards beneath, shelving on the walls, a clothes line attached to a pulley so it could be raised to the ceiling, a range with a kettle and pots and pans – she accidentally caught the eye of a thin, pale woman, near enough her mother's age, whose mouth twisted into a malicious smile.

She immediately dropped her gaze but it was too late.

'You're reckoning on that you don't know your own name? Must think we were all born yesterday.'

Now she should make a tearful denial but she was frozen. She could not even muster a sigh or shake of the head and every long and agonising second that passed in silence would only confirm their suspicions. Her lie was exposed, so quickly laid bare, and now the warden would ask her to leave the house and where would she go?

A dog barked, somewhere in the square, and the spell was broken.

'Leave her be, Winnie,' said another one of the women. 'The doctor will know what's what. You don't, that's for sure.'

She daren't look up to acknowledge the speaker. Probably only a second or two had passed. She could not maintain this pretence over the hours and days and weeks to come, not under such scrutiny. Despair filled her, and she finally expelled a long breath, her decision made. She lifted her head to look at Miss Barlow, who was sitting at a small table in the corner of the room, drinking tea and making a list on a piece of paper. She would tell her the truth, throw herself on the warden's mercy, ask for protection. As she was about to get to her feet, to go over to speak to Miss Barlow, the door opened and an old woman stepped in, sprightly and pink-cheeked from the cold.

Miss Barlow put down her pencil and gave the new arrival a narrow-eyed look.

'Good morning, Miss Barlow.'

'Good morning to you. We're full, Mrs Gunson. I had to chuck Amelia out of her bed last night. Again.'

The woman nodded equably. 'I'm alone, bringing only cheering news. The Mayor's wife has chosen this house for her charity of the year.'

She unbuttoned her cloak, draped it over a chair and sat in the remaining empty chair at the table. Mrs Gunson looked at the faces of the women, finally settling on hers.

'Ah, you must be Amelia's usurper? Good morning. I hope you are well, considering where you find yourself.'

Her mind was in turmoil but she seized on this opportunity to escape from the watchful eyes in the room. 'I have a terrible headache,' she whispered. 'I think I might return to bed.'

'Drink up your tea first,' said Miss Barlow.

The old lady raised an enquiring eyebrow at Miss Barlow.

'I can't introduce you, if that's what you're waiting for,' said the warden. 'The lass has no memory. Even her own name is beyond her grasp.'

'Oh dear. How awful. Well perhaps I can introduce myself to you.'

She removed her hat and scarf and pulled fine leather gloves from her fingers.

'My name is Charlotte Gunson and I am a volunteer agent for the house, guiding women to this little haven, if they are willing to come.' She glanced at the warden. 'Hence Miss Barlow's comment. It seems you found your own way here, and with your arrival we once again have a full house.'

Willing to come... found your own way here. Her gut twisted in fear. She had been dragged here, half-conscious. What if she was asked how she had heard about this House of Help? Her mind raced to find a plausible answer, then she remembered. As far as these women were concerned, she had no memory of anything at all before her arrival on the doorstep. She slumped in the chair, exhausted. The fissures made by her lies, like cracks in glazed pottery, would shatter her. She hadn't the strength for this.

Mrs Gunson reached across the table to pat her hand. She quickly withdrew it, clasping both hands in her lap. The old woman didn't seem perturbed. 'Can you not remember anything at all?'

'No.'

'Not how you got here? Nothing?'

The warden saved her.

'I've not had time to talk to the girl,' Miss Barlow said. 'I've got the doctor coming this morning. I think she's had the sense knocked out of her. There's a lump on her head the size of a seed potato.'

Now that she had been reminded of it, she became aware of the throbbing on the back of her head. It sent a dart of pain to the front of her skull with every heartbeat. She did not know what instrument he had used, only that she had been struggling with him in her bedroom one moment and was on the floor of his carriage the next. He'd told her, later, in the room at the tavern, that he'd put her limp body on the seat but she kept rolling off, so he'd thought it best to leave her on the floor of the carriage. He had laughed in a casual way about this, as if he was telling an amusing anecdote.

She raised her hand tentatively and touched the back of her head, finding the lump. He might have intended to kill her with that one blow. Snuff out a life – two lives – as easily as snuffing out a candle. Two lives. She clamped her teeth against a wave of nausea. There was another shock in store for these kind ladies, a secret that would reveal itself with or without her confession to it.

'Some cuts but nowt deep,' Miss Barlow was now telling Mrs Gunson. 'Swollen eye. We've seen a few of those, haven't we? I reckon it's no more nor less than that.'

'Well, Miss Barlow,' said Mrs Gunson, 'your background as a matron has to stand as a comfort to us all. I'm sure you will have dealt with far worse injuries than these.'

Miss Barlow frowned. 'Her memory'll come back to her. She's in the best place for now.'

Mrs Gunson turned to face her. 'How distressing for you, my dear.'

She glanced up. 'Yes.' Even acknowledging this much snatched her breath away.

'Wish I could forget my bleedin' name,' said a freckle-faced woman from the end of the table. Several of the women laughed.

'Mind your language, please,' said the warden.

Miss Barlow got up to sit beside Mrs Gunson and they engaged in quiet conversation, although she was aware she was under subtle scrutiny. The prickle of her skin told her so. She finished her tea as quickly as she could, by now desperate to escape the room.

'You. Girl.'

Her head jerked up. The young woman addressing her had been in the kitchen throughout breakfast but had not joined the others at the table, instead choosing to lean against the lip of the sink to eat her toast and drink her tea. She had the same thick, dark hair and strong jawline as the warden, and equally shrewd eyes. She gestured to the kettle.

'Want some more tea?'

When she shook her head, sparks danced across the room.

'Goodness me, Amelia,' said Mrs Gunson. 'We can't go about matters like this. My dear.'

She looked up, reluctantly.

'Is there a name you would have us call you?' Mrs Gunson smiled as if she was encouraging a baby to say its first words. 'Any name you can think of?'

'She might come up wi' her own,' said the girl Mrs Gunson had called Amelia.

Mrs Gunson tilted her head. 'That's rather flippant, but I wonder, if I asked you for your mother's name, could you recall it?'

Easily. Rose Hyde.

'Or I might ask you whether you can picture a sister or a brother, or both?'

I'm an only child, a beloved only child and I have no one to turn to.

She put trembling fingers to her throat to loosen her collar, then realised it was the chokehold of fear that tightened around her neck. The scratchy garment she wore, that her cousin had thrown at her in the dingy room of the tavern, had no collar. It had been filthy when she pulled it on, and she had slept in it. Her hair, that before

17

yesterday – only yesterday! – had been her pride and joy, now hung on either side of her face like the stamped-on straw in the stables. What did these women behold? A poor, stinking, ignorant girl.

She gripped the edge of the table, her fingers pressing into the rough wood. Her parents would be in the breakfast room now, being served devilled eggs on china plates, awaiting her arrival. Her father, growing impatient, would eventually send the maid to rouse her from her bed. He might comment on how uncommonly tired she had seemed for the past few weeks, prone to sleeping in. Her mother, on the maid's fretful return, would set down her teacup and go to investigate the empty bed for herself, a patient smile on her face, not yet overly concerned, and with no inkling of the misery that lay in wait.

Her mind swerved from that unbearable scene and fell on another. Her cousin, taking her hand, forcing her fingertips to the smooth barrel of the pistol he was holding, telling her without words her inevitable fate, should she refuse to comply. He told her he was taking her to this place in the north, where fallen women and reckless girls sought sanctuary and were given new lives. He'd heard about the place at his club, and seemed quite proud of himself, to have thought of it as a ready solution for a problem he insisted was hers alone. She was ruined and he had come to her rescue. It was as if he expected her to thank him.

'What do you think, then?' said Amelia. 'D'you like it?' She laughed. 'Look at her, she's miles away.'

Her heart lurched. They had been talking and she had not been listening.

Mrs Gunson spoke. 'Only until your memory is restored, which I am sure will be very soon.'

'Hope.' The warden's tone was brisk. 'That's the name Mrs Gunson has come up with.'

'It seems appropriate,' said Mrs Gunson. She sounded apologetic. 'If you don't like it, we can choose another, but we must call you something.'

She mustered a grateful smile. 'Hope would be apt.'

'Apt, eh?' said Miss Barlow.

Mrs Gunson raised an eyebrow but didn't speak.

'Can you read? Or would you like to learn?' This from the friendly, freckle-faced woman. 'We have a reading group tonight, if you're well enough.'

'She might be in the infirmary by then,' said another woman. 'Though I wouldn't want to be in hospital surrounded by all them that has the pox.'

'Hark at the voice of doom.'

'Well, I think she's got some colour in her cheeks.'

'Only colours I see are black an' blue.'

'Did Ethel get off all right this morning?'

'Aye, the station master sent a porter to collect her.'

'He's a saint, that man. He brought me 'ere.'

They chattered on, and she breathed out and released her grip on the table, clasping her hands in her lap.

'Does Ethel's departure free up a bed?' said Mrs Gunson.

'No,' said Miss Barlow, holding up her hand to forestall argument. 'I can't put up with another night of Amelia in mine. She nicks the covers.'

The girl laughed. 'At least I don't sound like a rumbling wheel, sister.' So, she was the warden's sister, not waif nor stray. That explained the strong resemblance they bore to one another, though Amelia's eyes were as brown and as pretty as a doe's and the warden's a cool blue.

Mrs Gunson said something she didn't catch. They were all looking at her again. What had she missed now?

'Yes, that's a grand idea,' said Miss Barlow. 'Get yourself back to bed, ready for the doctor.'

She rose to her feet, resting one hand on the table to still the tremor in her fingers. She met Mrs Gunson's sympathetic – but searching – gaze and fear swelled in her chest. Offering a weak smile, she walked from the room, and, out of view, paused on the small landing that led up to the ground floor hallway, desperate to learn whether her cousin's scheme was taking root.

'She talks like she's one step removed from royalty.' That was Miss Barlow.

There was gentle laughter from Mrs Gunson. 'But she's barely spoken two words together.'

'Even so.'

'That doesn't mean she isn't deserving of help. She clearly arrived in a terrible state.'

'She's not gone hungry, that's plain to see. She's a bonny girl.'

Winnie's strident voice was unmistakeable. 'How d'you know she's not pox-ridden and been chucked out of her lodgings?'

'The pox doesn't blacken your eye nor put a lump on your head.' This voice might belong to the freckle-faced woman, she couldn't be sure. 'And she's no spots on her face.'

'Wrecks your looks for good, the pox,' said Winnie, a note of triumph in her voice. 'Did you see the scars on the copper brought me in? You could dig for coal in them pits.'

Mrs Gunson's voice cut through the laughter that followed this remark. 'Miss Barlow, have we a set of clean clothes we can give to her?'

'Aye. Amelia, did you leave the underclothes on the bed?'

'Yes.'

'Good girl. You can fetch a dress from the clothes bin. But wait until the doctor's had a look at her. She might be in bed a day or two.'

She did not hear more. Startled by the sound of a chair being scraped across the floor, she hurried down the hallway. The dormitory was deserted. Each of the occupants had made up their bed – she had followed their lead, clumsily – before going for breakfast. It was the first time she had ever made a bed. In the life she had lost, she would throw back the covers, complete her toilet, dress and go down to breakfast. On her return, the sheets would be tucked in, pillows plumped and counterpane straightened. It was a small thing, but it brought home to her the chasm between her old life and the new one she must, somehow, carve out for herself.

On top of her bed lay a set of undergarments, thread-bare but clean. She took off the hateful uniform, keeping an eye on the door, balled it up and shoved it under the bed. She put on the knickers and chemise that had been provided, got into bed and pulled the covers over her body. She blew on her hands then rubbed them together and moved them tentatively across her belly. Was it her imagination or could she already feel the slightest dome beginning to rise between her hips? She had no idea how much time she would have before her condition became apparent. Her face was already rounder, her breasts swollen and sensitive.

Her body was changing and she was powerless to stop it.

She stared at the ceiling, convinced that sleep was beyond her, but must have nodded off because suddenly the warden and a portly, be-whiskered man were looming over her. They were talking quietly and she was able to observe them through the half-closed lid of the eye that was not swollen shut. She shuddered when the doctor laid a clammy palm on her forehead.

'Ah, she's awake,' he said.

His examination was perfunctory. He instructed her to lie on her side and pressed gently on the bump on the back of her head. He pinched between two fingers the rip on her earlobe. 'Earrings? Were you robbed?' She didn't reply – she could not speak past the bubble of terror in her throat – and he muttered something to himself and told her to roll onto her back. She stared up at the cracked plaster. The doctor leaned over her, lifting her chin to look at the marks on her neck. She tried not to inhale the onion scent of his breath.

'The cuts and grazes on her face are superficial, Miss Barlow,' he told the warden. 'She requires bed rest.' She was grateful when he moved away to rummage in his bag. 'Give her a spoonful of this now and another this evening.'

She coughed and whispered, 'What is in the medicine?' but they ignored her.

'Thank you,' said Miss Barlow. 'We're always so grateful for the support you give to our young ladies.'

He flapped his hand. 'I'm honoured to help. This one has been knocked about but is essentially healthy. Her colour is good. She looks well-nourished.'

He stepped away and gestured for Miss Barlow to follow him. He spoke to her in a low voice and waited where he stood when the warden returned to her side.

'Are your...' Miss Barlow paused. 'You wouldn't know if your courses are regular, would you?'

She tried to smile. 'The cramps have started this morning.'

'Then I'll get you some rags. The doctor wanted to spare you any further examination.'

This made her shudder again.

The warden nodded to the doctor, who returned to her bedside. 'You say, Miss Barlow, that she got up this morning and held down her breakfast and was able to converse?'

'Yes.'

He addressed her directly. 'You have a headache?'

'Yes, a terrible headache.'

'That's to be expected. Does anything else ail you, anything at all?'

'No.'

He patted her shoulder absently. 'Your memory loss is no doubt a result of the injury to your head. Allow some time and everything will return to you. Do not be frightened.'

She closed her eyes and turned her face away.

'I'm sure I can thank you on Miss Hope's behalf,' said the warden stiffly.

So there would be a short reprieve, a day, hopefully two, spent in bed, unbothered by her inquisitors. And what then? Wait. Wait for them to discover the truth about her. If she did not reveal herself, in error or deliberately, a further ordeal lay ahead. She would have to go through the rigmarole of pretending she didn't know she was carrying a child.

For how could she know that she was pregnant, having no memory?

'She can take a healthy dose now,' said the doctor.

She turned over to see the warden pouring thin liquid onto a spoon and she lifted her head and took it. It would seem suspicious to refuse. The medicine tasted bitter.

The voices of the doctor and the warden became muffled as consciousness slipped from her grasp. She must strive for simplicity. All she had to remember was that she could not remember anything.

Her cousin had told her that too.

Chapter 3

Attendance at the Bible class held each Sunday afternoon was not compulsory but, for the duration, the parlour opposite the warden's quarters was the only room in the main house in which a fire was lit. A day like today, when frost spread cold fingers along the inside of the window panes, often guaranteed a full turnout.

But Amelia wasn't in the main house. She'd crept past the parlour, a quick glance inside confirming the presence of all the girls and women in residence, along with one familiar face from the recent past. Sunday afternoon tea, laid on after the bible reading, was an opportunity for previous residents to visit. No doubt today's guest had something to boast about. Amelia had closed the door to the kitchen quietly behind her and breathed a sigh of relief. Mealtimes excepted, the kitchen was out of bounds to the transitory residents of the house unless they had been allocated cooking or cleaning duties.

Now, with the kettle whistling on the range, she took up a large knife to slice into the Victoria Cake donated by a supporter of the house, a baker in Norfolk Street whose jam sponges were lighter than a pickpocket's fingers. Amelia's mouth was already watering in anticipation. She divided the triple-layer cake into sixteen equal portions and was licking the blade clean of jam and cake crumbs when the door opened and Hope poked her head in.

Amelia dropped the knife on the floor, leaving a smear of cream and crumbs on the apron she wore.

'I could have sliced me tongue off!'

'I'm sorry.' Hope's wary smile made dimples in her cheeks. 'Perhaps I should have knocked. I came to help. Please, allow me.'

Hope got down on her knees to retrieve the knife from under the table. Amelia folded her arms and watched her lay it carefully beside the cake and brush her fingertips together. Hope was wearing a white high-necked blouse with long sleeves and pale blue buttons and piping, and a skirt in a rich dark blue. These were clothes that had been donated by one of the house's wealthier patrons and were beyond the budget of those who passed through and required more practical clothes for the next stage of their journey. Amelia begrudgingly admitted that Hope, with her blonde hair elegantly braided, looked quite the lady.

She returned Hope's smile. 'They've put you in clothes from the dressing up box, I see.'

'It's only that Miss Barlow wants to make a good impression. We've got a benefactor here today. Mr Deveraux.'

This one had been at the house a week and already talked like her feet were well and truly tucked under the table.

'You do like to make yoursen useful, don't you?'

Hope shrugged. 'I'm grateful to be here.'

Amelia studied her. The only remaining sign of Hope's trauma – physically, at least – was bruising around one eye that had already faded to a dirty yellow. Her memory had not returned, and Hetty had told Amelia not to pry, not that she was all that interested anyway. This one would soon disappear, like all the rest.

'Grateful, eh? Well, I can't wait to be shot of this place.' She gestured to the table. 'You can carry these plates and forks up. Then come back for the tea. Serve the bigwigs first, then my sister.' It did no harm to remind Hope that Hetty Barlow was her sibling. 'Then you lot.'

'All right. Are you coming?'

'Aye, I suppose so. Don't want her on the warpath.'

Amelia picked up the cake stand. She knew something this one didn't, something her sister had told her, something that would remind Hope that, in this house, Amelia was higher up the pecking order. She toyed with the idea of passing on the information now or waiting until after the tea party. It could wait. 'Can you get the door?'

In the crowded parlour, Charlotte Gunson was sitting on a worn chaise longue, conversing with Mr Deveraux, an exceptionally tall and gaunt man who looked uncomfortable on the low settee, with his knees up somewhere around his ears. Mrs Gunson smiled warmly at Amelia then turned an admiring gaze on Hope. Amelia straightened the bib of her apron – there was nothing she could do about the cream smeared on it – and tucked a lock of unruly hair behind her ear. Her braid never stayed tidy for long, but she knew she would look just as fine in the same get up as Hope.

'Good afternoon, Hope,' said Mrs Gunson. 'I must say you seem remarkably well.'

Hetty turned from where she was placing the leather-bound Bible back in its display case on the bureau in the corner of the room. 'She's being well looked after,' she said. 'We pray her memory will return to her soon.'

'It is a most curious case,' said Mr Deveraux. 'Most curious indeed.'

Hope busied herself with the plates. 'Will you have some cake, Mrs Gunson? And a cup of tea?'

'Serve our distinguished guest first,' said Mrs Gunson.

'No cake for me,' said Mr Deveraux, 'although it does look delicious. I'm dining at my club tonight.'

He rose to his feet, flexing his long legs with obvious relief, and began a conversation with Hetty about the friend with whom he'd arranged to spend the evening. This man had just bought some grand place on the outskirts of Doncaster, not far from the great ruin that was Conisbrough Castle. He had taken his butler and housekeeper with him from his previous residence, and said butler and housekeeper were tasked with finding new staff, from the maid of all work and stable boy to the lady's maid and cook, the idea being that a new broom sweeps clean. Mr Deveraux said the reason he was telling this tale was because he had persuaded the gentleman to consider taking on girls from the House of Help.

Hetty thanked him and said she was sure there would be many suitable candidates for on-the-job training. She looked around the room, and then pointed, and Amelia's gaze followed theirs to a girl who sat cross-legged on the carpet. Hope had gone over with a piece of cake and was trying to engage the girl in conversation. Good luck with that. The child was biddable but Amelia hadn't yet heard her string a whole sentence together. She knew the girl's story from Hetty. She was eleven years old, a rescue from the Kelham Island workhouse. Before her father left her there, she had looked after her sick mother for five years, right up to the day she died. Now, her father had broken up their home and gone to Liverpool in the hopes of finding work on the docks. It had been agreed the girl would be trained in domestic service and a live-in position found as soon as practicable.

Nobody expected the father to return.

'She's been no trouble,' Hetty said, 'and I reckon she can be fashioned into a hard-working servant.'

It seemed like Doncaster was on the cards for that one. Amelia decided she would buy her something for the journey from the spice shop on the corner, a roll of liquorice or a sugar mouse, or perhaps some fudge. Amelia licked her lips and, at that moment, a woman wearing a large bonnet bedecked with ostrich feathers swept past her shoulder like a flapping bird, descended on Mrs Gunson and commenced squawking.

'My favourite person in the world! I've brought you a gift. I said I'd come back, didn't I?'

Mrs Gunson rose to her feet and carefully set the tin of tea the woman had thrust into her hands onto the seat. 'How lovely to see you, Violet. And thank you. You seem to be faring very well.'

Violet cocked her head. 'Only head laundress at the Langham, on twenty-four pounds a year.' She made a show of recognising Amelia and pulled her close to kiss her cheek. She smelled of vinegar. 'My lovely! I remember you begging me to take you with me. Are you still here?'

'Aye, looks that way.'

'Amelia is a great help to her sister, and to the house,' said Mrs Gunson. 'We'd all be quite bereft without her.'

Amelia smiled tightly. The old woman meant well but it didn't help her cause. 'I won't be here forever. I'd give owt to visit London.'

'Then you should come back with me! Have you ever been on a train?'

'Aye, a'course.' She looked over to where Hetty was still deep in conversation with Mr Deveraux. 'We came here on the train, din't we, Hetty?'

Her sister folded her lips. Amelia knew she preferred to be addressed as Miss Barlow in company. She widened her eyes innocently.

'Mr Deveraux looks parched,' Hetty said. 'Are you doing the rounds with the tea?'

'Oh no,' he said. 'Thank you but I have already outstayed my welcome.' He cast about for somewhere to put down his cup. Hetty took it from him and handed it to Amelia.

'Will you start clearing up?'

'I've nowt better to do, have I?'

'I'm sorry.' Hetty was apologising as Amelia walked away. 'I don't know what's got into her today.'

The rising level of chatter combined with the cloying scent of the arrangement of white and pink lilies Mr Deveraux had brought to the tea party was giving Amelia a headache. Earlier, while ramming them into a vase, Hetty had complained to her that a basket of groceries to replenish the stores would have been far more helpful than flowers. Funeral flowers, at that.

Violet nudged her arm. Jam from the cake was smeared across her prominent front teeth. 'We can find you a job and a fiancé too, if you like. London is full of handsome fellas. Did you know I'm getting married next spring?'

Amelia kept her tart response – *How would I know that?* – to herself. She imagined running to the dorm, ripping off her servant's apron, dressing herself as finely in her own clothes as Hope was in her borrowed garment, and leaving with Violet on the train to London. And why shouldn't she? Hetty had displaced Amelia just as abruptly a few days after their mother's funeral, promising the world and delivering her a job as her sister's skivvy. She would tell Hetty as much, when she tried to prevent her from leaving. Excitement flared in her belly.

'I'll take a job if you have one for me,' she said as casually as she could. 'I can come back with you today, or next week. Whatever suits.'

Infuriatingly, Violet reached out to nip her cheek between finger and thumb. 'You are an impetuous girl. What would your sister do without you?'

'She'd find another slave,' said Amelia.

Violet laughed. 'You are such a sweet thing.'

Amelia realised Violet's offer had been empty, thrown at her to impress the other women. Humiliated, she smiled weakly and turned away. Picking up a tray, she set about retrieving empty teacups and saucers from around the room. She paused to assure a meek-voiced middle-aged woman that her spare set of underclothes would be dry by the following day, when she was due to leave to take up a position. Amelia would have to locate them in the forest of clothes horses and lines in the kitchen and scullery.

Hetty insisted that all donated clothing was washed and pressed under the flat iron before it was distributed. It seemed like a pointless task to Amelia, designed only to annoy her. The laundry woman came in three days a week to churn clothing, bedding, towels and flannels through the dolly tub and mangle, back-breaking work she began at six o'clock in the morning, finishing at six o'clock at night, with an hour off at noon to eat a cooked dinner. The woman's hands were as raw as slabs of meat.

Amelia and Clara, the general maid of the house, were expected to take up the slack the rest of the time.

She overheard a snatch of conversation about the closure of the free library and the cancellation by the Midland company of rail excursions to the town from Leeds. Two of the women of the house – Winnie and a newcomer whose name Amelia couldn't remember – were gossiping about the smallpox epidemic that had gripped the town and showed no sign of letting up. Winnie was crouched in front of the hearth, using a hand shovel to feed coal on to the fire while the other woman half-heartedly stoked it by poking an iron between the bars of the grate.

'Hear about that tram conductor thought he had the chickenpox?' said Winnie. 'He's another one that's died, I 'eard.'

'Oh dear, poor man. He'll have spread it round half the town.'

'Dozens in hospital, I 'eard. And I 'eard it's a horrible death.'

A third woman came over. 'You do 'ear a lot, don't you, Winnie? Miss Barlow says to leave the fire alone. The party's nearly over.'

Winnie leaned back on her heels. 'I'm only tellin' thee what's what.'

Silhouetted by the fading light from the window, Violet continued to hold court but the room was beginning to empty. Hetty was showing Mr Deveraux out, and Amelia could see no sign of Mrs Gunson or Hope. By the time all the clearing up had been done, it would be dark outside. She might spend the evening sitting in the armchair in Hetty's quarters, listening to her sister fret about this girl or that one. Then she'd go to her bed in the ground floor dormitory, then tomorrow it would all start again.

She carried a loaded tray from the room, ignoring Violet's 'Ta ta, dear', and stepped carefully along the hallway and down the few steps that led to the kitchen, pushing the door open with her hip.

As she turned, she saw Mrs Gunson quickly relinquish her hold on Hope's outstretched hands. The two women were sitting across from each other at the table, and both looked startled – and strangely guilty – to see her. Hope's tear-streaked cheeks flooded with colour.

'Don't mind me,' said Amelia. She took the tray through to the scullery where the maid was up to her ears in dirty crockery. 'Here's the rest, Clara.' She returned to the kitchen and flopped into the rocking chair by the range.

'Hidin' away, then? Don't blame you. I am sick to the back teeth of hearing Violet Hargreaves go on about her wonderful life. The woman whinnies like a horse.'

Gratifyingly, Mrs Gunson laughed. 'Amelia, don't be unkind.'

'Oh, I'm jealous, is all.' Amelia set the chair rocking. 'I might go back with her, you know, to London.'

Hope raised her eyebrows. 'Really?'

'Aye. Otherwise Hetty'll have me skivvying here to the end of me days.'

Hope's tone was grave. 'There are worse places than this house.'

'Oh aye? What would you know about that?' She tapped her skull. 'I thought you'd had your memory knocked out of you. Or is it coming back now?'

'It's unkind to press Hope so,' said Mrs Gunson.

Amelia threw up her hands. 'Two unkinds in the space of a minute. I should take meself off if I'm so disagreeable.'

Hope looked distressed. She got to her feet. 'You stay. I should go and take a cup of tea for Miss Barlow.'

'You know, you can't hide behind my sister's skirts forever,' said Amelia. 'Has she told you, by the way? Big day for you tomorrow.'

There. It was out. Hope was frowning at her, twisting in her hands the cloth she'd intended to use to pick up the handle of the kettle.

'What do you mean, Amelia?' said Mrs Gunson. 'And stop rocking so, would you?'

She planted her feet on the ground. 'Angus Deveraux has been asked to collect Hope in the morning and drive her to the police station at Castle Green.'

The colour drained from Hope's face. 'Who's Angus Deveraux? Why must I go to the police station?'

Mrs Gunson was frowning. 'He's the grandson of one of our benefactors, Mr Deveraux whom you met today. Why is he taking Hope there?'

Amelia sighed. Mrs Gunson was right. She'd been unkind. It was only frustration with her situation and she ought not to take it out on this poor girl.

'They're not lockin' you up, love,' she said to Hope. 'You're going to speak to a police constable, see whether anyone's been reported missing, spread the word about you. They'll help you return to your kin. So it's a good thing, in't it?'

Hope's chest hitched with what Amelia at first thought was a sob, of relief or fear, she didn't know. But then, in a series of quick and graceful movements, Hope placed the towel on the table, ran through the scullery to the back door, opened it, sank to her knees and vomited in the dirt of the alleyway. Clara stood at the sink, her mouth hanging open.

'Too much cake,' said Amelia. She helped Mrs Gunson guide Hope back into the kitchen to sit once again at the table. Hope closed her eyes and cradled her belly.

Amelia saw the truth in the old woman's eyes.

Mrs Gunson began to speak, and Amelia cut her off.

'It's not my business, but you're showing, love.' She looked from Hope, who had now covered her face with her hands, to Clara who was studiously washing and stacking the crockery. 'I'll fetch the bucket, shall I? And we'll get that lot swilled away before my sister sees it.'

Chapter 4

She had wordlessly accepted a creased felt bonnet, a wool shawl and a muff that had seen better days from Miss Barlow. The two of them waited in the porch for her transport to the town hall to arrive, gazing out through the open door onto a swirl of snowflakes.

In any other circumstances, she would find this view mesmerising. There was something magical about the first snowfall of winter, something that reminded her of the innocence of childhood. But she was unable to prevent herself from repeatedly glancing at the pastel stripes of the paper on the hallway walls. It was precisely the pattern that adorned the walls of her bedroom at home. She half-closed her eyes, and almost moaned aloud in desperation. Her yearning for a life that had been destroyed was a physical ache in her gut. How could she face a police interview if mere wallpaper could reduce her to this? Perhaps there was a way out. If she faked a swoon, she might be returned to bed and today's appointment postponed.

She was reaching for the wall, for that pastel stripe, preparing to cry out, to sink to her knees, when a cabriolet clattered to a halt at the foot of the steps. Too late. She might have managed it if only Miss Barlow had been present to witness a faked collapse. Add others to the mix and it became a scene. Nausea tightened her throat and the truth tasted bitter on her tongue, as bitter as the medicine she had taken on her first night in the House of Help. She could not withstand the interrogation to come. She hadn't been strong enough to fend off her cousin and she was not strong enough to maintain the ruse he had devised.

She glanced again at the wallpaper, as if in the space of a blink some magic could be wrought and she would find herself in her childhood bed, cocooned between the soft mattress and lace-edged covers. She imagined pulling the sheets over her head, hiding from the world.

'About time,' muttered Miss Barlow. She called to the young man who was holding the reins of two handsome chestnut horses. 'Good day, Mr Deveraux.'

His tone was amused, his voice muffled by a scarf that covered half his face. 'For a sleigh ride, I'll grant you.'

A woman poked her head from the cover that protected the passenger seats from the elements, wearing pince-nez on her beaky nose, her hands, gloved in black kid, tugging higher the collar of her cape. 'Come, come, before this gets any worse.'

'Mrs Shaw,' called Miss Barlow. 'Thank you for chaperoning Miss Hope.' She stepped back and made a gesture as if she was shooing geese out of her path. 'Down you go, now. Be careful of the steps. It's starting to settle.'

'Good morning,' said the man the warden had called Mr Deveraux, as she pulled herself up and into the cab. She forced her mouth into the semblance of a smile. Inside, Mrs Shaw indicated the cushioned seat beside her. The compartment smelled of the floral scent the older woman wore, and of damp clothes, and horse dung. The well-upholstered interior was cramped, their bodies touching from shoulder to hip and thigh as the cab set off.

She sensed the woman disliked their proximity and shrank into herself.

But when she glimpsed the stone bulk and spire of a church on the left as they ascended a narrow, cobbled lane, she could not help but shuffle forward to peer out. This was her first sight of the town. She'd listened to the women at the house talk of place names that were foreign to her – Castle Folds, the Wicker, Lady's Bridge, Barker Pool – and of the men and women, and children, who worked in the great factories in the basin of the town that shipped steel all over the world.

She clutched at the handrail of the gig as it turned left onto what must be the high street, the horses trotting past the front of the church, and the businesses and shops in mismatched buildings on both sides of the street, some towering and imposing with columns and arches and ornate brick and iron work, some squat by comparison – although still two, three and four storeys tall – topped with giant advertisement signs for tobacco, cigars, wine, brandy. There were chandleries, drapers, coffee houses, print shops. Colourfully striped awnings disappeared into the distance as the street sloped away. And people everywhere, hurrying across the street, some holding umbrellas although they were little use in the swirling snow, standing on corners, pushing barrows, tightening harnesses, waiting to board omnibuses.

She couldn't see any factories but guessed they would be the source of the peculiar burnt smell of the town, as if treacle toffee had been thrown onto a coal fire. That wasn't quite right, but it was the closest she could come to it.

'Please sit back,' said Mrs Shaw. 'Or we shall die of pneumonia.'

She obeyed, retreating into the black well of the compartment. For a few moments, she had forgotten about their destination, had been caught up in the clamour of the town.

'Thankfully we are only a short distance away,' said Mrs Shaw.

She nodded.

'I only hope your visit will be brief as Mr Deveraux must deliver me back to Hallam Gate afterwards. God forbid we get trapped in town by this. Snow was *not* in the forecast for today.'

She fought the impulse to apologise for the weather. 'I'm grateful for your assistance.'

Mrs Shaw leaned away so she could fully scrutinise her face. She braced herself for the inevitable question.

'No memory at all, then? You've no idea who you are, where you came from?'

She shook her head, and pressed her fingertips against the sudden throbbing of a vein in her temple. 'I'm afraid not.'

'Remarkable.' Mrs Shaw removed her pince-nez, yawned widely and tucked her chin into the top of her cloak. 'Well, you should save your story, such as it is, for the constable. I'll hear it then.'

Mr Deveraux helped the women alight from the carriage on the cobbles outside the police station. She looked up at the redbrick edifice, wondering whether, once she entered this fortress, she'd be permitted to leave again. The snow was settling now, and falling more densely, so she could see little of her surroundings through the milky screen, except for the wet brick of the building. She could not suppress a shudder when Mr Deveraux's gloved hand enveloped hers, clenching her teeth against the memory of another man's touch, a predator's touch. Mr Deveraux made sure she had found her feet on the treacherous surface, and jumped back onto the box, explaining he had an errand to run, would return in an hour, and the two ladies should wait inside by the fire once the interview was over.

He bent to catch her eye. His were green, with friendly crinkles at the corners. 'Good luck. I'm sure you have nothing to be anxious about. I hope the police will help you find some answers.'

'Thank you, Mr Deveraux,' said Mrs Shaw, steering her away. 'The sooner we get inside the sooner we shall be finished.'

The two women were met in the lobby, where people milled about in front of the warm orange glow of a fireplace. She kept her eyes lowered while Mrs Shaw spoke to the gentleman who had intercepted them. Eventually, Mrs Shaw took her elbow and guided her through a set of double doors and down a tiled corridor. She looked blindly at the pictures on the walls, failing to comprehend the slightest detail. Mrs Shaw brought her to a halt at a wooden bench outside a closed door, and the two women sat.

'I wonder,' said Mrs Shaw, with a theatrical shiver of her shoulders, 'whether there are any men or women of the criminal class under our feet.'

She looked at her shoes. 'What do you mean?'

'There are basement cells, directly beneath us. Crooks waiting to be removed to the jails in Wakefield or Leeds.'

Would her deception be classed as a criminal offence? If she revealed her true identity today, would she be handcuffed and marched to a cold, damp cell to await her fate? Her cousin might be sent to collect her, on behalf of her father. He would drive her to a forest, slit her throat and leave her body under pine needles for foxes to snuffle out… *Stop*. This time she could not suppress the shudder that ran up her spine.

'You might well shiver,' said Mrs Shaw. 'There are people in this town who are a disgrace to humanity,' she said. 'At the house, we are seeing young girls, children under the age of twelve, who have been grievously sinned against. Flogging is too good for those wrongdoers.'

Hope thought about how she had been wronged, how she had been harmed, and the condition in which she had been left. She considered the idea of revealing the truth about what had happened to her. She could not imagine uttering her cousin's name, but she might be believed, here, by people who were strangers to her, who would not wish to silence her in order to avoid a scandal.

She turned to Mrs Shaw. 'What happens to them, to the men who… to the wrongdoers?'

'Well, my dear, I'd like to say they all get hard labour, but more often than not they escape justice.'

She nodded, dismayed. That would be the way of it.

Mrs Shaw continued. 'It's not just the men. Some of the mothers are lacking too. We have utterly destitute young women come to us who want to go into service but they don't even know how to make up a bed because they've been raised by slip-shod mothers.' She paused. 'I'm telling you this because I want you to appreciate how fortunate you were, fetching up on our doorstep.'

Some sort of response was required. 'I am indeed very lucky,' she said. 'Can I ask, what is your role within the house?'

'Why, I'm the honorary secretary to the board of trustees. Did Miss Barlow not give you this information?'

The warden hadn't. 'I may have forgotten it.'

'Well, the board exists for the likes of you, my dear. The friendless girls. We have already checked the downward course of many young women, some of whom, I have to say, were of very ill repute. Indeed, we—'

'Mrs Shaw?' A man wearing the blue uniform of a police officer was striding towards them. Beside him hurried another man, wearing a black waistcoat over a high-collared and decidedly grubby-looking shirt and carrying a large, flat case under one arm. 'I took the liberty of inviting our court artist. Would you like to come in, ladies?'

He opened the door they had been sitting outside and ushered them in, directing them to chairs facing a cluttered desk. The second man perched on a stool under the window and rested his case on his lap. He unbuckled it and brought out a sheet of card, a sheaf of paper and a slim pack of pencils.

With mounting dismay, she realised that he intended to sketch her likeness. She focused her attention on the constable.

'There have been no reports of missing people in the town who match your description,' he said. 'The house warden said you arrived wearing the uniform of a buffer girl.'

She raised her eyebrows. 'I didn't know that. I mean to say, I didn't know that's what the garment was.'

'Do you remember working in a factory?' said Mrs Shaw, eagerly.

The constable scratched his nose. 'Mrs… er…'

'Mrs William Shaw.'

'Yes. Thank you. If you'll permit me to question the young lady.' He turned to her. 'If I may say, you don't have the demeanour of a factory worker. None that I've come across, at least. Although you're the right age. Around eighteen, nineteen?'

'Twenty?' said Mrs Shaw.

The constable scratched his nose again. She wondered whether it was a habit or a tic brought on by Mrs Shaw's interruptions.

'I don't know how old I am.' *Strive for simplicity.* 'I've no memory of working in a factory.'

'And when you arrived at the house, you had nothing with you, no possessions whatsoever?'

She confirmed this with a nod. *All I have to remember is that I have no memory.*

'And no idea how you came to be left at the house.'

'No. I can't recall anything before I was let in. I can remember Miss Barlow putting me to bed and feeling exhausted and dizzy.'

Did this sound over-rehearsed? The man sitting under the window was examining her face, eyes narrowed. She looked away and he continued to sketch with his pencil. She had been drawn before, with her parents, she and her mother seated on a chaise longue, dressed in their finest gowns, her father standing behind them. She recalled the warmth and weight of her father's hand on her shoulder, the light touch of her mother's hand on her arm. Their precious daughter, now brought so low. She remembered the celebration when the oil portrait was hung on the wall, the glass of red wine she had been permitted, her cousin catching her eye, the wolfish smile she mistook for affection. It had led to her ruin.

Would they read the truth in this man's drawing?

You have no memory. How she wished her memory was impaired. She could forget the journey to the house, during which she remained convinced her cousin meant

43

to kill her. When the carriage jerked to a halt, she had tumbled forward, striking her head, leaving her stunned. Her wrists had been seized and she'd been hauled from her seat. Her cousin had half-carried, half-dragged her across a dark open space, her toes stubbing against slabs of stone. He'd wrapped his hand in her hair, his fingers clamping the nape of her neck, and pulled her up the steps to the house. He'd shoved her so her cheek was flattened against the door. When he reached over her for the doorknocker, his ragged breathing was hot and loud in her ear, transporting her back to that fallow field of dandelions and nettles where her fingers had dug into the dirt.

He'd left her on the doorstep of the House of Help as suddenly as he'd fled from that field. She felt his absence as a cold draught against the back of her legs. She had used all her strength to brace herself against the wall, so that she would not fall backwards and tumble down the stairs.

He hadn't spoken a word. He hadn't killed her as she feared he would. But Emma Hyde died that night nonetheless.

'Your amnesia remains total?'

'Yes.'

'But the doctor believes your memory will return, in time.'

She could not continue to meet the constable's frank gaze and dipped her head. 'I hope so.' She twisted her hands together. 'I must have a family somewhere who will be desperate to know where I am.' Her voice dropped to a whisper and the truth was almost too painful to speak. 'A mother who is missing me, who might think I ran away from home because of some disgrace.'

'Why might your mother think that?' said the constable.

'I don't know.' She had said too much. *Keep it simple.* 'I suppose I'm speculating.'

He was studying her face. 'Did you run away from home? Are you remembering something about—'

Mrs Shaw interrupted. '*Did* you bring disgrace on your family?'

She shook her head. 'I don't know. No.'

Mrs Shaw clicked her tongue. 'You *say* no but you can't be sure, can you?'

Her face burned with what they would take to be shame. There were a few seconds of silence then the sketch artist got to his feet and put a sheet of paper down in front of the constable.

'Finished,' he said. 'I'll take it down the road, shall I?'

The constable picked up the paper. 'Thank you. It's a good likeness.' He showed it to the two women. 'What do you think?'

She nodded, relieved that there was no real resemblance. Her hair was shaded in so that it appeared much darker than it was, her nose too snub and her chin too round. It was an unremarkable portrait, the eyes blank, containing no hint of the inner turmoil. Mrs Shaw made noises of approval and asked the constable what would happen next. He explained the sketch would be printed in the town's newspapers with a description and an appeal for information. A poster would be made and circulated to other police forces both inside and outside the county.

'Oh dear,' said Mrs Shaw, and gave a tinkling laugh. 'Hope, your face will be pasted here, there and everywhere, just like one of those wanted posters for criminals.'

The constable smiled at her. 'I'm sure the young lady is wanted, somewhere.'

–

Mrs Shaw's fears about being snowed in had not been realised, although a couple of inches now blanketed every undisturbed surface. The wheels of wagons and carriage threw out grey spray and pedestrians winced and grimaced as if they were stepping on hot coals. Mrs Shaw advised Mr Deveraux to drive more slowly back to the house.

All was quiet on her return and Hope went straight to the dormitory where she lay down and curled on her side, watching snowflakes blur across the window, and trying – and failing – to still the whirl of her mind. She whipped her head around when the door opened. There was no peace to be found in this house.

Amelia strode in, flung herself onto the bed next to hers and lay staring at the ceiling.

'We had three leave while you were out gallivanting,' Amelia said, eventually. 'Little Sarah and the other one, the mousy thing whose name I can never remember – doesn't matter now, does it. Anyhow, they got carted off by a driver from that fancy place in Doncaster, would you believe it. Off to be scullery maids. Oh, and you'll be glad to hear your friend Winnie has gone. She's been taken in by relatives somewhere or other.'

She recalled the woman she had first encountered at breakfast on her first morning in the house, the one who had challenged her. 'Winnie isn't my friend.'

'I know.' Amelia sighed. 'But even you in the state you're in would have to feel sorry for her. D'you know what brought her here?'

'No.' She turned to face the window again, to resume her study of the falling flakes.

It seemed Amelia wouldn't be deterred. 'Then I'll tell thee. Our Winnie found out that the man she thought was going to marry her was already hitched to another woman. What do you think about that? Winnie had her suspicions, though. So one day she follows him across town, to see where he's going.' Amelia stopped. 'Are you listenin'?'

Hope turned over to face Amelia. 'What happened?'

'She ends up gettin' a right battering from the wife for her trouble. Chased off. Kicked from here to kingdom come, was how Winnie put it. He'd been payin' her rent and a bit extra. So that stopped. And she ended up here.' Amelia made a clucking noise with her tongue. 'Some people get themselves into reight messes, don't they?'

She made a non-committal sound.

When Amelia sat up, so, wearily, did she. They faced each other, knees almost touching.

Amelia cocked her head. 'I'll just come straight out wi' it, love. How many courses have you missed?'

She clamped her lips together. The answer was four but she could not reveal it. She shook her head and allowed her hair, which she'd unpinned before lying down on the bed, to fall across her face, a shield to hide behind.

'Oh. I suppose you wouldn't know, would you, having amnesia and all that. But I know you're gipping a fair bit so I'd say three months, maybe four. Your tummy will settle but then,' she leaned forward and gently lifted the curtain of hair to find her eyes, 'you'll really start to show. What will you do?'

'I haven't thought about it.'

'Well, you can't ignore it.'

47

'How do you know so much about it?'

Amelia sat back and gave a mock-shudder. 'Not from experience, I can tell thee that.' She gestured around the room. 'From you lot, a'course. Can't help but listen to your stories.'

Her throat thickened and she gulped. She would not cry. If she did, she'd never stop. She got up and went to the window, resting her forearms on the cold sash. The snow had cleaned the square to a gleaming white, and, its work completed, had stopped.

'Tell you what,' said Amelia. 'Let's talk about something else. What do you think of our Angus Deveraux?'

She turned around. 'What do you mean?'

'He's a looker, in't he?'

She thought about the friendly crinkles around his eyes. 'I didn't notice.'

'Oh aye, you did.'

'I really did not!'

Amelia laughed, and the sound of her laughter brought a smile to her face. 'Come on, hopeless Hope, bundle yoursen up and let's go and make footprints in the snow before my sister finds us and gives us summat to do.'

'That's a good idea. I should like some fresh air.'

'In this town? Are you havin' me on?'

'Where shall we go?'

'Anywhere.' The light left Amelia's eyes. 'Anywhere but this place.'

Chapter 5

By the following afternoon, the cold snap had hardened the snow into a sparkling blanket on the rooftops around the square. Less pleasantly, on the ground, passing traffic had reduced nature's handiwork to brittle slush that slid like eels into Hetty's boots.

She entered the house from the back yard into the scullery and crossed the threshold into the kitchen, where Cook and three of the house residents were preparing a small afternoon tea.

The sweet aroma of freshly baked scones filled the room.

'Have we cream for those?' said Hetty.

'I've just finished it, Miss Barlow.' One of the girls, eager to please, tilted the contents of the mixing bowl towards Hetty. 'We've got jam too.'

'An' egg sandwiches,' said Cook. 'We were left a dozen on the doorstep this mornin'.'

Hetty nodded, satisfied. The headmaster of a private school in the square kept hens in his garden and regularly delivered eggs to the house. The butcher, too, was generous with scrag ends to make soup and liver and lights to fry. She had no complaints about the generosity of those who populated the square.

She was about to express her surprise that the hens were still laying in the depths of winter when there came a series of raps on the front door.

'They're early,' said Cook. 'Worried about getting snowed in, I don't doubt. There's more forecast for later. Come on, girls. Get thee skates on.'

Hetty sighed and trotted up the short flight of stairs. She'd hoped for time to change out of her boots and stockings. As it was, she'd barely completed her report. She had intended a last read through before handing it to the secretary and treasurer of the trustees, who would present it a week from today at the annual general meeting at Cutlers Hall. As warden, she was not required to attend this meeting, and was thankful for it.

On her way to the front door, she nipped into the parlour and left the package she'd purchased from the sweet shop and tobacconists in Campo Lane on a side table. Wrapped in a sheet of newspaper and tied with string, the package contained a selection of Christmas cards, one for each of the girls and women who would be resident on Christmas Day. In addition, they would each receive a bag of homemade bon-bons. It had been Hope's idea, and a good one. The difficulty had lain in choosing cards that did not show happy family scenes, or cats, dogs, floppy-eared bunnies and caged birds. Hetty maintained a strict *no pets* policy at the house. In the end, she had settled for an illustration of a young woman, garlanded in ivy and holly berries, with an inscription beneath that read *Love & Peace With Thee Abide*. That should be safe enough.

When she opened the front door, an immediate sense of relief – she had been expecting the treasurer and the secretary, and it was neither one – was quickly overtaken by irritation. A porter from the station stood on the wet pavement clutching the bar of a handcart on which balanced a large and battered leather case, buckles tightened against the straining seams like a portly gentleman's braces over his belly. A young man stood beside the porter, his hand resting on the case, a confident smile – some might even call it cocky – on his face. He lifted his hat.

'Good afternoon, my name is Linus Harmon and I have—'

'Wait.' Hetty held up both hands, palms out. 'I'm sorry but I don't have time for hawkers today. Or any day, really.' She rubbed her forehead. 'Unless you're donating to us whatever it is you've got in there.'

The hawker nodded to the porter, who quickly obeyed the unspoken signal to unload the case. Hetty shook her head. 'I wasn't inviting you in.'

'A place like this needs security,' the hawker said, slightly breathlessly, as the two men lifted the case up the steps. Hetty stepped out of the way as they deposited it inside the threshold, still shaking her head.

'I said, there's nowt we need. You've blocked the way.'

The hawker mumbled an apology and shoved the case further in, towards the foot of the stairs. 'Have you ever heard of Legge locks, famed throughout Staffordshire, Yorkshire, Lancashire and Wales?'

Hetty gestured to the porter who had straightened up and was pressing both hands into the small of his back. 'If he's told you about this house then you should know our door is always open.'

'Our locks fit safes as well as doors.'

'We keep nowt worth stealing.'

Not to be deterred, the hawker set about unbuckling the case. She had to admire his persistence. 'Then you might be interested in the other wares I have to show you. The newest steel pens, paper knives, beautiful card cases. Elastic bands!' He smiled up at her. 'My cousin has a stationery business.'

'Good for him, but…'

At that moment, one of the girls who had been helping in the kitchen emerged holding a platter of sandwiches in one hand and a stack of plates in the other. She began to walk carefully down the hall towards them.

'Goodness me.' The hawker clapped his hands and rubbed them together. 'You shouldn't have gone to this amount of trouble just for me.'

Hetty laughed. She couldn't help herself. 'The parlour,' she told the girl, who obediently veered through the open door of the room Hetty was indicating. 'Mr Harper…'

'Har*mon*. Linus Harmon, at your service.'

'Our stationery needs are well catered for, at cost, by a local business who sympathises with our cause. They're situated in this very square.' She paused when the sound of plates chinking together came from the parlour. She hoped the girl had not smashed a piece of their best – their only – china. 'I'm sorry but you've wasted your time. If you could take your leave now,' she gestured to the case on the ground, 'I'm expecting guests.'

The hawker wasn't listening to her. She followed his gaze, which was fastened on the young woman descending the staircase. It was Amelia, carrying an empty coal scuttle. Hetty saw her through the young man's eyes, an attractive girl with large brown eyes, a braid of glossy hair framing a cream-coloured complexion. She was lovely looking and Hetty marvelled for a moment that they were related at all. Thank goodness Amelia lived in a house full of women. She'd soon be lost to her otherwise, and Hetty, having taken Amelia under her wing less than a year ago, was determined not to release her too quickly. She had rescued the girl, although she knew Amelia didn't see it in quite the same light.

'Need a help?' The hawker bounded up and took the scuttle from her. Amelia raised an eyebrow.

'Thank you, mister...'

'Harmon. Mr Linus Harmon. At your service.' He winked. 'Very definitely at your service, Miss...'

'Barlow,' said Amelia. 'Amelia Barlow.'

'A lovely name to match a lovely face.'

The hawker was undeniably handsome but, Hetty believed, the sort who practised before the mirror the charming smile that made dimples in his strong jaw, who deliberately narrowed his gaze to increase its intensity. Surely, Amelia would see that too... She frowned when she saw the coy smile playing on Amelia's lips. It was time to see this young man off.

'I don't know what sort of house you think I run, Mr Harmon, but you're being forward in the extreme, and I won't have that, not under my roof.' She gave Amelia what she hoped was a meaningful look.

Amelia ignored her. 'What have you come to sell us, Mr Harmon?'

The hawker lifted the lid of the case. 'Let me show you.'

'Locks and pens and bits of paper,' said Hetty. 'Nowt that would interest you, Amelia. Mr Harmon, you should chance your arm elsewhere. You'll have no luck here.'

'I think this might turn out to be the luckiest day of my life,' he said, his eyes never leaving Amelia's face. 'I have items to sell, but I freely give my heart to you.'

Amelia tilted her head. 'Do you get very far with blether like that, Mr Harmon?'

'I hope to.'

Hetty raised her eyes to the ceiling when the pair of them burst out laughing. She was about to throw the hawker out on his ear when she felt a gentle tug on her sleeve. It was the girl who had carried up the sandwiches, a pale and timid creature, orphaned by the pox. She was capable enough in her quiet way and had been found an excellent situation as an assistant cook at a house on the outskirts of town. Hetty hoped she would find a friend there. What was the name of the house? It had slipped her mind. She sighed. She had enough on, without Amelia delaying the departure of the hawker purely because she knew Hetty wanted him gone.

'Is there owt else needs doing?' the girl whispered.

'Ask Cook,' said Hetty. The girl set off down the hallway. 'Wait. You might come back and pour the tea when my visitors arrive. Put on a clean apron first and brush those lugs out of your hair.'

When she turned back, Amelia had a pen in her hand and was examining its nib. When she caught Hetty's eye, she handed it back to the hawker. 'Hetty might take one of these. She's always scribbling in that ledger of hers.'

The hawker pressed something into Amelia's hand and closed her fingers over it.

'What's that?' said Hetty sharply.

Amelia opened her palm to reveal a perfume sachet. She raised it to her nose and sniffed. 'Lavender. It smells like bees in summer.'

'A gift, for you,' the hawker said. 'You ought to put it under your pillow for dreams as sweet as you are.'

'Oh, give over!'

Amelia might well protest but Hetty could see how pleased she was, and how she now examined Linus Harmon's face with interest. Amelia blushed when he looked directly at her but didn't look away. Hetty coughed and folded her arms.

Finally, he turned his attention back to the suitcase, but instead of fastening it up, he lifted out a sheaf of notepaper and used the pen Amelia had returned to him to write on the top sheet. Hetty gave him an enquiring look.

'Jotting a note to myself,' he murmured, 'then I'll be on my way.'

It was another salesman's ploy. 'There's no need to faff about with that,' said Hetty. 'I don't require a new pen.'

He grinned at her. 'I'll get out from under your feet then. Where's my man gone?'

Hetty rose onto her toes to peer outside. The porter was leaning against the handle of the handcart, tamping tobacco into a pipe. A carriage rattled into the square, horses snorting clouds of moisture into the freezing air. It pulled up behind the porter, who nodded to the driver. Hetty caught a blur of movement through the fogged-up window of the carriage. It was the secretary to the trustees, Mrs Shaw, waving a greeting. A man leaned forward from his seat beside her and smiled at Hetty. Mr Wallace, the treasurer.

–

Hetty and Mr Wallace sipped their tea and carefully avoided making eye contact. She knew if their eyes met she would be unable to prevent a mischievous smile from spreading across her face, and she knew that he was experiencing the same difficulty. On the surface, they were politely listening to Mrs Shaw's tirade on the unsuitability of light amusements for children in the poorer classes. Underneath, the usual mirth invoked by these lectures was bubbling away like a saucepan on the kitchen range.

Mrs Shaw seemed to be nearing the end.

She brushed cake crumbs from her jacket. 'All I will say is, there are hundreds of children who would do better in life if they were given a good meal and introduced to the wondrous cleaning abilities of a facecloth.' She looked around for a napkin and, finding none, patted the corners of her mouth with her fingertips. 'You can be sure I shall be saying as much at the meeting. I know the friends of the house mean well but don't give us tickets for the circus. Give us...' she looked blank for a moment, '...some improving literature.'

'I rather enjoy the circus,' said Mr Wallace.

'As do I.' Mrs Shaw took a gulp of her tea and clattered her cup into its saucer. 'But an example must be set. When the lower classes throw away what little money they have on entertainments... well, why not enjoy a bracing family walk instead? This town is surrounded by the beauty of the countryside that can be enjoyed free of charge.'

Mr Wallace examined the toes of his shoes. Hetty noted one was darker than the other, still soaked through from stepping into the slushy gutter as he helped Mrs Shaw from the carriage.

'You'd need to be equipped with the correct footwear,' he said, 'and a good coat, especially in a climate such as ours where the day can start with sunshine, move through a gale and end in a downpour. Waterproofs, too. A good Mackintosh. They're not cheap.' He gazed out of the window, a faint smile on his lips. 'At this time of year, skating is a pleasant outdoor pursuit. I was always a clumsy oaf, even in the best skates money could buy. There's always a cost involved somewhere, isn't there?'

Hetty looked away, fixing her gaze on the bible that was propped up in its display case, so that Mrs Shaw wouldn't see the merriment in her eyes.

'On our journey here, we saw several children engaged in snowball fights,' said Mrs Shaw. 'No cost there. Just good, clean fun in the outdoors.'

'I do recall your complaining about them playing in the middle of the street and blocking our route.' Mr Wallace delivered his jibe with the kindest of smiles. Mrs Shaw would have taken offence if Hetty had spoken to her like that.

'Well, all I will say to end the argument is this. Nobody,' said Mrs Shaw, 'betters themselves by having access to cheap entertainment.'

Hetty wondered whether betterment was the aim of the circus but thought it prudent to keep that thought to herself. 'Shall I go through the main points of my report?'

'Please do,' said Mr Wallace, with an encouraging smile.

She took a breath. 'It was my pleasure to take up the position of warden some seven months ago. I was given the reins of a well-run household. I have since sent thirty-five women to the local training home, and double that number went straight to situations, all with suitable clothing. We put eighteen women in the workhouse.'

She didn't say that some of the girls sent to the workhouse had been expecting, and, in the absence of the father, had been turfed out of the family home. Undoubtedly, another lecture from Mrs Shaw would have followed.

'We had five girls who were too young to train. Three went to orphanages, and two of those...' she paused, 'to the workhouse.'

'The workhouse?' said Mr Wallace.

'Aye, the orphanages wouldn't take them because they suffered mental weakness. It's a sad fact that we could not help them.'

Mrs Shaw sighed. 'It's unfortunate that some are unwilling to help themselves.'

'Or unable to help themselves,' said Hetty. 'Shall I continue?'

'Please do,' said Mr Wallace.

'I believe it is self-evident that the house is providing a vital service and has set hundreds of young women on the right path. The experiment is working, in my very humble opinion.'

She took another breath and continued on.

'Our volunteer agents are rescuing girls from the courts who would otherwise no doubt continue a life of crime. The older women tend to find their own way to our door. They might be getting clouted... I mean to say, suffering in the domestic arena, or they have found themselves in a strange town and need a refuge for a night or two. The station porters point them in our direction. We've also built a working relationship with the bobbies, who bring us those souls who are in dire straits, girls and women they believe we can manage.'

'You are doing commendable work, no doubt about it,' said Mr Wallace. 'Might I say a word about our finances?' He took out his pocketbook. 'Our income this year from subscriptions and donations is two hundred and forty-seven pounds.'

'And our expenditure?' said Mrs Shaw. She gave Hetty a knowing look.

'Two hundred and forty-eight pounds.' He closed his book.

'A difference of just one pound?' said Hetty. 'I don't see an issue. We're not setting out to make a profit.'

Mr Wallace grimaced. 'Unfortunately, we are still in debt from establishing the house, to the tune of three hundred pounds. We require substantially more funding if corners are not to be cut.'

Hetty immediately thought of Amelia on a maid of all work's wage while effectively carrying out the duties of a housekeeper, and without even a bed of her own. She slept in the downstairs dorm with the residents, and when a bed was needed urgently, in Hetty's bed. The warden's salary was meagre, too. It was the reason there had not been many candidates for the job. The house could not manage without a cook or maid, even with the residents helping out and they, anyway, were transient and some incapable of completing the simplest of tasks. It was an ongoing challenge to provide nourishing meals and keep within the grocery budget. Amelia reported this on an almost daily basis. Hetty frequently heard the scrape of the shovel over the bare stone floor of the cellar, the sound of the scullery maid fishing out the last few pieces of coal from the corners. There were never enough blankets to satisfy the residents, and winter was only just getting into its stride.

Mrs Shaw interrupted this train of thought. 'We ought to show off our achievements to attract more donations. When did we last parade our successes before potential benefactors, hmm?'

'What do you mean by parade?' said Hetty. Wasn't it enough that benefactors could invade the house every Sunday, drink tea, eat cake and slyly inspect the residents?

Mrs Shaw ignored her question. 'I believe it was before your time, Miss Barlow, when the archdeacon invited young ladies who had benefited from our services to afternoon tea.'

She took a small bite from an egg sandwich, chewed and swallowed and, with lips pursed, laid a fragment of shell on her plate. 'What an afternoon tea that was! The archdeacon's wife told me that all the wives present were pleasantly surprised by our young ladies' respectability and modest demeanour. Didn't we receive a substantial donation as a result of that, Mr Wallace?'

'We did, indeed,' said Mr Wallace. He turned to Hetty. 'Please be assured the trustees are grateful for your hard work. To have secured the services of a former matron is a coup, indeed. I am sorry we cannot remunerate you more generously.' He paused. 'I believe we promised you an assistant, if funds allowed, or a deputy.'

'Aye, I could use both,' said Hetty.

'Oh, that reminds me!' Mrs Shaw reached for a scone, dropping it delicately onto her plate. 'Do you know, Miss Barlow, that the widow of one of our former trustees trained and worked as a matron in the Winter Street hospital many years ago? She married the surgeon there.'

'Ah, you're talking about Mrs John Calver,' said Mr Wallace. 'A fine lady.'

'Yes, Mr Calver dropped dead of a heart attack a week before we opened our doors,' said Mrs Shaw. 'God bless his soul. Anyway, I must introduce you to her. You have so much in common and I know she'd be most interested in taking a look around the house.'

'I believe she's been quite lonely since Mr Calver passed,' said Mr Wallace, 'and you, Miss Barlow, being new to the town... Perhaps there is a friendship to be had?'

Hetty's mind flew to the documents she kept in the bottom drawer of her desk, those excellent references she had presented to the trustees to secure the job of warden. She had worked in a hospital, there was no lie in that, but she'd been mopping the floors and not the brows of the patients. Sometimes she reflected on what path her life, and Amelia's, would have taken if she had sought out the House of Help when they arrived in the town, instead of finding a room in a boarding house. After a few weeks in that hellhole, she'd seen the job advertisement in the local newspaper and it had been kind Mr Wallace who interviewed her for the post of warden.

'They're looking for a housekeeper too,' she'd said to Amelia. 'I can recommend you for the job.'

Growing up, Amelia had been told her sister had an important job in a hospital many miles from home. There had been no reason for Amelia not to believe the necessary lie. Her mother gave her busy role as the reason Hetty never visited. At least she had been able to put the confection to good use. An ex-convict living in the same lodgings had agreed to forge references in return for the rest of the coin she had on her. She took a gamble, and it had, so far, paid off.

A probing question from a former matron might wreck all her careful work.

Mr Wallace coughed. 'Of course, I wouldn't presume to force a friendship on you.'

Hetty attempted to lift the corners of her mouth into a smile. 'It's only that I'm run off my feet all day every day. Perhaps you might show her around, Mrs Shaw.'

Mrs Shaw widened her eyes in surprise. 'I thought you'd welcome the opportunity to talk to somebody with whom you have so much in common.'

'I was in a hospital at Whitby.'

Mrs Shaw tilted her head quizzically. 'But a matron is a matron, wherever she hails from?'

Hetty smiled politely, having not the first idea what to say. She needed to be alone, to think, to consider whether she faced a real threat, or was over-reacting. The truth was that people liked to talk about themselves, and rarely listened.

The late surgeon's wife would be no different.

Chapter 6

When Hetty stepped outside to greet her visitors, Linus Harmon had taken the piece of notepaper he'd been scribbling on, neatly folded it and folded it again into a square hardly bigger than a postage stamp and pressed it into Amelia's hand. He'd bent her fingers over it, turned her hand over and kissed the back of it.

Nothing like this had ever happened to Amelia during the sheltered life she'd led on the estuary with her mother and aunt. She could almost forgive Hetty for bringing her here and setting her to work.

Thinking again of the touch of his lips on her skin, a thrill coursed through her body.

Hetty would be horrified. Amelia believed her sister had brought her here to keep her away from men, determined she too would live out her life as a spinster. Well, *she* was determined not to grow old and bitter. She flattened the notepaper on the desk in Hetty's quarters, listening out for footsteps in the hall. She traced the creases Linus had made when he had folded the paper. They were like the creases in the palm of her hand. What fortunes would those lines tell? Which crease spelled out marriage and which children? She ran her finger over the central crease. This one, she decided, signified a long and happy life. As Linus's wife.

She examined the notepaper. It looked expensive, coloured a pale blue with a tiny sprig of purple and yellow wildflowers in the top right-hand corner. His handwriting was larger than Hetty's script, which was cramped and as sharp as pins. Linus's handwriting was giddy with swirls and loops. It had been written in a hurry but she believed his script would be this extravagant, this alive, even if he'd had all the time in the world to pen his note to her.

She tracked the outline of her name with the nail of her little finger. She had watched him write *Amelia*, a smile on his lips, and her breath had caught in her throat. By the time Hetty had re-entered the house with an older woman who was fussing about the weather, followed by a short and kindly-looking man shaking a trouser hem that was soaked through, the note was concealed in Amelia's hand. Linus had bowed and then stood back to allow the visitors to pass, smiling over their heads at Amelia. She'd folded her lips to prevent the bubble of joy in her throat from escaping.

She had interpreted as much of this precious piece of paper as she could. Now, she needed help. Amelia pushed back Hetty's chair and stood, pressing the note against her chest. There was really only one person she could go to.

-

In the store room next to the coal cellar, the earthy smell of potatoes and carrots mingled with the sharper scents of milk and cheese. There was nowhere to sit so they stood facing each other on the bare stone floor in the narrow passageway between the shelves. Amelia held the candle. If they were discovered, she had the ready excuse that she had needed another pair of hands to help carry the makings of tonight's meal to the kitchen.

But now that Hope was standing before her, Amelia didn't know how to begin. Heat rose into her cheeks, despite the chill in the air, and the concerned frown on Hope's brow deepened.

'Are you in trouble?'

'No!' Amelia said. 'Nothin' like the trouble you're in.' She immediately regretted speaking so harshly but would not explain the reason why. Hope would not understand the humiliation she felt in making this request. 'Sorry.'

Hope looked behind her, although the door remained closed and no sounds filtered down from the house. When she faced Amelia again her eyes were wary. 'What is it?'

'You prob'ly went to school, din't you?' She shook her head, impatient with herself and with Hope, for not understanding. 'I know, I know, you don't remember.' She held out the notepaper. 'I've got this. I can't make out some of the words. I saw you reading to little Tilly and I thought...'

Hope took it from her. 'Give me the candle,' she said.

Amelia laughed nervously. 'Whatever you do, don't set it alight.'

Hope stood the tray that held the candle on a shelf by her shoulder. Her eyes were dark pools in the flickering light. 'It's addressed to you,' she said.

'Aye, I know that,' said Amelia, impatience getting the better of her. 'And I've already got the gist of it. Can you tell me the rest?'

Hope scanned the sheet. 'Oh,' she said.

'Don't you dare tell anybody about this,' said Amelia.

'Of course not. I thought... I've seen you read out Cook's list to the grocer and pay the coalman.'

'Well, I can manage that sort of thing!' said Amelia. 'A few words, a bit of countin'. I'm not completely daft.

Just tell me what it says. Every word. And be quick-sharp about it, before some nosy parker comes.'

Hope cleared her throat and began to read.

Miss Amelia, forgive me for being as presumptuous as the lady of the house suggests...

'Presumptuous. What a word.'

'It means...'

'I know what it means.' Amelia smiled. 'And Hetty didn't just suggest it. She came right out and said he was forward. She was right, too. Bold as brass, he was. He didn't take his eyes off me once.' She took a breath. 'D'you believe in love at first sight?'

Hope swallowed. 'I don't know.'

'Well, I do. I din't, but I do now.'

'What did he say to you?'

'Oh, this and that. It was more the way he looked at me.' She stabbed at the notepaper. 'Read the letter, would you?'

Hope read on.

> *But I hope you will consider starting a correspond-*
> *ence with a view to allowing me to escort you and*
> *your chaperone...*

Amelia stifled a burst of laughter. 'My chaperone!'

> *...to tea at the Red Lion Hotel in Campo Lane.*

Hope looked up. 'Where is that?'

'Two minutes away. Around the corner. Is that it? Is there more?'

'Not much. It's certainly short and sweet.'

'He was in a hurry. Finish it.'

Yours in fervent hope and anticipation,
      Linus Harmon.

'And his address.' She squinted at the sheet of paper. 'He lives in a place called Tamworth. Goodness me. I can't tell from your face whether this pleases you or not.'

Standing with her fists clenched under her chin, biting her lip, Amelia was frozen for a long moment. Then she threw her arms around Hope, who gave a weak cry of alarm. Amelia stepped away, snatched the notepaper back and pressed it against her chest. This flimsy piece of paper was her ticket to a different life, as wife to a travelling salesman, a businessman. They'd set up home in Tamworth, wherever that was. It could be on the moon for all she cared. Amelia Harmon. Pleased to make your acquaintance. My name is Mrs Amelia Harmon.

Hope was smiling at her. 'Is he as handsome as you purport Mr Angus Deveraux to be?'

'More so. Wickedly handsome.'

Hope looked uncertain.

'What's that face for?'

'You'll need to tell Miss Barlow about this, won't you?'

'Hetty? She's my sister, not my mother. It's nowt to do with her, is it?'

She picked up the basket she'd grabbed from the scullery on her way to the store room. 'We'd better do what we reckoned to have come down here to do. Cook's making a meat and potato pie for tea.' She bent to pick at the tie on a sack of potatoes. 'You get the butter and flour and the salt…'

Instructing Hope on what to collect in the basket, Amelia's mind was occupied elsewhere. Should she wait and see whether Linus Harmon really was a serious prospect before telling her sister anything about it? Somehow, Hetty would manage to scupper her chance at happiness. Or was she being too harsh on her sister? She'd gone with Hetty willingly enough, on the promise of a better life. If she was being truthful, after their mother's death, and their aunt's attempts to resurrect her – Amelia shuddered at the thought – she'd never been so glad to see her sister. She shook clods of earth from a carrot. The exhilaration of leaving the estuary for the first time in her life had soon waned.

They filled the basket and when Hope spoke, it was as if she had read Amelia's mind.

'You and Miss Barlow always seem to be at loggerheads. Can I help carry that?'

Amelia shook her head and waved Hope ahead of her. 'I can manage.'

Hope picked up the candle and snuffed it out. 'I only mean to say that you have somebody, a sister.'

'If you're about to tell me to count my blessings, don't bother.'

The scullery was empty and Amelia set down the basket on the counter beside the stone sink with a sigh.

'I never really knew Hetty,' she said. 'She's so much older than me. And she moved to a different town, a faraway place I was told, when I was a babe in arms. She would have come back for our father's funeral, but I was too young to remember.' She shrugged.

'Yet here you are together now?'

'Aye. Aye, we are. She came home eight months ago, for our mother's funeral.'

She recalled the chill of the chapel that spring morning, the handful of mourners that would have barely filled a pew, if they'd all been sitting together, which they weren't.

Her aunt had explained to her that her mother had lost contact with most of the people she knew when they moved to a different district of town not long after Amelia was born. The reason for the flit was never given.

Hetty hadn't said much at all, but Amelia was aware of being under scrutiny. Every time she looked at Hetty across the aisle, her sister looked away.

Hope touched her sleeve hesitantly. 'I'm sorry you lost your mother.'

'Aye. Well.' Amelia nodded briskly and cleared her throat, and when she felt she had herself under control, continued. 'She caused a bit of a ruckus, got into an argument with our aunt, and disappeared off again. Then she turns up a week later, tells me we're moving away, makin' a fresh start. I remember my aunt saying no good had come of her and no good would come of me, either.'

'Oh dear,' said Hope.

Amelia shrugged. 'It's all right. She's a bit of a barmpot, my aunt. Anyway, we came here and Hetty found a job – this job – and there was a position for me.' Amelia frowned. 'I don't know why I'm telling you all this.'

'What about your aunt?' said Hope.

'She's still in the house I grew up in. She's from my father's side o' the family and moved in after he died, so she's allus been there, I suppose.'

'That must have been nice.' Hope sounded wistful.

'Not especially.' Amelia gazed at the whitewashed wall. It needed repainting. She would no doubt end up doing it herself. 'I was always gettin' under her feet. I would catch her looking at me, critical like, but she never said owt. Anyhow, I'm blethering on.'

She wanted to end what was becoming a difficult conversation. Her aunt had let her go with Hetty without a murmur of protest, as if she was glad to see the back of the girl she'd helped raise. Amelia had felt unwanted, a burden that her aunt was glad to be rid of. That was the truth of it.

'It's over and done with,' she said.

'I suppose there's no point dwelling on the past,' said Hope. 'We must make the most of the lot we're given.'

She sounded like she was trying to convince herself.

'Aye,' said Amelia. 'Let's get this lot into the kitchen, shall we?'

–

Amelia and Hope had fallen into the habit of going for a short walk after tea, provided Hetty hadn't dished out chores for them to complete. They always took the same route, walking around all four sides of the square, then through the ginnel towards St Peter's, up the slight incline of Church Street and back. Occasionally, they reversed direction, and sometimes, if there were men standing outside the Q on the Corner tavern, they would cut diagonally across the square to avoid passing them and enduring ribald comments. Once, when the pavement outside the Q was empty, they had stood in the shadows and listened to the fiddlers playing within, until the cold drove them on.

For Amelia, it was a brief escape from all the women and the clamour of the house. She assumed Hope enjoyed being away from the scrutiny she seemed always to be under as the mysterious woman with no past. Occasionally, one of the other women would invite herself along. Amelia hoped that on this occasion the cold wind rattling the window panes would put off any interlopers.

As soon as the residents allocated to clear away the dishes that evening had scraped back their chairs, Amelia jerked her head towards the door. Hope nodded. She had probably already guessed what Amelia wanted to ask. She was sharp as a tack, that one, for all her loss of memory.

Still, it took a while for her to pluck up the courage to ask Hope the question that had been on her mind ever since she'd heard the contents of Linus's letter.

The night air caught in the back of her throat and the pavements gleamed in the pools of light cast by the streetlamps. It was impossible to tell whether the ground beneath their feet was coated in black ice or was simply wet, and they progressed slowly, arm in arm. The air was sharp and smoky, the town's central church a blacker bulk against the impenetrable night sky. They turned right onto the small incline of Church Street, the church, its tall spire and all its dead now behind them.

'Do you think we'll have more snow?' said Hope.

'Nah, it's too cold for snow.' Amelia cleared her throat. 'I've been wonderin'… about your situation. Has Mrs Gunson given you any advice? Does anybody else know?'

'I think she's trying to come up with a scheme that will keep me out of the workhouse. I haven't worked up the courage to tell Miss Barlow yet, but I will. Very soon.'

'All right, then. And nowt coming back? No memories?'

'No.' Hope paused. 'No. Nothing.'

A few seconds passed in silence, then Hope spoke again. 'Amelia, would you like me to write to Mr Harmon on your behalf? You ought to give him an answer, one way or the other.'

The woman was being irritatingly tactful, but Amelia knew she might never have got around to asking for the favour. She pretended to consider the suggestion as they turned right again onto the street that would bring them back to the square. Lights shone from the windows of tightly packed terraced dwellings and the air was full of the scent of coalsmoke. There were few passers-by. Most people, thought Amelia, would be warming their feet by the fire or swilling ale in one of the taverns that decorated every street corner.

'What do you think?' said Hope.

'That's an idea,' she said. 'I wish I'd thought of it.'

Hope squeezed her arm.

Amelia returned the pressure. 'I could tell thee what to write. It'll be like you're a clerk taking dictation from your gaffer. You know, some of the steelworks bosses can barely read or write but that's not to say they don't know how to build an empire.'

'That's what clerks are there for,' said Hope. 'To cross the t's and dot the i's.'

'It takes all kinds.'

'That's settled then.'

'Aye.' Amelia strengthened her grip on Hope's arm when her feet slid on the pavement, and kept them both from tumbling. 'Watch yourself, love. A fall's the last thing you need.'

Hope stopped suddenly, in the shadows between two lampposts and disengaged her arm from Amelia's, hiding her face behind her gloved fingers. Amelia waited for a long moment then gently took her wrists and lowered her hands. It was too dark to make out Hope's features.

'What's up?'

Hope laughed shakily. 'Nothing. It's nothing. It's only when you mentioned a fall... I'm sorry.' She shook her head. 'This will sound melodramatic but I've already fallen, haven't I? I've fallen about as far as you can fall.' Her breath hitched. 'I've heard about the workhouses, how you have to wear a uniform that marks you out. What if Miss Barlow sends me there?'

Her breath hitched again and she collapsed against Amelia's shoulder and began to sob. Surprised by the show of emotion, for Hope had always appeared so reserved, Amelia took her into her arms and awkwardly patted her back.

'Don't talk daft.' She was out of her depth. Mrs Gunson would find the right words of comfort. What would that lady say? 'It'll all work out, in the end.'

Hope's face remained buried in her shoulder.

'My child born in a workhouse. I can't stand to think of it. What will become of us, Amelia? What will become of us?'

Chapter 7

Over the course of a couple of weeks, a room on the second floor that had originally been used as a library, and latterly a junk room, was stripped out and cleaned from top to toe. A cheap set of curtains and nets were purchased from a house clearance to hang in the window. Chairs and stools were scrounged from here and there, mismatched but no matter. An appeal was made for blackboard easels and chalk and these were duly donated. The built-in library shelves were stacked with books, paper and pencils, pens and ink, sewing tins and paint-boxes and brushes, purchased wholesale from the new budget for *Education and Improvement* that had been devised thanks to the persuasive urging of the honourable secretary, Mrs Shaw.

Even Amelia was caught up in the excitement. The house was to get a dedicated classroom for reading, writing and arithmetic, needlework, bible studies and craft work. The final item to be installed was a long oak table, sold off cheaply by a department store. It had been used on the shop floor as a display table and was only slightly damaged, a nick in the wood here and there, some scratches and dents on the surface.

Mr Wallace had purchased it for a song, Hetty told Amelia.

'Shame you couldn't get some of the weight taken off it, an' all,' Amelia grumbled as she helped Hetty, Clara, the wagon driver who had delivered it, and a new arrival – who had preceded the table by minutes only – manoeuvre it up the stairs.

This new arrival was a young woman who had turned up that morning carrying a bulky valise in both hands. She was wearing a red cloak trimmed in black fur and certainly didn't look destitute. Nothing about her was conventionally pretty. Her large eyes were hooded and her nose a sharp blade, reminding Amelia of a bird of prey. Her lips were red – painted, surely – and her neck was as long as a swan's – yet she was striking to look at. Amelia couldn't take her eyes off her.

In a voice that commanded attention, the woman explained her trunk had been delivered straight to the Theatre Royal.

'You're an actress!' said Amelia.

'I am indeed.' She laughed, then arranged her small mouth into an even smaller pout. 'And without a place to stay in town. I don't get paid enough to afford hotel accommodation. If you can put me up, I'll try and secure some free tickets for the pantomime.'

'Pantomime?' said Amelia.

The woman struck a pose, one hand behind her head, the other on her hip. 'I'm the star attraction.' She raised her voice, theatrically. '*The Fair One with the Golden Locks.*'

'You're never the fair one?' said Amelia.

'I wear a wig, of course.'

'If you really have nowhere you can stay...' Hetty began to say.

'I know nobody at all in the town! I won't be paid until the production is over.'

'…then we have a bed for you. How long would you require it?'

'Oh, thank you, I'm so grateful. Three weeks, only. A week's rehearsing then the show runs for two weeks.'

Hetty had sent Amelia to show her where she could sleep – the bed Winnie had occupied in the attic dorm – and opened a new page in the ledger. Anneliese Titterton. What a mouthful, Amelia thought. She wondered whether it was a stage name. She couldn't wait to tell Hope all about her, right after Hope had written the promised letter to Linus.

Amelia had told Hetty a few days earlier that she wanted to improve her reading and writing but didn't want to join the evening classes run for the women of the house. Hope, she said, had offered private lessons. She did not tell Hetty that she had no intention of learning more than she already knew, which she considered to be adequate. She did, however, need to get some private time with Hope.

She had lain in bed trying and failing to compose her reply, stewing in the snores and snuffles of the women around her, her determination to get away stronger than ever.

'You and Hope have become thick as thieves,' Hetty had remarked.

Amelia frowned. 'I wouldn't say so. No point making friends with any of this lot, they all disappear, don't they?'

'I'm here.'

'Hmm.'

'I'm sorry I didn't come home more often, when you were little.'

'And you being the favourite child, and all.'

'Don't be daft. What makes you say that?'

'Well,' Amelia paused. 'They never really bothered with me, did they? You got schooled. I never. I never even had any friends, neither. They wouldn't let me go to Sunday school like the neighbours' kids because of Auntie Gertie's beliefs. You should have seen that lot, gettin' to play in the field after, and sometimes they'd get given spice. And there's me, sittin' in the window gawping at them.'

This was the most she had ever told Hetty about her life before their mother died.

'Then you should be glad I took you away,' Hetty had replied tartly. 'You won't get far on self-pity.' And she marched off before Amelia could respond.

Now, they stood with Anneliese Titterton, the wagon driver and Clara the maid, surveying the room, all slightly out of breath.

'We have a classroom,' said Hetty, looking around with a satisfied smile.

'You're doing good work at this house,' the wagon driver said.

'Thank you,' said Hetty. 'I take it you'll be waiving the delivery charge?'

He scratched his head. 'Er… aye, all right.'

Tonight, thought Amelia. She would ask Hope to write the letter tonight, after everyone else had gone to bed. As if she had conjured her up just by thinking about her, Hope appeared on the threshold.

'There's a strange noise coming from upstairs,' she said. 'A horrible wailing. Can anyone hear it?' She looked around the room. 'My goodness, this is perfect.'

Anneliese threw up her hands theatrically and hurried towards the door. 'Oh dear. Jenkins will be so cross. I'll be back in a flash.'

'Who's Jenkins?' said Amelia.

'I have no idea,' said Hetty. 'But listening to that racket, I do have my suspicions.'

'I'll be off then,' said the wagon driver. Clara followed him from the room, muttering about finding fresh sheets for the actress's bed.

The house's newest resident was true to her word, reappearing only minutes later with the valise held, once again, in two hands out before her, as if there was a heavy weight inside. The contents of the bag shifted, bulging first in one corner and then the other. Amelia could guess what would emerge. Anneliese put the valise on a chair and unfastened the clasp, making gentle noises with pursed red lips. She lifted out a sleek black cat and held it up for inspection, a proud smile on her face.

'Isn't he marvellous? I know you won't be able to resist him, Miss Barlow.' She stroked the animal between its ears and set it down on the floorboards. The cat sat still as a sphinx then examined a paw and proceeded to wash its face. 'Jenkins goes everywhere with me.'

'I can barely believe this is the creature that was making such an ungodly noise,' said Hope, bending to pet the animal.

Anneliese put out a warning hand. 'I wouldn't,' she said. 'He's liable to scratch. Cat scratches can be dangerous to ladies who are in a delicate condition.'

For a split-second, Hope froze as she straightened up, and Amelia darted a quick glance at Hetty, who was frowning at the cat named Jenkins and seemed not to have heard. Amelia saw with fresh eyes that the housedress Hope was wearing no longer fit. It stretched too tightly over her belly, and the buttons on the blouse she wore were barely holding the garment together.

'He's a very well-behaved boy,' said Anneliese. 'He won't make any mess.'

Hetty shook her head.

'We don't accept animals,' she said. 'That's the rule.'

'Oh dear, I was so afraid of this,' said Anneliese. 'It's why I smuggled him in.' She winked at Amelia. 'It's harder to throw out a cat than let one in, don't you find? I've always had Jenkins, since I was a little girl.'

'Males aren't allowed in this house,' said Amelia, amused.

They all watched the cat move across the floor, stretching his back legs out behind him, one then the other, his body coiling and pooling like molten iron.

'Come on then,' said Anneliese, reluctantly scooping up the cat. She looked at Hetty, an appeal in her eyes. 'I suppose we'll have to find somewhere else to take us. I shall be exhausted before rehearsal even starts.'

Hetty shook her head, more in resignation than denial.

Anneliese evidently saw the chink in her armour. 'We'll be model housemates,' she said.

'He's probably a fine mouser,' said Hope. She had pulled out one of the chairs to sit in. She put one hand to her mouth and burped. 'Oh dear. Do excuse me.'

Hetty frowned at Hope then returned her attention to the actress. 'I suppose we can always use a mouser,' she said. She looked startled when Anneliese released the cat onto the floorboards, took hold of Hetty's elbows and kissed her on both cheeks.

'No more surprises, Miss Titterton,' Hetty said. 'All right?'

But now Anneliese was studying Hope, her head tilted sympathetically. 'Can I fetch you some water? My mother told me she went all the way to the very day of my birth feeling like she'd upchuck at any moment. I have to say that she was prone to exaggeration.'

'No. I'll be all right. Thank you.' Hope spoke quietly, her eyes darting from Amelia to Hetty and back to Amelia, widening in a plea for help. What did she expect her to do? She grimaced sympathetically.

Hetty caught Amelia's eye and slowly shook her head. She had guessed the truth. Now there would be ructions.

Anneliese seemed immune to the tension in the air. She patted Hope's arm.

'Tell me, when are you due?' she said. 'No, don't tell me. I'm going to guess springtime.' She clapped her hands together. 'A May baby! That's lovely, isn't it? Isn't that perfection, Miss Barlow?'

Chapter 8

Hope had known this day would arrive but wished she'd had time to prepare herself before she had to face the warden, to rehearse what she might say, how she might plead her case. She descended the stairs slowly, down to the first floor, along the hall, down to the ground floor, Miss Barlow following behind. She was reluctant to relinquish her grip on the bannister rail at the bottom. She had adapted to the life of the house, had made herself useful. Was it really possible she could find herself in the workhouse before the end of the day?

Miss Barlow tapped her shoulder. 'The parlour,' she said.

The warden followed her into the room, gently closed the door behind them and remained standing by it. Hope stood in the middle of the room, her arms hanging by her sides.

'I think it's time you came clean with me, Hope.'

'May I sit?' Her eyes filled with tears that she blinked away. She had learned enough about Miss Barlow to know she would not be sympathetic to an emotional outburst.

'Aye, go on then.' The warden remained standing by the door.

Hope found the nearest armchair and sat in it. Nausea swelled in her gut. She longed to rest her head back against the antimacassar, to gently doze, to have her mother place a cool palm against her forehead. She made her hands into fists in her lap as if they could anchor her against a wave of homesickness that was so strong it dizzied her.

'Are you with child?'

'I think so.' Her voice was thick with despair.

'You think so. Shall I send for the doctor to examine you?'

She shook her head. The coldness in the warden's voice sent a trickle of ice down her spine. She realised she might have had all the time in the world to prepare herself for this moment, it would still come down to this. Disapproval. Disappointment. It was unbearable.

'I intended to tell you…'

'Oh aye?' There was a note of amusement in Miss Barlow's voice. 'When?'

'Soon. I was afraid.' She paused. 'I was afraid you would send me away. I feel safe here. I thought to stay, if you would have me. You have so much to do. I thought I could help.'

She realised the hopelessness of her situation even as she spoke the words. She had read all about the workhouses, where women were left to give birth alone in squalor, and no doctor if there were complications. Her heart was racing.

'Who is the father?'

She stared into her lap, her fingers worrying the folds of her dress. She had nothing. Not even the clothes on her back belonged to her. She truly was a destitute case, and foolish to think she had anything to offer this house.

'You don't know, of course, because you have no memory beyond your arrival at the house.' Miss Barlow's tone softened. 'You were certainly in a state when you turned up on the doorstep, I remember that. Does anybody else know?'

'I confided in Mrs Gunson, and Amelia guessed it.'

'Did she now? And never thought to tell me.'

'Please don't be angry with her.'

There was a long silence. Eventually, she plucked up the courage to raise her eyes to Miss Barlow's face, but the other woman was deep in thought, gazing towards the window. She waited.

'Well then,' said Miss Barlow eventually. 'I'm walking Tilly over to Mrs Gunson's tomorrow. She wants an extra pair of hands to help get the house ready for their Christmas party. You'll come with us and if Mrs Gunson is at home we'll have a talk about what can be done with you.'

Miss Barlow turned to leave the room, glancing back to ask: 'Is that all right?'

'Of course. Thank you.' She stood up, panicked anew. 'What shall I do now?'

'Well, it's nearly tea time. I take it you want to keep out of the road of the rest of them, especially our Miss Titterton?'

She nodded. 'I can't face anybody, just at the moment.'

'Then go to your bed. I'll send Amelia up with a tray and tell them you're feeling poorly.'

'Thank you, thank you so much.'

'Don't thank me yet. You lot will be the death of me.'

And the warden was gone, leaving the door into the hallway open.

Hope let out a shaky breath and leaned back in the chair, cupping her belly with one hand. The reprieve was temporary and she had no idea what lay ahead, but for now, she was content to fall into a semi-stupor, to allow her eyelids to droop, her thoughts to dim like a wick being turned low. She wasn't sure how much time had passed before she became aware of several pairs of feet descending the stairs, residents on their way to the kitchen for tea. She prayed for a few moments' grace, that no one would enter the parlour and she would be able to creep across the hall to the dormitory unnoticed. She kept her eyes closed, feigning sleep, and imagined herself sitting across from her mother, discussing names for the baby, the wedding band on her finger catching the light from a roaring fire. Her father would be standing at the mantelpiece, sipping brandy and smoking a cigar, conversing with the suitable match he had found for his only child. She tried to conjure a face for this mythical husband but could not. No matter. She focused on her father's handsomely stern profile rising from a starched collar, the blonde curls falling around her mother's face, the flames licking at the grate.

In this story, her cousin had never lured her away to the field at the edge of the estate. Instead, he had moved to London with his fiancée. His visits home would be few and far between, but they would remain friends. There would be no cause for rancour. In this story, he had never told her how she had teased him, how she had been the one at fault. She squeezed her eyes more tightly closed, to prevent the fantasy from falling apart. But the cosy fireside scene had dissolved and now her cousin's face swam before her, his sneering mouth and eyes obliterating all else. It was no good.

Her old life had never felt further away. She wasn't a respectably married young woman awaiting the birth of her child. Instead, she was one of the destitute, one of the *You lot* the warden had remarked upon. Her past was violent and her fate as uncertain as theirs.

To the casual observer, they might look members of a close-knit family, a little girl standing between her mother and aunt, all bathed in the orange glow of the window of Cole Brothers merchants. Miss Barlow had allowed the detour so that Tilly could examine the baubles, candied fruits and music boxes on display.

Darkness had already descended, blotting out the smoke that rose from the factory stacks in the bottom of the valley. All the stars had fallen from the heavens, through the clouds and the smoke, and become trapped behind the panes of the shopfronts on the high street and Fargate and Church Street. She smiled to herself but then caught Miss Barlow's gaze in the reflection through the glass and dropped her eyes, the spell broken.

'I like that one,' said Tilly shyly.

She had pressed her fingertip against the glass to point to a tin bauble, about the size of an apple, with a beautifully-wrought illustration of a child in a red dress against a background of green boughs. The child was holding a hoop in one hand and a doll in the other.

'It's lovely,' said Hope.

'Miss Barlow, will we have a Christmas tree at the house?'

The anticipation in her voice was heart-breaking.

'Aye, we always do, and you can come and visit and help us decorate it with coloured paper hoops.' Miss Barlow waved her hand at the display as if she could make it disappear. 'None of this expensive rubbish.' She stepped away from the window display. 'Come on, let's get you to Mrs Gunson.'

Tilly would be in service before Christmas, perhaps with a permanent position at Mrs Gunson's house if she performed her duties well over the next couple of days. She was a tiny creature who looked considerably younger than her thirteen years, brought to the house in threadbare clothes that were too small even on her thin frame. Her mother had six children – Tilly was the oldest – and had recently remarried and inherited another three mouths to feed. She couldn't afford to keep Tilly. She had assured the warden that the girl wasn't as frail as she looked, and more than old enough to be trained in service.

Hope had witnessed the mother leave, hugging the girl hard against her, whispering in a voice made harsh with pain that she must do as she was told, and turning away before Tilly could see the tears on her face. Miss Barlow had asked her to take the girl into the kitchen, where Cook gave her bread and butter and a cup of tea, and Hope explained to her about the house and how she would be helped towards a better life. Later, she had tucked Tilly into bed and gone to her own, and for the first time felt that sense of peace found in purpose that her mother had always talked about.

Now, she took Tilly's hand to cross a busy intersection, their breath pluming and mingling in the cold air. 'We're nearly there,' said Miss Barlow.

Inside the townhouse on Division Street, piano music filled the air. Someone was playing the gentle notes of a piece so familiar that her fingers twitched in response and a deep melancholy swept through her. She had sat with her mother, side by side on the cushion of the piano stool, and they had played this sonata together, that began so beautifully and so mournfully. She closed her eyes and saw her mother's slender fingers alongside her own moving over the ivory and ebony keys.

How long ago it seemed, now that she answered to a name that was not her own.

'Wake up, Hope.'

Miss Barlow indicated with a curt nod that they should follow the maid who had let them into the house. Hope trod over the rich carpeting in the wood-panelled hall, and down a darkened corridor of linseed and beeswax-scented polished planks. The music was a lamentation she could hardly bear, drowning her senses. She was relieved when the haunting notes faded as she entered the kitchen behind Tilly and Miss Barlow and clicked the door closed behind her. Shutting out the music that stirred the grief she tried so hard to hold at bay felt like a small victory.

The scene before her was chaotic. The cook, a round-faced woman whose doughy features were reddened by the heat of the room, was supervising another, younger woman who was using a dishcloth to pull a joint of meat from the range. 'One or two slices each with potatoes and peas and asparagus. The rest is for tomorrow,' she said, ignoring the newcomers. 'Go on, get the next one bunged in.'

The kitchen table and the countertops were invisible beneath boxes and trays of fruit and vegetables, pastries and cakes. The aroma of freshly baked bread mingled with the stronger, equally delicious, smell of cooked meat.

She was suddenly ravenous.

'Have a seat, Miss Barlow,' said the maid, 'if you can stand the heat in here.'

'We're here to see the housekeeper about Tilly here,' said the warden, 'but I'd like a word with Mrs Gunson too, if she isn't busy.'

Tilly had been staring about her, open-mouthed. Now she snapped to attention. 'I'm to help with the party tomorrow.'

The maid – she looked not much older than Tilly – smiled at her. 'Aye. I've made a bed up for thee in the scullery.' She turned to Miss Barlow. 'Mrs Bennett is due back any minute. I'll go and tell Mrs Gunson you're here.'

The cook rapped her knuckles on the table. 'Now you're here, lass, you can start by sorting these deliveries. I can't be doing with all this clutter.'

'Me?' said Tilly.

'Unless you've got summat better to do,' said the cook. 'You've come from that house to make yoursen useful, haven't you?'

Hope gave Tilly an encouraging nod.

When the maid returned, she invited Miss Barlow and her companion to find their own way to the parlour, which lay behind the second door on the left-hand side of the vestibule. She would follow with a pot of tea and the selection of pastries Mrs Gunson had requested.

The cook grumbled about having nothing left for the party if certain people continued to pick at the food. Tilly had her hands in a box, lifting out a bag of plums, and she didn't look up as they left the kitchen.

–

Hope complimented Mrs Gunson on her piano playing skills.

'The first movement is easy,' Mrs Gunson replied. 'Do you know it?'

She tried to ignore the desperate ache in the pit of her stomach. She was on dangerous ground here, skating over thin ice that would crack beneath her and send her hurtling down, to drown in her deception. She suddenly wanted only to return to the House of Help.

'No, I don't know it,' she said, and sighed, weary of the duplicity. However small this lie was it added to the discomfort of all the other deceptions she practised, sticking to her like a burr she could not brush away.

Mrs Gunson's voice was gentle. 'Do you play, I wonder?'

She shook her head minutely.

'It's only,' said Mrs Gunson, 'that you seem the sort of young lady who might be proficient. The sonata I was playing...' she paused as if waiting for her to supply the title of it, to name the composer, and, horrifyingly, she almost fell into the trap. 'Well,' said Mrs Gunson, 'it reminds me of a time my little boy was poorly and he lay wrapped up in blankets just where you sit, Miss Barlow, and I lulled him to sleep. It was a long time ago but it might have been only yesterday.' She smiled. 'Music can unlock memories we think are long-buried, and make them fresh again.'

'Give it a try, Hope,' said Miss Barlow. 'You never know.'

She rose obediently and sat at the piano, and gingerly depressed a key – G sharp – with one finger. The urge to spread both hands across the keys, to walk her fingers through the chords, find the melody, was overwhelming. She was acutely aware of being under observation, like some exotic animal in a menagerie, and wondered anew how she had ended up here. She ought to be seated at the piano at home, caressing those keys. Not these, not in a stranger's house, not with the threat of the workhouse hanging over her.

She shook her head and got up and returned to her seat next to Miss Barlow.

'There's nothing familiar there,' she said, and looked at the warden. Now, surely, Miss Barlow would finally speak of their reason for visiting. She was both wanting it over and done with and dreading the verdict.

'Never mind, my dear,' said Mrs Gunson. 'Miss Barlow, let me tell you about the idea the trustees have had for raising money for the house.'

She began to talk about a grand bazaar that was planned for the springtime, to be held in the grounds of Tylecote, which was the Master Cutler's residence at Ranmoor. A committee was being established to organise it. Mrs Gunson would chair this committee and keep the warden up to date with the particulars.

'It will be a large affair,' she said, 'but we have many months to prepare and plenty of willing ladies and their daughters. We're going to endeavour to pay off the debt with funds to spare. I wondered whether, perhaps, Hope could join our committee. I'm convinced she would be an invaluable member of the team.'

Hope, who had lowered her gaze to her clasped hands, looked up gratefully. It occurred to her that Mrs Gunson was deliberately steering the conversation in a direction that might help secure her position at the house.

'I should be very glad to join your committee,' she said, 'and do whatever I can to help with the bazaar.'

Miss Barlow blew air through her lips. 'That's all well and good, Mrs Gunson, but you know why I've brought Hope to you today and it's not to talk about piano playing or bazaars. Why didn't you tell me?'

Mrs Gunson smiled sympathetically at Hope. 'It was up to Hope to tell you, and she would have had to, sooner or later.'

'All this going on under my roof, and I'm the last to know,' said Miss Barlow.

Mrs Gunson moved to sit beside Hope, so she was hemmed in between the two women. 'For all we know, this is a respectably married young woman.'

'She wasn't wearing a wedding band when she turned up,' said Miss Barlow, 'although she might have been robbed. I remember the doctor thought she might have been wearing earrings, and had them ripped out.'

Sitting between them, she shivered, and pushed the memory away.

'You'd like to stay at the house,' said Mrs Gunson kindly.

She nodded, twisting her hands. Mrs Gunson put a hand over hers to still them.

'Certainly,' she said, 'I'm told you have a way with the other young ladies, and with the little girls too. You're a help, it seems?'

'Aye,' said Miss Barlow, 'she is, and more than she knows it. But we can't have a baby in the house, and that's that.'

She struggled to speak through a throat that was raw with suppressed tears. 'I'm sorry... I'm sorry to be a burden. I don't mean to be.'

Mrs Gunson squeezed her hands. 'You're not!'

'Maybe a little bit, eh?' said Mrs Barlow, nudging her arm.

She spluttered, surprised into laughter that eased some of the tension knotting up her insides, even if there was a slightly hysterical edge to it.

'All right,' said Miss Barlow, serious again. 'There is a role in the house that remains unfilled. I think Hope here could manage it. Lord knows I need the help.'

'You're thinking of the deputy warden's role,' said Mrs Gunson. 'Funds don't allow...'

'For a paid position. I know. Perhaps in return for room and board, and with the promise of a weekly wage in the future.' Miss Barlow paused. 'But as I've said we can't have babies in the house.'

'I agree that it might open the floodgates,' said Mrs Gunson. 'The house would not cope. In addition, and I do not wish to insult you, Hope, the taint of scandal might attach itself to the house. Donations are already thin on the ground.'

Miss Barlow nodded in agreement. 'People are quick to judge.'

These women were kind-hearted but she was alone, she knew that now. Where could she go? Not home. Her mind baulked at that. He was there, and if she revealed the truth he would fabricate a story and there was no doubt he'd be believed over a foolish young girl with a baby in her belly. She could hear him now. *She read too many of those penny dreadfuls and got herself into trouble with some rough sort, and is now pinning the crime on me. Desperation has driven her to this. Please, don't be too harsh on the poor girl.* He'd be magnanimous about it, offer his help to her distraught parents. *My fiancée and I will take her to live with us, we'll even adopt the child and your daughter can return to her old life once the fuss has died down.* She'd be forever listening for his tread on the stairs, the creak of the hinges of her bedroom door. Or perhaps he'd be fearful the child might resemble him. He'd kill her before the baby could be born.

She suppressed a shudder, her mind a whirlpool of horror, and was dimly aware of Mrs Gunson putting a shawl around her shoulders, of the two women murmuring over her head. She would never see her mother again. It was as if she was coming to this realisation for the first time, and her breath came in quick gasps.

'Hope,' said Mrs Gunson.

Miss Barlow repeated it. 'Hope!'

She remembered this was her name and looked up fearfully.

'Listen,' said Miss Barlow. 'We won't abandon you, all right? The police are sharing your information and I'm sure your people will come for you in no time, or you'll get your memory back. It's only a matter of time, the doctor said.'

Mrs Gunson took over. 'Until such a time, you can remain at the house and take up a role as Miss Barlow's deputy, if you're agreeable to that. It's unpaid, but you will be safe and sound with us. Such a worthy employment can only improve your state of mind. I shall clear it with the trustees.'

She stared at the rug through tear-filled eyes, the bright colours of fern and poppy bleeding into each other, not daring to believe her ears, but knowing that there was more to come. She pressed her hands against her belly.

'And when the time is right,' said Miss Barlow, 'you leave the house, or remain, and be made very welcome as a permanent member of staff, but give the baby up.'

She whispered the words. 'An orphanage?'

Mrs Gunson spoke hurriedly. 'No, no. Not an orphanage, of course not. A family. A respectable couple who will give your child the best start in life, far better than being raised in a halfway house. And the child will have a father.'

This was the closest Mrs Gunson would come to pointing out that, if she kept the baby, the label of bastard would taint its life.

Miss Barlow nodded her agreement. 'It's not right, keeping a child in the house. All we know about our inmates is what they tell us, unless they have a champion. We knew nowt at all about you.' She looked away as if she was talking to herself. 'Still don't, come to that.'

A respectable family. Worthy employment. The phrases swam in her head.

'If you'll forgive me for keeping this from you, from both of you,' said Mrs Gunson, 'but I've already discussed your circumstances with friends of mine, a lovely couple who have never been able to have children of their own. They raised their nephew after his mother abandoned him. Now he is grown and gone and they miss him dreadfully.'

'And they'll take on a stranger's child?' said Miss Barlow. 'Just like that?'

'Why not? I can vouch for them. I didn't want to say anything until I was certain they might help, and it turns out they would be thrilled to raise a child from infancy.' Mrs Gunson took Hope's cold hand in hers. 'Is this something you'd countenance, Hope?'

She looked around the room, at the lush green fern in the corner, the rosewood piano, the richly textured rug under her feet, and the swag of the velvet curtains. She could be in the smaller parlour of her parents' house. Perhaps that was where she was, curled up in an armchair, fast asleep. Mrs Gunson's parlour was the dream. She could not be sitting here with a life inside her, talking about donating a baby to a barren couple. This was not her life. It could not be.

'Are they… are they kind people?' she said.

'The kindest,' said Mrs Gunson. She turned to Miss Barlow. 'I offer this as a potential solution, if Hope does not regain her memory and nobody comes forward to claim her by the time she has the baby.'

Miss Barlow nodded, tight-lipped. 'Hope is my responsibility now. We need to do right by her, and right by the bairn she's carrying.'

Chapter 9

On the winter solstice, her father would have his groundsman pin evergreen boughs to the front door and a fir brought inside to stand in the corner of the parlour, or 'wither' as he preferred to describe it. Her parents would bicker good-naturedly, her father wondering why a healthy tree had to be uprooted only for it to die indoors, shedding needles all over the carpet. Her mother would remind him that he wouldn't be the one clearing them up, or lifting a finger to help decorate the tree, and he would tell the story of his early days as a magistrate when a man came before him for putting a harness around his wife's neck and trying to sell her at the Saturday market, for being too sharp with her tongue.

Hope had felt the onset of a headache when the boughs of a fir were spread in the hallway of the House of Help and the residents tasked with decorating it, the younger girls hopping up and down in excitement when the Christmas box came out. Jenkins had prowled around the large black pot the tree stood in, raising his black velvet nose to sniff suspiciously at the lower branches. 'It's only a matter of time before he attempts to climb it,' Anneliese exclaimed cheerfully.

Mrs Gunson's new maid of all work, Tilly, returned for a visit, as Miss Barlow had promised she might. She seemed older, having grown in confidence, and gossiped away about all the fine ladies and gentlemen who had attended the Gunsons' Christmas party. The work was hard – Tilly was up at six to light the fires and was the last allowed to bed, as it was her task to ensure all the lamps had been snuffed out and the grates dampened – but the Gunsons were generous employers and Tilly was given both Saturday *and* Sunday afternoons off.

In all the clamour, nobody noticed Hope slip away but it wasn't long before Amelia found her curled under the covers. The mattress sank as Amelia sat on it.

'Have you decided yet? What you're going to do? Hetty says you'll probably give the baby away to this couple in the town.'

She feigned sleep.

Amelia shook her shoulder. 'Stop pretending you're kippin' or I'll get under these covers and tickle you to death.'

'I hate being tickled,' she mumbled.

'Get up then.'

Hope sighed and sat up, picking at her braid with fingers that were clumsy with fatigue. 'Is it the letter?'

Amelia threw up her hands. 'Aye, of course it's the letter. Hetty's busy with that tree. We'll have an hour or more to ourselves, I reckon.'

She rubbed her eyes. 'I really was falling asleep. I have a headache.'

'Liggin' about in bed and feeling sorry for yoursen won't do you any good.'

She conceded Amelia was probably right about that.

'Will you re-braid my hair first?'

'Quick, then.' Amelia got up to find a hairbrush, plonked herself back down and began to make long sweeping strokes through Hope's hair. 'This is easy. Yours isn't half as thick as mine, and it's a lovely shade. I always wished I had blonde hair.'

'No, it's the colour of straw,' said Hope. 'I'd rather have your beautiful dark hair.'

'Nah, you wouldn't!' Amelia seemed pleased, nonetheless, and hummed a tune as she plaited. 'Done.'

Amelia came around the bed to face her and fished about in the pocket of her apron. There was triumph in her smile as she lined up on the counterpane the items she'd taken from the warden's desk – a gummed envelope, blank where the address would be printed but with a penny stamp already in the top right-hand corner, pen, wiper and inkpot, a piece of blotting paper and several sheets of white paper.

'In case you make a mistake,' she said. She looked uncertainly at the paper. 'Do you think this is all right? A bit plain? Compared to this?'

She extracted from her bodice the folded sheet of blue paper Linus Harmon had scribbled his note on. She opened it up – it was looking decidedly dog-eared – and pointed at the sprig of flowers drawn in the top corner.

Vulgar, her father would say. Any colour other than white with a black letterhead is vulgar and mawkish.

'I think plain white paper is quite elegant,' she said. 'Are you posting it today?'

'Aye, when we go for a wander after tea.' She fanned her face with the coloured notepaper. 'There's a pillar box at the bottom of the square. You can stand look-out. Come on, we have to do this now.'

'I can't very well write it on the bed, Amelia. I need a hard surface to rest on. Why don't we go up to the classroom?'

'Because,' Amelia said, 'we'd have to get past a stair-case full of women decorating for Christmas, and end up pinning streamers and doing goodness knows what else. I've waited so long for you to write this letter!'

Hope laughed. 'Have you a hard cover book, then, that I can rest on?'

Amelia cast about her then sprinted to the bureau that held the washing bowl, jug and the clean stack of flannels for the morning and moved them onto the floorboards. 'This'll do,' she said.

'That's too tall for a chair.'

'Stand, then!'

She laughed. 'All right, I will. You're so agitated.'

Amelia's eyes were sparkling with excitement but there was trepidation in her expression too. 'I have to get this right,' she said. 'It's important.'

She touched Amelia's arm. 'Because there's a lot at stake.'

'Aye.'

She took up the pen, leaned her elbow on the bureau, and raised her eyebrows. 'What should I write?'

'I don't know,' wailed Amelia. 'I've been trying and trying to think.'

Hope furrowed her brow. 'Let me see.' She inscribed *Dear Mr Harmon* at the top of the page. 'My goodness, this is nerve-wracking.'

'Now you see why I'm in this state,' said Amelia.

She bent over the paper, pen poised. 'It should be written as if he is standing here before us, before you. What would you say to him?' She faced Amelia and straightened her back. 'I'm Linus Harmon.'

Amelia cocked her head and gave her an appraising look. 'I'd say you're being as bold as brass, but you're so handsome you can get away with it. I accept your invitation. Wait. Should the paper be perfumed?'

'Do you have any?'

'No.'

'Does Miss Barlow wear scent?'

Amelia scoffed. 'Hetty?'

'Well, unless you want to turn the house upside down in search of a bottle of perfume I'd say there's your answer.'

'You sound like my sister.'

'I'm going to take that as a compliment,' said Hope. She continued to write. 'Dear Mr Harmon. Your note was as thrilling as it was surprising to receive. Yes?'

Amelia wrinkled her nose. 'Is that a bit much?'

'Are you, or are you not, in a state of delight and excitement?'

Amelia put her hand over her mouth and nodded.

'Then don't play the coquette.' She dipped the pen and continued writing. 'I am pleased to accept your invitation and, before we meet, I look forward to receiving a lengthier letter than time allowed during your visit.'

Amelia was nodding her head. 'Yes, that's all right.'

'It's only that you should correspond once or twice before you see each other again,' she said.

Amelia snorted. 'Maybe in the world you live in.'

Lived in. Hope wrote the final line and read it aloud. 'I pray you have not altered your mind since then.' She glanced at Amelia. 'This gives him the opportunity to pay you boundless compliments. With great respect and all good wishes, Miss Amelia Barlow.' She blotted the sheet and handed it to Amelia. 'There you are.'

Amelia scanned the letter, placed it on the bureau and embraced her.

'You are now my sister,' she said, 'and there should be no secrets between us.'

After a slight hesitation, she returned the embrace.

Hope was crossing the hall a few days later when the door knocker clacked, once, twice, thrice. It was a common enough sound, in this house, but she paused by the stair bannister, cupping the smooth round top of the newel post in her palm. Only two nights before, she had dreamed that she opened this door to her father, and had fallen sobbing into his arms. He had patted her back and told her the drive up had been horrendous, which made her laugh and cry even harder. Her face had been wet with tears when she woke.

She'd had nightmares too, recurring nightmares about her cousin returning, rampaging through the house, shouting for her – *Come to me! I'll find you!* – or screaming that he was going to kill her, or calling in a sing-song voice – *Where are you, my sweet girl* – as if they were playing a game of hide and seek. She hurtled through the house, always just out of reach of his grasping hands. She always ended up, panting and terrified, in the coal cellar, where she pressed herself against the wall, trying to remain as silent as the spiders spinning their thick webs that drooped from the ceiling and caught in her hair. She was safe.

Always before she woke, she felt his hot breath tickle her cheek.

In the cold light of day, she knew there was no reason for her cousin to return, that it made no sense at all for him to do so. He must know he had frightened her sufficiently to save his skin.

'Is anybody going to get that?' The call came from the kitchen. It was Cook. 'Or do I have to do every sodding thing around here?'

Hope let go of the bannister and smiled. She was safe here and her nightmares could not tell her otherwise. 'I'll get it!'

But Amelia had already emerged from Miss Barlow's quarters. 'I've got it,' she said, and opened the door.

Hope's stomach plunged as if the ground had dropped away from beneath her feet. A cry of alarm filled her throat, choking her. She could not move, could not draw in nor release a breath. She was looking down a tunnel towards a familiar face, a hateful leer, that grew and grew until it filled her vision. It was her cousin, his sneer making his face the ugliest thing she had ever seen. The cry that was trapped in her throat was finally released as a scream as he stepped over the threshold and came towards her.

She knew this was a dream – a different version of her nightmare. She was taking an afternoon nap. In a moment she would wake and all would be well. *Wake up!*

She staggered backwards and fell against the bannister – all too solid, all too real – landing in a heap on the stairs, a high-pitched whine in her ears. It seemed futile to lift her head, to do anything at all. She was overcome with the certainty that she was about to die. She could hear Amelia's voice, raised in alarm, but she couldn't make out the words. Now his voice, reasonable in tone. He would tell Amelia that he was her husband and she a disgraced wife, escaped from a lunatic asylum, and he would drag her from the house and that would be the end of her. It was only what she had been waiting for, all these long weeks. She felt the gentle touch of a hand on her hair. She had wanted to wake. Now she willed sleep to take her. She would not open her eyes, would not look on him again. A shudder ran through her body. She curled her fingers around the spindle on the bottom stair, and held on tightly. He wouldn't have her.

A breath on her face. Her eyes snapped open. Amelia's concerned face was inches from hers.

'Hope?'

'Don't believe a word he says,' she whispered. She retightened her grip on the bannister. 'Don't let him take me.'

But Amelia was looking away, speaking to somebody else. To him. 'I think she fainted or had a fit, some sort of conniption. Can you carry her?'

His quiet voice. 'I can certainly try.'

She was dimly aware of an arm sliding under her thighs, another across her back, and she was raised up. She marvelled, in a distant way, at how easily the spindle of the bannister slipped from her grasp. It was of no consequence. There was no point fighting. She had tried her best and it had all been for nought and she was so very weary. Her head lolled against her cousin's shoulder, the rough fabric of his greatcoat damp against her skin, a button pressing into her cheek, the smell of outdoors, of smoke and rain, the hopelessness of it all.

Then, mercifully, everything went away.

She came to on her bed, her head sunk in the pillow. It seemed hours must have passed but Amelia, sitting on the edge of the mattress, assured her it had been a few minutes only.

'Poor Mr Deveraux,' she said. 'I think he's done his back in carting you about. You're no lightweight, you know.'

'Mr...'

'You know. The handsome grandson. Angus. You've met the lad. You should see the Christmas treats and tranklements he brought in his fancy little wicker basket.'

She raised herself up into a sitting position and glanced at the door, gasping when she saw it stood ajar. 'Is he here? Is he somewhere in the house?'

'He's waiting in the parlour. He won't leave until he's certain you're all right. I reckon he's soft on thee.'

Hope rubbed her forehead. 'Are you talking about Angus Deveraux?'

'Aye. Who else would I be talking about?'

'My... my cousin...'

'Your *cousin?*'

She grasped Amelia's hand. 'He brought me here. He knows I'm here.' She collapsed back onto her pillow.

'Eh?' said Amelia. She leaned forward, her eyes eager. 'Do you remember summat? Was it your cousin left you here?' Now her eyes narrowed. 'Why would he do that?'

'I can't...' She put her hand over her mouth, the horror of what she had revealed creeping over her, paralysing her limbs.

'Hope, have you got your memory back?' Amelia's voice shook with excitement. 'Tell me what you remember, quick-sharp. In case you forget it again.' She squeezed Hope's hand. 'Or should I run and fetch Hetty?'

'No! Don't bother Miss Barlow. It doesn't mean anything.' She tried to smile. She knew it would look a weak and pathetic attempt. 'I was dreaming and got confused. I don't remember a man. I dreamt him up.'

'You mentioned a cousin,' said Amelia.

'Did I?' Somehow, she managed to laugh. 'I'm sorry if I frightened you. It was nonsense talk.'

Amelia frowned, then leaned back, extracting her hand from Hope's. 'You can say that again, love. I'll go and tell our Mr Deveraux that you're awake, but have gone insane.'

'I think just telling him I'm awake would do.'

Amelia got to her feet. 'And then I will go and fetch Hetty and we'll get the doctor to you.'

'No!' She grasped Amelia's wrist. 'I don't need the doctor and please don't tell Miss Barlow anything about this, or about my silly ramblings. I'm really as right as rain. I promise I am.'

Amelia looked away.

'Please. Amelia. Can we just forget this happened?'

Amelia gently detached herself and stepped back. She spoke in a whisper. 'You never lost your memory at all, did you?'

Hope covered her face with her hands. 'You have no idea how much I wish I had.'

She felt the mattress give as Amelia sat on the edge of it.

'Who are you? Where have you come from?'

Her words echoed the warden's on the terrible night she had arrived at the house. She dropped her hands and looked into the other woman's large brown eyes. Could she be trusted? She had no choice in the matter. 'I will tell you. I'll tell you everything. I'll tell you tonight, if you can promise to keep my secret. Can you promise?'

'Aye,' said Amelia. 'I promise.'

–

They crept out of the dorm with their blankets bundled in their arms, feeling their way in the pitch dark towards the parlour. Once inside, and with the door closed behind them, Amelia lit a lamp and put it on the floor behind an armchair, giving them just enough light to see each other's faces. They curled up together in the armchair, nibbling at gingerbread stars dusted with icing sugar.

'These are wonderful,' said Hope.

'The last few,' said Amelia. 'He brought satsumas too, for the tree. They won't last two minutes either, not in this house. And candles in fancy little holders but Hetty has flat refused to put those on the tree. She's worried the house will burn down.'

'What did he say about... about what happened?'

'Not much,' said Amelia. 'He's a man. He probably thinks all women faint away at the drop of a hat. You should have seen it when he swept you into his arms. Bet you wanted him to revive you with a kiss, eh?'

'Oh, Amelia!'

'Keep your voice down. My sister's only across the hall.' Amelia's eyes glittered in the dark. 'So, then.'

She wondered how she should start, and where.

'Start at the beginning.' It was as if Amelia had read her mind.

'I must extract your solemn promise not to tell. Not Miss Barlow, not anyone. Ever.'

'You're not after a blood pact, are you?' Amelia extracted a hand from the folds of her blanket – it was pale, ghostly and insubstantial in the darkness of the room – and placed it over her heart. 'I won't tell.'

'If I'm to start at the beginning,' she cleared her throat, 'I'll start with my mother's sister. My aunt had been a widow for a year when she married a man recently divorced from his wife.'

'Divorced!'

'Yes, it was quite the scandal. Anyway, this man has a son, who I was encouraged to call cousin. My mother explained that we must make him feel like one of the family, what with his mother running off to Europe.'

Amelia gasped. 'She ran off to *Europe*?'

Hope giggled. 'To Paris.'

'No!'

'To live with an impoverished artist.'

'Are you making this up?'

'Only the last part.'

'So, her son. This is the cousin you mistook poor Angus Deveraux for.'

Hope laid her head on Amelia's shoulder.

'Yes. My aunt and her new husband went travelling. My new cousin came to stay.'

'What's the name of this so-called cousin?'

She shivered and clutched her blanket tightly against her chin. 'What does it matter? I can't say his name. I won't utter it, ever.'

'All right.'

She would never admit this to Amelia, or to anybody, but she had found her new cousin attractive, at first, and good company. They went riding together, and ice skating, played chess and backgammon, and gossiped about their parents and the friends of their parents.

'He's not much older than me,' she said, 'but he seemed so much more sophisticated. He'd been given a high-up position in his father's bank and was sensitive to claims of nepotism.'

'What's nepotism?'

'Where someone influential, like his father, will give jobs to friends or relatives, like my cousin. So, he was determined to prove himself worthy of the role he'd been given. Then he got engaged to the daughter of a papermill owner.'

She paused. She had been dismayed, at first, by this news because she had harboured romantic ideas about him. She was anxious, too, about how his engagement would affect their friendship. How naïve she had been.

'Then what happened?' said Amelia.

'I think he was a little in awe of this girl. He confided in me that he was worried he wouldn't measure up. She'd come from a wealthy, respectable family and his mother had run away.' Hope sighed. 'I'm such a fool.'

'No, you're not.' Amelia stroked her hair. 'You're the cleverest person I know, Hope.'

'That's kind, but untrue. Anyway, he said I was the only one he could talk to about it. I said flattering things, to boost his confidence.' She was glad Amelia could not see her cheeks blush. 'He told me about brothels he'd visited.'

'Brothels! And he told you all this?'

'Yes. He said the women there were paid to say nice things to him. He trusted me to be truthful because I was pure. That's what he told me.'

'Ugh,' said Amelia.

'He wanted to kiss me, to kiss me properly, you understand? I told him no. He was engaged. I thought I was being noble.'

She did not tell Amelia that he had crept into her bedroom one night, not long after this conversation, and woken her with rough kisses on her mouth. He had pinned her arms by her sides and had bitten and sucked at her neck. She had been frozen by fear, nauseated by the tickle of his moustache on her skin, crushed by the weight of his body. A door had slammed somewhere in the house and he'd released her and stumbled out. She did not sleep for the rest of the night.

The following morning, the maid who came in to wake her asked her how she was feeling. When she looked in her mirror, there were purple blotches on her neck. She put on the highest-necked blouse she could find. When she confronted him, he had laughed it off, had blamed the bottle of whisky he'd consumed, had chastised *her* for being so desirable. He was contrite when she told him of the bruises on her neck and on her arms and swore he would never do anything like that again.

Weeks passed without event, but she was wary now, and their friendship began to sour.

'After I rejected his advances, he became cruel,' she said. 'He would look for opportunities to put me down. If I won a board game he would, in front of everyone, accuse me of cheating. He was always there.' She gulped. 'I couldn't get away from him. I began to hate him as much as he appeared to hate me.'

One evening, a woman walking home alone was attacked. Her parents discussed the incident over dinner, in a conversation intended as a warning to her. 'She was reckless,' her father said, 'and should not have put herself in that position. I see this sort of thing all the time. Men are like beasts who cannot help themselves. A woman's honour is a frail thing and it is her duty to protect it at all costs.'

The smile on her cousin's face during this lecture had chilled her to the bone.

'My father was – is – very enamoured of him,' she told Amelia. 'In his eyes, my cousin can do no wrong. At the end of the summer, he asked me to accept his apologies for the way he had been treating me. He said he had been under a lot of stress and oughtn't to have taken it out on me. He wanted to make amends.' She swallowed. 'He asked me if I would join him and his fiancée at a picnic site we often went to. It's on the edge of my parent's estate.'

She had politely declined. He'd pleaded with her, telling her he was distressed by their estrangement, and ashamed of himself for creating the distance between them. Of course, there was no picnic, no fiancée. He intercepted her as she took their regular short cut through a fallow field.

'It was a trap,' she told Amelia.

'What happened?'

'What do you think?' She had spoken more harshly than she intended. She rubbed at her forehead as if she could erase the memory. 'The thing that might have happened when he came into my bedroom if a door hadn't slammed. Afterwards, he wouldn't let me go. He put his hand around my throat.' She shuddered. 'He told me nobody would believe my story. He said I'd be accused of making up fantasies to destroy his engagement, because I was secretly in love with him.'

'No!' said Amelia.

'Yes. My earlier devotion to him had been apparent. He said even if I was believed, I'd be soiled goods. No man of repute would have me.' She laughed hollowly. 'It was no secret I'd held him in high esteem when he first came into our lives. I should have told my mother the night he came into my bedroom. I should have spoken out.'

'But you didn't,' said Amelia gently, 'and you didn't say anything about... about what happened in the field.'

'No. I tried to forget it. And he became distant after that. He moved into rented chambers near his place of work. We saw very little of him. I was relieved, for a short while.'

'You were pregnant.'

'Yes. My courses stopped. I was certain of it too, as I always suffer greatly from the pains. I panicked.'

'What did you do?'

She sighed. 'This is exhausting.'

'I know it is, love, but you can't stop there.'

'I didn't know what to do. In the end, I went to his office. I sat across the desk from him as if I was just another customer at the bank.'

'Oh, Hope.'

'He wouldn't look at me. He said he wouldn't break off his engagement to marry me – as if that was what I wanted! He told me to sort out my own mess and to never come to his place of work again.'

'What did you do?'

'Short of making a scene, there was nothing I could do. I left.'

She had gone home and shut herself into the library, where she took a book down blindly and sat by the window. Her father had popped his head in and asked her what she was reading. She'd held the book up so he could see the spine. To this day, she couldn't name the title but he must have approved of it for he smiled and disappeared again. There were novels she was not permitted to read. When her mother brought home the volumes of Elizabeth Gaskell's novel *Ruth*, he had thrown them on the fire. It was one of the few times she'd seen him speak angrily to her mother. He claimed the book glamorised illegitimacy, and painted women who had children out of wedlock as victims, not the loose fools or calculating harlots they were.

Which was she?

'You didn't tell your mother or father,' said Amelia.

'No.'

'How did you end up here?'

'He still had his key,' she said. 'He came for me that night. That very night.'

She had been sitting at her dressing table, staring into space, unable to summon the strength even to brush her hair, when the lamp was snuffed out and a hand clamped over her mouth. She knew immediately. She would never forget the overwhelming scent of the cologne he wore.

'He had a pistol,' she said. 'He told me I had to go with him. I was convinced he was going to kill me.'

'To get you out of the way.'

'Yes.'

Amelia laughed shakily. 'This is like something out of a penny dreadful. You're making it up.'

'I wish I was. Do you want to hear the rest?'

'I don't know. You're frightening me.'

Another hollow laugh forced its way out of her throat. 'Imagine how I felt.'

He had driven her to a house where a woman wearing a shawl over a long, loose shift was waiting on the pavement. She carried no light. Her cousin had cursed when he jumped down from the carriage and stumbled in the dark. He had dragged her out, one hand squeezing her bicep and the other clamped on the back of her neck, and pushed her past the woman and into the house. Once the door was closed behind them, her despair deepened when she saw there was no sympathy in the woman's eyes. Her painted mouth curved downward and she muttered about having only just got out of the nick and she'd better not land back in it.

'I didn't know what the nick was,' she said.

'It's prison,' said Amelia.

'Yes, I know that now. He told her to stop wasting her breath and help him.'

She had been begging, trying to appeal to each of them in turn, to let her go. They had ignored her pleas. The two of them had manhandled her into a shabby room dominated by a large four-poster bed. There were items of clothing scattered on the floor and flung over chairs. Empty bottles and dirty plates were piled on a card table. She had gasped when she saw a knife, a slender blade with a mother-of-pearl handle, among the detritus on a dressing table. He'd shoved her onto the bed.

'I didn't know what was happening. This woman gave him a garment, the rough thing I was brought here wearing. She asked him about payment and he...' she stopped, took a deep breath, and blew the air out slowly. 'He gave her my earrings.'

He had leaned down and ripped them away, dropping them into the woman's open palm. He had gripped her by the throat and ordered her to take off her dress and all her underclothes and put on the garment the woman had supplied.

'He said I had five minutes or woe betide me. He went out with the woman and locked the door.'

'What did you do?'

'What could I do? I did as I was told.'

She would never tell anyone how she had debased herself when he returned. She had begged him to take her home, sworn on her mother's life that she would never reveal what had happened, never betray him. She had flung herself at him and he had caught her wrists and laughed in her face. The woman ignored her completely

– she was holding her silk dress against her body, stroking the material. 'That belongs to me,' she had cried and he had lashed out.

'The next thing I remember was waking up on the floor of his carriage, listening to the thundering of his horses' hooves,' she said. 'And here I am.'

Telling her story had left her curiously empty. It was as if it had happened to somebody else.

Amelia's face was a white disc in the gloom.

'Oh, Hope,' she said. 'Oh, Hope.'

'Oh indeed.'

'What will you do about the baby?'

'I'll give it up for adoption. It's what Mrs Gunson and Miss Barlow want.'

Amelia spoke so softly that she barely registered the words. 'But what do you want?'

'I don't know.' It was the truth. 'I don't know what I want.' Having Amelia stroke her hair was comforting at the same time as it was a painful reminder of what she'd lost. 'I want my mother.'

'Me too,' whispered Amelia.

A whistle blew, somewhere, and a bird set up a fretful cawing that was answered by another.

'It's nearly morning,' said Amelia. She lifted Hope's head away from her shoulder, stood up and stretched, and held out a hand for Hope to take.

The two women stood in the middle of the room. Hope spread her arms wide. 'So now you know. That's it. That's everything.'

Amelia embraced her. She was suddenly so weary she felt she could sleep for a week.

'That's not everything, though, is it?' Amelia said. She disengaged herself from their embrace and stood back and stuck out her hand. 'Pleased to meet you. I'm Amelia Barlow.'

She shook the offered hand and released a tremulous breath.

'My name is Emma Hyde. I'd be pleased if you would call me Hope.'

PART TWO

Spring 1888

Chapter 10

Hetty set down her pen and pinched the bridge of her nose between thumb and index finger.

'Yes, come in. What is it?'

Hope stepped into the room, her nightgown stretched over the large dome of her belly. Her plump feet were bare, her rounded cheeks rosy and the hair Hetty recalled had been matted and limp when she arrived at the house had thickened, shining like gold in the light reflected from the wall sconce.

She seemed to have accepted her new life. The police officer who had interviewed her all those months ago had returned to visit twice, on both occasions to report that he had no news. On his second visit, he'd had the good grace to seem thoroughly embarrassed by the lack of progress and the house hadn't seen hide nor hair of him since.

Hope had been examined by several doctors who showed an interest in her amnesia. One of these gentlemen had suggested that her apparent sanguinity about giving up the child she was carrying might indicate more than memory loss. He thought that perhaps the part of the brain that dealt in emotional regulation had been damaged too.

Hetty preferred to believe the evidence of her own eyes and ears. Hope was wonderfully intuitive with the inmates of the house, especially the younger girls. She knew when they needed support and when they needed to be left alone. It was Hope the inmates sought out when they were fearful or needed advice, whatever age they were.

As for her pregnancy, Hope said she wanted to do what was best for all concerned, though Hetty knew what a wrench giving up her child would be, come the hour.

Now, an anxious frown twisted Hope's brow. 'I'm sorry to disturb you. Would you come and look at Miss Millthorpe?'

'Now? At this hour?'

'She came in to wake me. She's sick, and she's worried she has smallpox.'

'Smallpox?' The word sent a shiver down her spine. She pushed back her chair. 'Not in my house.'

Hetty had been dreading this day since the epidemic began. She had issued a directive that anyone arriving on the doorstep who showed signs of the disease should be sent straight to the quarantine hospital. Under no circumstances should they be allowed over the threshold.

'Is she still up there?'

'I put her in the parlour to keep her away from the others.'

'Good.'

She found the girl's page in the ledger and quickly scanned it.

Jane Millthorpe, a strapping lass of nineteen, had come off a farm looking for work. She hadn't a penny to her name and was given a bed while she searched for a job and lodgings. She'd been at the house for six days. A pleasant girl, her situation was uncomplicated, and Hetty now cursed herself for her complacency in believing there would be no drama around this one.

She'd been given a bed in a room on the second floor of the house, across from the classroom. There were four other women sharing the same space. Hetty had no idea how smallpox was transmitted but the fact that two isolation hospitals had been hurriedly built in the town over the past year did not bode well for anybody who had come into contact with Jane Millthorpe.

'She's babbling,' said Hope, following her along the hall towards the parlour. 'She says the tramp brought it in with him and this is the thanks she gets for helping him. I felt her forehead. She's hot.'

'Did you wash your hands afterwards?' said Hetty sharply. 'Go and scrub them now.'

A couple of days ago, Jane had taken pity on a homeless creature she had found huddled on the back doorstep of the house during a thunderstorm. She had brought him inside, given him a mug of tea and let him sit by the kitchen range until the worst of the storm had passed. He hadn't said much – Hetty thought he was simple – but she recalled he'd been shivering violently. She'd been glad to see the back of the filthy creature and afterwards had reminded Jane the house was open to girls and women in need, not men, and that went for tramps off the street too.

The light was dim in the parlour, but the glow from a small table lamp revealed a hunched shape on the edge of the chaise longue. The sour smell of vomit reached Hetty's nostrils. She approached the girl, who she could now see had her arms wrapped tightly around her middle.

'Miss Millthorpe,' she said, stopping a couple of feet away and lifting her lamp to shine as much light as possible onto the girl's face. Her eyes were bright spots in a mottled mask, a dense rash that covered her cheeks, forehead and chin, and extended down her neck and onto the part of her collarbone that was visible above the ties of her nightgown. The garment clung wetly to her skin. Hetty had never witnessed an active case of smallpox before. She'd only seen the pockmarks and deeper disfigurations left behind on the faces of those who survived the disease.

She shivered. Survivors were sometimes left blinded.

The girl looked up at Hetty and wiped spittle from the corner of her mouth with a trembling hand. 'I know about that pox hospital. You can't send me there. I'll never come out.'

'You need to be looked after in the best place for it,' said Hetty gently. *You need to be out of my house.*

She glanced over her shoulder when Hope entered the room. She was rubbing her belly protectively.

'Is it smallpox?' said Hope.

'I've no idea, love. I think it might be.'

'But can't you tell? Weren't you a nurse?' Hope's tone was sharp. She was afraid.

Not half as afraid as I am, and not just about the pox. Amelia was clamouring to visit their aunt, telling Hetty she needed to retrieve certain items left behind in their hasty departure – a locket, a photograph of their mother, a tapestry she had made. She wanted to breathe fresh air again, to escape from the stinking, pox-ridden town for a few days. What reason could Hetty give to deny her? She could not tell Amelia the truth, that she was terrified her aunt would, out of sheer malice, reveal her deepest secret. *Out of sight, out of mind.* Hetty was counting on that adage.

Hope's voice wrenched her back to the task at hand. 'You must have cared for patients with smallpox.'

'Aye,' Hetty said shortly. 'It's the pox. Go and wake Clara. Tell her to strip Miss Millthorpe's bed and bring me a clean sheet.' She took a step back as Jane moaned and leaned further forward, her mouth hanging open. 'Bring the bucket. If you can't find it, ask Clara.' The bucket was always going missing. 'And bring her pillow. She might as well have it. We'll get the doctor to her first thing. Go on now.'

Hope hurried out of the room, closing the door behind her. Hetty watched the girl cover her mouth with her hand and retch into it. She sighed again. This was going to be a long night.

–

All the talk around the breakfast table the next morning was of Jane Millthorpe and how weak she had been when she'd been carted off to hospital, barely able to walk. Hope didn't join in the chatter, or eat any breakfast, Hetty noted. The night before, Clara had brought in the items Hetty had requested and muttered darkly about the speckled monster and various herbal potions that kept it at bay. Hope had looked stricken and Hetty had told Clara to focus on the task at hand and stop talking nonsense.

She rose from her small table in the corner of the kitchen, reminded those who had been enrolled in the training house of the time, and walked through the house to the parlour. The rug had already been lifted. Doused in bicarbonate of soda, it was swinging from the clothes line in the backyard, ready to be beaten.

Clara was on her knees, a bowl full of soapy water on the floorboards beside her, scrubbing the chaise longue with a fat-bristled brush.

'Morning,' said Hetty.

'Morning, ma'am.'

She walked to the window and looked out into the square. It was bathed in sunshine and those going about their business had a lightness in their step. Hetty watched a young couple stride past the glass and china shop, arm in arm, chatting animatedly to each other. The posters obscuring the windows of the printing office at the bottom of the square were bleached white flags in the sun's glare. A lad stepped out from the awning of the butcher's shop and turned his face to the sky. The butcher followed, a cleaver in his hand, and called the boy inside, but then remained on the pavement for another moment and took a deep breath of the morning air.

She pushed up the sash as far as it would go and leaned out. A cool breeze caressed her cheeks and carried to her nostrils the scent of the armfuls of spring flowers being sold in the square, mingling with the ever-present smell of coalsmoke. She sneezed, and sneezed again.

'Bless you,' muttered Clara.

She spoke without turning. 'When you've finished there, you should open all the windows in the house. Air it out.'

'Amelia's already told me.'

The landlord of the Q in the Corner, which was a few doors down, tucked into the closed corner of the square, emerged onto the cobbles, hauling another man by the arm. 'Next time tha passes out drunk, Albie, I'll not be leaving thee to sleep it off. Tha'll be slung out for the thieves and foxes.'

The man staggered and laughed. 'I've more to fear from the wife.'

'Aye, she'll have tha guts for garters, that's for sure. Get home now.'

The man staggered past her window. He touched his cap when he saw Hetty watching him, an act that sent him spinning. She smiled and shook her head, then turned reluctantly from the view of the square. She had forgotten something.

Only those residents with jobs to do at the house remained in the kitchen, four women and one young girl, along with Hope and Amelia who were deep in conversation.

'Hope,' said Hetty, 'would you mind delivering a message to Mr Wallace? He has an office on Norfolk Street. It's not far.'

'I'll go with her,' said Amelia. She made a show of holding her nose. 'I could use a rest from this plague-ridden house.'

'Amelia!' Hetty's admonishment was drowned out by cries of dismay from the others. Hope looked as though she might burst into tears. 'Yes, go, go with Hope. Wait.'

She took hold of Amelia's wrist and examined her face.

'What's up?' said Amelia.

'Nothing.' She relinquished her grip. The girl's complexion was clear, no tell-tale rash, no sheen of sweat on her brow. 'I'll write a note for you to give to Mr Wallace.'

She looked around the room. 'If any of you begin to feel unwell, you're to tell me straightaway. Do you understand?'

They all nodded solemnly.

'What are the symptoms?' said Hope.

'It doesn't matter what they are,' said Hetty. 'Come to find me if you feel unwell in any way whatsoever.'

As it turned out, Mr Wallace, after reading the note, discovered he hadn't time to visit the house. Instead, would Miss Barlow be free to come to his office at three o'clock that afternoon? The treasurer had an appointment with a third party whom he was sure she would like to meet.

'Is that all he said?' Hetty adjusted her bonnet in the mirror, a suspicion growing in her mind about who that *third party* might be.

'Aye, that's it,' said Amelia. 'He did say summat about hoping you were in good health. Fit as a fiddle, I told him, and he told *me* how much he enjoyed your company. Hetty, I think our Mr Wallace has got designs on you.'

Hetty snorted.

'Either that,' said Amelia, 'or he doesn't want to catch the filthy pox off you.'

'Amelia, I wish you would stop,' said Hope. 'This is growing tiresome.'

Both Hetty and Amelia looked at her in surprise. Then Amelia's eyes flashed in anger.

'Hark at you,' she said. 'And pardon me for breathing, mi'lady. Found your own kind on that committee, haven't you?'

'Own kind?' said Hetty. She knew Amelia was jealous of Hope's involvement in the organisation of the fete being held in aid of the house. She herself was sick of hearing about the grand bazaar. It was all the trustees talked about. But Amelia had declined when Hope suggested she volunteer her services.

Amelia flapped a hand dismissively. 'Nowt. I'm talking rubbish, as per.'

An expression Hetty couldn't decipher came over Hope's face. It was only later, as she walked into the Norfolk Street edifice containing the offices of Wallace & Sons accounting firm, that she realised it had been fear.

Mr Wallace looked delighted when Hetty was shown into his office. He was sitting behind a large walnut desk, facing a woman she didn't recognise who turned and offered a friendly smile. She was striking-looking, with pure white hair and dark, straight brows over narrow eyes and high cheekbones. She wore an expensive burgundy-coloured cape with a large green jewelled clasp. Hetty was glad she had taken the time to change into her best dress – a dark blue jacket and skirt that flattered her complexion – but still felt drab and plain by comparison.

The clerk retreated, closing the door behind him.

'Ah, I'm so glad you could spare the time, Miss Barlow.' Mr Wallace got to his feet. 'Can I introduce you to Mrs John Calver, one of our volunteers. Mrs Calver, this is Miss Henrietta Barlow, the warden of the house.'

The two women exchanged *how do you dos*. 'Oh, how remiss of me,' said Mr Wallace. 'Let me get you a chair. We don't stand on ceremony here.'

He came out from behind the desk – *bustled* out – and wheeled a leather upholstered chair from the corner of the room where a bookcase crammed with leather-bound tomes stretched from floor to ceiling. Hetty thanked him and sat. She couldn't hold the other woman's appraising gaze and looked away, pretending interest in the elaborately framed watercolour painting above the fireplace. It depicted the curved frontage of a glasshouse, half-hidden by lush foliage.

'The botanical gardens,' said Mr Wallace. 'Have you visited?'

'No,' said Hetty. 'I'm sorry to say I haven't. I don't know how I would find the time.'

'Ah, but all work and no play make Jack a dull boy,' said Mr Wallace, smiling broadly.

'And I'd say to that, a woman's work is never done,' she replied, softening the comment with a smile.

He bowed before resuming his seat. 'Touché.'

Mrs Calver had twisted her body to examine the painting. She turned back to Hetty. 'Miss Barlow speaks the truth but I must admit I have visited the gardens. This really is a delightful rendering.'

Mr Wallace beamed. 'My daughter is the artist. Flora has been a great comfort to me since Mrs Wallace passed.' He leaned forward, towards Hetty. 'You know, this gives me an idea, Miss Barlow. We ought to organise a trip for your ladies. It's most instructional.' He smiled at her conspiratorially. 'I'm sure even our honourable secretary would find no fault in that.'

'Can I say I'm very pleased to finally meet you.' Mrs Calver's voice was intelligent, modulated at a low pitch. Here was a woman accustomed to giving commands and having them obeyed. 'I'm sorry to hear you have a case of smallpox at the house?'

It was phrased as a question. 'Yes,' said Hetty. 'Almost certainly so. The girl's skin is covered in pustules.' She saw out of the corner of her eye Mr Wallace try to suppress a shudder. 'We've had her removed to the quarantine hospital.'

'Mrs Calver had some business to transact here and I thought this would be a good opportunity for you to meet,' said Mr Wallace, 'and perhaps arrange a tour of the house.' He paused. 'At a more convenient time.'

'As I speak, the house is being cleaned from top to toe,' said Hetty. 'The residents are instructed to inform me if they so much as develop a runny nose. All the staff were re-vaccinated at the start of the outbreak.'

'Good, good,' murmured Mr Wallace.

'Can we say the same for all the residents?' said Mrs Calver.

She turned to Mrs Calver. 'The deputy warden has been tasked with ensuring any new arrivals who are expected to stay for more than a night or two will be taken for a vaccination.'

Mr Wallace said: 'And the young lady who has fallen sick?'

'I have her details and have already written to notify her next of kin. She's in isolation but if her condition worsens then relatives may be allowed in to see her, so I've been told.'

'We pray she makes a full recovery,' said Mrs Calver. 'You know, I've been made aware that at the Lodge Moor quarantine hospital the nurses are living, eating and sleeping under the same roof as the smallpox patients, but a concession has been made for servants. They're allowed to leave the premises at the discretion of the matron.'

She shook her head but Hetty couldn't tell whether this was a mark of disapproval or admiration. Some sort of response was required.

'That seems inappropriate,' she said, 'but I'm sure the matron knows what she is doing.'

'They're not all as competent as you and I,' said Mrs Calver. 'Of course, the surgeons come and go as they see fit, and no porter's book is kept. I would not allow it, would you, Miss Barlow, as a matron, allow such shoddy management?'

Was she being tested? Perhaps this woman had been shown her credentials and recognised them as forgeries.

Hetty was being played with, like a cat plays with a mouse. She kept her voice steady. 'I would not.'

Mrs Calver nodded sagely. 'Then we agree, two matrons together, that access to places where the disease is rife should not be allowed.'

Hetty's gut clenched. 'It's not rife at the house. We've had one case. Miss Millthorpe hasn't even been properly diagnosed yet.'

'But it *is* smallpox.'

'The doctor thinks so.' Her voice rose. She couldn't help it. 'Would you have us close our doors?'

'Oh my goodness, no,' said Mr Wallace. 'Nobody is suggesting that.' He looked at Mrs Calver. 'Are we?'

'I think Miss Barlow is best placed to answer that question,' said Mrs Calver. 'I'm sure she has plenty of experience in dealing with infectious disease. The house is in good hands.' She smiled at Hetty. 'Which hospital were you at, my dear, before you took on the House of Help?'

She managed to raise a tight smile. 'Latterly, the new women's hospital at Whitby.'

Mrs Calver frowned. 'I don't think I am acquainted with anybody at that establishment. I was here in the town, at Winter Street, but retired some years ago. You must have been appointed matron at a young age, if I may say?'

'Twenty-six.' She covered her mouth then dropped her hand into her lap. Her neck itched and she resisted the temptation to scratch it. Twenty-six was the age printed on the forged documents so that, at thirty-eight, she would appear to have ample experience under her belt. At the age of twenty-six, she had been on her hands and knees scrubbing floors in the labour ward.

'We were lucky to secure Miss Barlow's services,' said Mr Wallace. 'With her sister, we got two for the price of one.' He laughed. 'I jest, of course. Both ladies are remunerated. Not handsomely, but...' he trailed off and gave Hetty a sympathetic grimace.

'How fortuitous,' said Mrs Calver. 'I wonder, though, and forgive me for asking, why you left the profession? Nursing is a calling, a vocation, and not easily given up.'

'Perhaps that's your experience,' said Hetty. 'You miss the work?'

'Indeed, I do. I'm sure you'll agree that overseeing the day-to-day running of a hospital is a challenging but extremely rewarding career. Sometimes a struggle, of course, convincing our betters to follow our path.'

Hetty did not believe Mrs Calver had ever struggled to assert her authority over any doctor she encountered.

The clerk sidled in, whispered in Mr Wallace's ear and left again.

'Do forgive me, ladies,' he said. 'Duty calls. I'm glad I was able to effect this introduction. Miss Barlow, I do appreciate how busy you are and I hope you don't consider me an interfering old fool, but I thought Mrs Calver might be able to help you.'

Mrs Calver put her hand on Hetty's arm. 'Miss Barlow, you might make use of my skills, if you are so inclined. I do relish a challenge and I find myself with too much time on my hands since my husband passed. I know you are new to the town and I'd like to extend the hand of friendship, if I may.'

With a shock, she realised that the former matron was volunteering her services; she wasn't attempting to catch Hetty out in a lie. And – a further realisation struck her – why would she attempt such a thing in the first place?

Hetty's guilty conscience had coloured her interpretation of their conversation. She had been a fool to fret over it at all. It was clear that Mrs Calver was not the sort of woman who in retirement could devote her days to her grandchildren. She was touched by the offer of a friendship.

Still, she wouldn't have this woman in the house. The risk of Hetty's lie being exposed was too great.

'A fine suggestion,' said Mr Wallace heartily. 'Miss Barlow, if another case presents itself we should seek the advice of the sanitation officer, but for now I think we keep our doors open, yes?'

She stiffened her back against the relief that flooded her body. 'Yes.'

'Then that's settled.'

Minutes later, Hetty was back on Norfolk Street. On her departure, she had made encouraging noises about having Mrs Calver to the house but managed to avoid actually setting a date. More importantly, the house would remain open, for now. Even a temporary closure could be disastrous. It might spell the end of the experiment – those philanthropists whose money established it might turn their attention towards another worthy cause – and then what would become of her, and Amelia?

There was the aunt, of course, and a house, but Hetty hoped never to have to deal with that woman again. What to do about Amelia? Hetty looked up at the sky, as if the heavens beyond the pale blue canopy could give her an answer.

She set off north along the busy street, deciding on the spur of the moment to take a circuitous route back to the house. She skirted a group of children, their feet blackened, who were clambering on the railings outside the Wesleyan chapel, and paused to allow two men, carrying a large wooden crate between them, to exit a winery. She passed the Methodist church and walked into the shadow thrown by the tall soot-blackened brick walls of a cutlers works and back into sunshine again.

Across the street, blocking the pavement in front of a terrace of shops – Boyd's tailors, Shaw's sweet shop and the chemist's – worked a gang of navvies, fifteen men or thereabouts in shirts with the sleeves rolled up to their biceps, waistcoats and caps covered in dust and dirt, digging up the road. They could be preparing the ground for new tramlines or the laying of telephone cables, which was going on all over town. She wondered idly whether the house would one day have a telephone set. It seemed far too exotic even to consider. Who would she ring? The Queen?

She considered continuing on to Market Hall. One of the previous residents of the house had found employment at a bookbinder's in the market. Hetty could picture her, a flame-haired girl named Beatrice Mellows. But in the end, she cut through Change Alley onto the high street and walked up towards St Peter's. Church Street was thronged. Townspeople strolled along in the sunshine, or hurried to whatever important business they had. Old and young sat on benches observing the world go by, relishing the warmth of the day. Costermongers pulled or pushed their barrows along the road, weaving in and out to avoid crowded omnibuses, gigs and horseback riders.

Hetty reached the ginnel that led onto Paradise Square, turned the corner onto the square and stopped in her tracks.

Amelia and that hawker, Linus Harmon, were sitting on the steps of the house, heads together like children conjuring up some mischief. A cold rock settled in Hetty's stomach.

'Miss Barlow!' Linus dropped Amelia's hand like a hot coal and leapt to his feet. 'Amelia thought it best to sit out here because of the pox in the house.'

She sighed. 'Tell the whole square, why don't you?'

Amelia stood up and brushed dust from the back of her skirt. She tapped Linus's arm playfully and slipped her hand into his. 'Sitting out here was your idea, Lenny.' Hetty raised an eyebrow. Lenny, was it? 'And the pox is not in the house, anyway. Its been removed to the hospital inside poor Miss Millthorpe.'

Hetty pursed her lips. 'Stop pawing at him, Amelia. This is a respectable house.'

'I know, I know.' Amelia let go of the hawker's hand. 'We were only sitting. We weren't kissin' or anything.'

'Amelia!'

Linus held up both hands. 'I'm sorry, Miss Barlow. I'm going to take myself off from under your feet.'

Amelia pouted. 'You don't have to leave just because my sister is back.'

He took her hands then glanced at Hetty and dropped them. 'I still have calls to make before the train and if I leave the porter in the Q any longer he won't be fit to pull the cart,' he said. 'Next time I'm here, we'll go to the boating lake. What do you say?'

'I say that I should like to visit Tamworth.'

'I promise you will. One day soon.'

'You keep promising.'

Hetty shook her head and turned away to climb the steps to the door. The interior of the house was dim compared to the brightness outside and smelled strongly of soap and vinegar. She untied her bonnet and hung it on a peg in the porch and went to her quarters, where she shrugged off her jacket and sat at her desk. A few seconds later, Amelia came in without knocking and stood over Hetty, arms folded, a face like fury. She had been expecting this and fought the urge to laugh. It would only further infuriate the girl.

'Why are you so bloomin' rude to Linus?'

'I don't think I am,' she said mildly, 'but I'm entitled to have certain reservations.'

'No, you're not. It's none of your business.'

Instead of flouncing out, as Hetty had expected, Amelia went to the window and perched on the ledge. She folded her arms. 'All right, then, let's have it. What *reservations*, sister?'

Hetty knew that anything she might say to discourage the courtship would only strengthen Amelia's resolve to marry this man. Hetty didn't trust him. He had paid several visits to the house but had not yet invited Amelia to visit his home, to meet his parents, with whom he reckoned to live. It wasn't enough that he kept repeating that, once wed, the couple would live in Tamworth. He was probably stringing along women in Chesterfield, Halifax and Leeds, and there'd be women in some of these places offering him more than chaste kisses.

So she held her tongue.

Amelia threw up her hands.

'It's the same old story, isn't it?' she said. 'You don't want me to have a life of my own. Why can't you just be happy for me?' She made a strangled sound of frustration. 'I'm not a child and I'll do what I want without your say-so.'

'I only want what's best for you. I want to protect you.' Hetty considered whether to continue, then decided she would. 'It's why I came back to take you away from that mad old woman.'

Amelia shook her head dismissively. She wasn't interested in talking about their father's sister. 'I'll tell you something, shall I? I can admit that I saw Linus as a way to escape from this house, from you ordering me about. But I love him, Hetty. I think I loved him from the moment I clapped eyes on him, and he feels the same. What do you know about love?'

Hetty smiled grimly. 'More than you think.'

'Give over.' Amelia narrowed her eyes. 'You try and control me. You don't want me going home. What's Auntie Gertie got on you? Are you scared of her, or summat?'

Hetty's stomach dropped. 'You're talking rubbish now and I won't have it.'

Amelia looked pleased to have got a reaction. 'Linus is saving up for us to wed. Imagine if I told him I had a share in a house on the coast.'

'You know that mother left the house to her, and the old witch has written us out of her will,' said Hetty. 'I'm sorry to say this, Amelia, but she was glad to see the back of us, both of us.'

Amelia had a mulish look on her face. 'She's still family and she won't turn me away.'

Oh, I hope she does. She might do worse than that.

Hetty wracked her brain for something less incendiary that she could say aloud, and then it didn't matter, because Amelia had swept out of the room, slamming the door behind her.

Chapter 11

Amelia moved her paisley shawl up from where she had draped it around her arms, shivering in the early morning chill, and fed the last of the carrot ends to the coal cart horse. The fog curling up from the bottom of the valley made ghosts of the buildings at the foot of Paradise Square. Any minute now, a man's shape would emerge from the shadows down there. He would raise a hand in greeting and quicken his step to reach her sooner. The anticipation of his appearance, even before she had clapped eyes on him, made Amelia's heart race.

She'd been standing outside the house for five minutes. It felt like longer.

'Up early,' the coalman said, returning with his shovel over his shoulder.

'Aye, big day today.'

'Oh aye?'

'My fiancé is taking me to the fair.'

Amelia's cheeks reddened a little but she was confident the coalman wouldn't notice her discomfort. Although she enjoyed uttering the word *fiancé*, she wasn't yet betrothed. Linus had talked of visiting the jeweller to purchase a gold wedding band, and of building up his little pot of savings so they could rent their own place in Tamworth, but he hadn't yet formally asked her to marry him. Amelia had told him she didn't need an expensive ring and she'd be happy living with his parents, for a short while anyway, but he was having none of it. It had to be done properly. He would not allow his sweetheart any less.

Perhaps today would be the day he presented her with that ring.

The horse snuffled damply against the palm of her hand. 'I've no more,' she said, gently scratching the soft hair between the animal's eyes. 'They should have gone in the stew so you can count yoursen lucky.'

In his latest letter, Linus had said he would travel up the night before Whitsun and stay at the Red Lion in New Queen's Street. Amelia had the gist of the letter before Hope read it to her but she liked to hear his words spoken aloud in Hope's soft voice. Linus planned to take her for breakfast at the King's Head Hotel, which he assured her was very grand, and then he would escort her to the annual Whitsun fair.

A proposal over breakfast in one of the town's fanciest hotels would be just the thing. The Whitsun fair, which was all anybody had talked about for weeks, she could take or leave. If Linus proposed to her this morning, all she would want to do was rush back and deliver the news to Hetty and Hope.

She peered into the gloom. He wouldn't be long. He had promised her this day and she knew he'd be true to his word, whatever Hetty's loaded silences might have to say about it.

'This fog'll burn off in no time,' said the coalman.

'Let's hope so.' She hugged her elbows. She had bought a new dress for this day – an apple-green linen bodice that emphasised her tiny waist, and matching skirt. The colour went well with the paisley. Her bonnet was new, with a wide white-satin ribbon to match the trim on the buttoned-down cuffs and collar of her shirt. With board at the house included, along with any meals she shared with the women, she could afford to dress herself relatively well, and now she had a reason to discard her grubby apron for something that befit a young wife, one half of an up-and-coming couple.

Mrs Amelia Harmon. She'd be married before the summer was out. She had offered Hope a bet on it. Typically, Hope had declined. Sometimes, that girl could be a smidge too po-faced for Amelia's liking.

When a man appeared at the east side of the square, she caught her breath but her hopeful smile soon faded. He came ahead of another man, both wearing greatcoats and bowlers and pulling between them a handcart that they carefully manoeuvred onto the cobbles. Those employed at the solicitors and insurance firms in the square and on Campo Lane and St James's Street would buy their coffee and pipe tobacco from this stall when they arrived for work.

A finger of doubt crept into Amelia's mind. What if she was still standing here when premises around the square began opening for business? The idea of retreating into the house was untenable. If Linus didn't show up – and the thought made her heart trip – she'd have to take herself off for a walk to save face. Later, after she had collected herself and rehearsed the lie, she could tell Hetty she had mixed up the dates. Although that wouldn't work, as this was the Whitsun fair weekend and it was the Whitsun fair he'd promised. She could picture her sister's face. She'd not be able to hide her triumph. *I told you so.* Amelia didn't need to come up with an excuse. He would turn up. Any moment now.

She stared at the corner of the square Linus would emerge onto, where the lines of brickwork were coming into sharper focus as the fog lifted, as if she could will him into existence.

If she had to, she'd walk all the way to Crookes and back to avoid Hetty's judgemental look. What did her sister know about love? She'd never married, never even had a beau as far as Amelia knew, and now she was an old spinster of thirty-eight. She could never understand the ache in Amelia's gut whenever Linus was absent, or the jolt she felt when after each long pause in their courting she first saw his face, and returned the smile he reserved for her alone, the smile he'd gifted her the day they met.

Hetty was probably watching her now. Amelia looked over her shoulder, expecting to see a curtain twitch back in place, or a figure swiftly retreat into shadow, but the house presented a blank, disinterested face. How she longed to be away for good from this place her sister had brought her to, and imprisoned her in.

When she turned back to face the square, he was there, standing right before her, and she yelped and flung her arms around his neck without thinking.

'Whoah, girl.'

Linus held her at arm's length and looked her up and down, finally examining the contours of her face as if it had been years and not weeks since he had last seen her. 'You're a sight for sore eyes, all right. Ready for some grub?'

At the King's Head Hotel, they were seated at a table for two in a corner of the dining room, near the entrance to the kitchen. Amelia ordered whitebait, toast and a pot of tea. She sipped nervously from her china cup, afraid of spilling liquid on a tablecloth of blinding white linen.

She thought about telling Linus that this was a step up – a whole staircase up! – from the oilcloth on the kitchen table at the house, but decided she would seem unsophisticated. He probably ate from tables like this all the time.

Much of the wood-panelled room was hidden behind the pillar beside their table. She leaned sideways and glimpsed a large fireplace in which stood a glass vase filled with long-stemmed flowers that reached almost to the underside of the high mantel. She recognised the cluster of light purple petals on the top of each tapering stalk.

'My mother grew those in her garden,' she whispered, afraid to raise her voice in a room where the chink of cutlery and sounds of conversation were subdued, as if she had water in her ears. She frowned. 'They don't flower this early, though.'

'I bet they're as artificial as the daisy on your hat,' said Linus.

She touched the brim hesitantly. 'Don't you like my hat?'

'It's a lovely hat, sitting on a lovely head.' He pointed to the fireplace with his knife. 'What are those flowers called, then?'

'Chimney bellflowers.'

'Chimneys, eh? Sounds about right for this town.'

Linus smacked his lips and speared a black pudding sausage on his fork.

'When we get to the fair,' he said, 'I'll take you for a ride on the Sea-on-Land.'

'The what?'

He spelled out the letters. 'Have you ever seen it?'

She shook her head. 'We weren't here last Whitsun.'

'But you must have had travelling fairs where you're from?'

'Aye, I suppose. I never went to one.' She nibbled on a slice of toast. 'What else will there be, at the fair?'

'Swings and roundabouts and all sorts! Drink up your tea and you'll find out.'

The streets leading towards the cattle market on the banks of the river Don were teeming with people. Amelia took the arm Linus offered and they joined the throng. The flat, open site where the fair had pitched wasn't yet visible. All Amelia could see was the familiar backdrop across the river, of factory stacks billowing smoke into the blue sky, from white through every shade of grey to black.

They joined the queue at the bottleneck entrance to the fair. Linus put his arm across her shoulders to protect her from the jostling crowd and when she tilted her head up to smile at him, he ducked his head and brushed his lips against hers. It was a touch as light as a butterfly's and just as quickly gone. Somebody whistled. Amelia ducked her head, elated and mortified in equal measure. The queue shuffled forward and Linus placed her before him, his torso pressing against her back. She looked at the expectant faces around her.

Nobody could be as happy as she was, in this moment. She leaned back slightly, against his body. She could stand in this queue forever.

Linus paid their threepenny bit entry fee and they emerged onto the rush-strewn fairground and into a cacophony of colour and noise. Directly before her, painted statues of horses, frozen in the act of galloping, followed each other around a giant circular rotating disc, skewered by colourfully striped poles that disappeared into the canopy above and the boards beneath. One of the riders, a small child, let go of her pole to wave to by-standers and Amelia waved back, her heart in her mouth. A man held a cone-shaped trumpet to his mouth. *Hold on tight!* The horses galloped faster.

Linus bent to shout in her ear that there was a better roundabout further in, and he wanted to take her on the Sea-on-Land too, and she wondered where he got all this knowledge from. Had this fair been to Tamworth and had he taken another girl there? She dismissed the idea. Hetty was infecting her with her bitterness.

She raised herself onto her tiptoes, using his arm for support. There were more roundabout canopies visible amongst the stalls and booths. To the left of where they stood, a row of small boats suspended from an immense wooden frame swung backwards and forwards, their occupants facing each other and controlling the movement by pulling on a rope. She pointed to it.

'Shuggy boats!' said Linus. 'Come on.'

The boat swing, though exhilarating, was a gentle ride compared to the Sea-on-Land, which featured garish replicas of seafaring vessels, steam-driven. 'This'll pitch and toss like any boat on the sea,' the man who operated it told her, and he was as good as his word. She was afraid her legs would not hold her up when she disembarked this ride and she clung to Linus, who was laughing at a man's assertion that the steam-driven attractions would result in an explosion, and kill scores of people. 'Give it a try yourself!' Linus told him. 'If these weak women can manage it, I'm sure you can.'

She slapped his arm. 'Weak, eh? Where's the next one?'

He laughed and lifted her off her feet, swinging her around. 'I'll find you a ride that'll send us flying into the middle of next week.'

Later, lying in bed, the snores of the women around her dimmed as she recalled the strength of his hands on her waist when he lifted her and placed her onto the thin wooden planks of a roundabout ride, the euphoria of flying through the air on the swing boat, and the lingering kisses they had shared behind the hoopla stall when he had held her so tightly against his body she couldn't catch her breath.

Linus had a train to catch at three o'clock and declined her invitation to come into the house. They stood on the steps, the elation she'd felt at the fair slipping away. She tried to quell the feeling that she was being abandoned forever. Linus had been unusually quiet on the walk back, while she babbled on about the rides they had been on and which were her favourites. He hadn't wanted anything from the bag of spice he'd bought for her so she finished off the aniseed balls and sugar mice and fudge squares. Perhaps he'd spent more money than he'd intended. But wasn't she worth his hard-earned coin?

'When will I see you next?' she said, trying and failing to keep the impatience from her voice.

Linus reached inside his coat. For one thrilling moment she thought he would bring out a ring, and the narky mood she was nursing into a full-blown bad temper evaporated. But instead he produced a flat package about the size of a paperback book, wrapped in brown paper. He offered it and she took it from him, and raised a quizzical eyebrow.

'What's this?'

'Don't open it now,' he said. 'I'd be mortified.' He hopped down to the pavement. 'I should like you to come and meet my parents soon. I'll write. I'll put pen to paper as soon as I get home.'

'Make sure you do,' she said. She ran up the steps then turned, came back down and kissed him, boldly, right on the mouth. To hell with anyone who might be watching, from the house or from the street. 'I had a lovely time.'

She had no sooner got inside than Hope pounced on her like a fox on a rabbit. She wanted to know whether the order had gone to the grocers, when they would start on the mountain of mending that needed to be done, and when would Amelia find replacements for the two oil lamps that had been broken during the spring clean?

Holding the package in one hand, Amelia untied her bonnet with the other and shook off her paisley shawl. 'Thank you for asking. We had a reight lovely time at the fair.'

'Oh, my goodness, I'm so sorry.' Hope's round cheeks had already been flushed. The colour deepened. 'I'm so exhausted. I can't seem to keep track of everything. Miss Barlow is in a foul temper and I have no idea why. I just want to…'

'Do your best for Miss Barlow. I know.'

She was fed up of hearing Hope's constant refrain that she didn't mind working for free, that she was giving something back to the house that had saved her. It rankled that Hope now outranked Amelia in the hierarchy of the house.

'Listen, Hope. Your job's to help Hetty look after these women. Leave the housekeeping to me.'

'Of course, I will.'

'Well, I've got to say you've brought me back down to earth with a bang.'

'I am sorry.' Hope tried to embrace her, but her bulk and Amelia's full hands made it awkward and she stepped back. 'What do you have there?'

'My new bonnet and shawl are going in the wardrobe.' Amelia nodded to the row of pegs that had been knocked into a board and hung on the wall of the porch. 'Too many light-fingered lasses around here for my liking.'

Hope sighed. She got cross when Amelia said disparaging things about the residents. 'I meant the package.'

'I know you did.' Amelia laughed. 'Linus gave it to me. I have no idea what's inside. Do you want to see? Is there anybody in our dorm?'

'No, they're all out.' Hope's eyes sparkled. 'Of course, I want to see.'

'Come on then.'

'Now?' Hope looked behind her. 'I've so much to...'

'Now or never, love. I'm not waitin' on you to open it.'

It was pleasantly cool in the dorm, the light breeze coming through the open sash carrying the sounds of the square with it. Amelia sat on the edge of her bed and began to pick at the string wrapped around the package. Linus had said *I'd be mortified*. Thinking about this made her fingers clumsy.

Hope lowered herself onto her mattress, lay down on her back and groaned.

'I feel like every organ in my body is being crushed under a door,' she said. 'Did you know, centuries ago, that was a form of torture and execution, for witches and wicked women.'

'You are a barmpot,' Amelia muttered, finally overcoming the knots, pulling the string away from the package and opening the leaves of brown paper.

She saw what was inside and glanced at Hope, who struggled into a sitting position against the headboard.

'What did he give you?'

'It's a picture.'

'You sound disappointed.'

'I don't know why he gave me a picture.'

She studied the framed print. Beneath the glass, a central verse was decorated with red roses in the margins. She recognised the words *red* and *lass* and *ten* and one or two others, but they were jumbled up with strange words she couldn't interpret, and a complete sentence eluded her.

'Emma…'

Hope sighed. 'I asked you not to call me that.'

Amelia stuck out her tongue. 'I'm only teasing. It's only because…' she stopped. She would not admit that she hated feeling beholden to anybody, that she wished she did not have to rely on Hope. If she admitted that, then Hope, or Emma, or whatever she wanted to call herself, would suggest she learn properly to read and write. The worst of it was, she'd be making a good point. Amelia ought to swallow her pride and attend Hope's Thursday night class with the women from the house.

'It's a poem or a song. I don't know. Will you read it to me?'

'I'd love to.'

Amelia put the print in Hope's hands and studied her face. Hope's eyes were glassy with tears when she looked up at her.

'Amelia, this is a lovely thing Linus has given you. It was written by a Scotsman. He is one of my father's favourite poets.' Her gaze fell sideways, to the bedcovers, although Amelia knew the counterpane wasn't what she saw. She was lost in a memory.

Amelia waited and after a long moment Hope looked up, startled, as if she had found herself in an unfamiliar place.

'I'm sorry. Sometimes…' she trailed off.

'You're allus apologising,' said Amelia. 'An' it's not you should be sorry. It's him, that cousin of yours.'

Hope shook her head impatiently. Her tone, when she spoke again, was brisk. 'It's written in dialect, so it isn't all that easy to understand. I won't be able to do the language justice. My father would.'

'But you can read it?'

'Yes, yes, it's a song. You might know it. It's very famous.'

Hope laid the print face-down on the mattress. She rested her hands on her belly and looked at the ceiling, then back at Amelia. 'I'll try to sing it without sounding like a thousand cats being strangled to death.'

Amelia laughed to cover her nervousness. She had never been sung to before and didn't know what to do with herself. She settled for staring at the floor as Hope began singing in a tremulous voice.

'O my love is like a red, red rose,
That's newly sprung in June.
O my love is like the melody
That's sweetly played in tune.'

Amelia was held by Hope's musical voice and didn't realise someone had stepped into the room until a second voice joined Hope's for the last line of the verse. *That's sweetly played in tune.* She whipped her head around. She didn't recognise the woman who had entered the room, who perched on the edge of Hope's bed.

'This is Mrs Henderson,' said Hope. 'She's travelling through the town and requires a bed for tonight.'

'You have a gem here in Miss Hope,' the woman said. 'She's a good listener. And it looks like she can hold a melody too. Do you know the next verse?'

Amelia shook her head. 'I've never heard the song before.'

Hope and the woman continued in unison.

'As fair are thou, my bonny lass,
So deep in love am I;
And I will love thee still, my dear,
Til all the sea's gang dry.'

This love song had been gifted to her, by Linus. She pictured him on the train, returning home. Was he thinking of her in this same moment, as the landscape rushed by? She wished with all her heart that she was sitting beside him, that they were journeying together, his fingers gripping hers, now and forevermore. She clasped her hands together.

'It's lovely.'

The woman smiled. 'There's more,' she said. She cleared her throat.

'Till all the seas gang dry, my dear,
And the rocks melt with the sun,
I will love thee still, my dear,
While the sands of life shall run.'

Hope tried to join in, but the tears were falling freely now, and she shook her head in defeat. The woman took her hand and continued to sing.

'And fare thee well, my only love,
And fare thee well, a while.
And I will come again, my love.
Though it were ten thousand mile!'

A lump had risen in Amelia's throat and she daren't trust herself to speak. Instead, she clapped her hands in applause then picked up the print. *And fare thee well, my only love.* Linus was telling her that he would return, over and over, and that she was his one true love.

She became aware of the two women watching her, one indulgently and the other with a tremulous smile on her face.

'He's a romantic fool, isn't he?' she said.

She took the print from the mattress and laid it in the drawer of her bedside table. In only a few short months, she'd be hanging it above the marital bed where she'd lie in Linus's arms, secure in the knowledge that she was his only love.

Chapter 12

Word had spread about Hope's Thursday evening reading and writing class and the decision had been taken to admit pupils from outside the house, those pupils to pay a shilling a time.

'It all adds up,' Miss Barlow told her, 'and goodness knows we need all the pennies we can scrape together. I can find more chairs, don't fret yourself about that. They can sit on the floor if need be.'

Hope had agreed without a murmur. She knew that her employer was preoccupied with something beyond the ongoing struggle to maintain the house on a shoestring. Miss Barlow had asked her whether she could step into her shoes for a few days, oversee the welfare of the residents while she dealt with a family matter. 'It might come to naught,' Miss Barlow had said, 'and it can wait until after.' She'd nodded at Hope's belly.

Hope was preoccupied herself, growing increasingly fearful about giving birth. Teaching was a welcome distraction, and, happily, she'd discovered she had an aptitude for it, quickly realising a one size fits all approach would not work. She had been privately schooled by a governess whose skills she hoped to emulate. Patience, she had in abundance. Pupils, the same. Any spare time she could scrimp was spent tailoring her classes to suit a range of needs, from helping those who had never picked up a pencil to the eager students who brought their own pen and ink. She reminded herself she must tell Miss Barlow that pupils who supplied their own materials could probably afford to pay more than a shilling a lesson.

On this particular evening, Hope stood before a class comprised of nine girls and women who were presently residing in the house, an adolescent who turned out to be a steelwork apprentice, this boy's father, a woman Hope recognised as the proprietor of a sweet shop in Norfolk Street, three young women and one young man who had appeared for the first time the previous week, and, incongruously, Angus Deveraux, who sat cross-legged on the floor at the back of the room alongside two of the house girls. They were giving him sidelong glances and giggling behind their hands.

'You don't mind, do you, if I observe?' he'd said when he entered the room. 'Only my grandfather has taken a keen interest in your night school. Unfortunately, he hasn't been able to find a free Thursday evening to come along.'

'I don't mind at all,' said Hope, but his presence unaccountably had her fidgeting as she stood at the front of the room and explained what tonight's class would involve. She felt his eyes on her, and stood as straight-backed as she could, considering.

She paired two of the house women who could read and write perfectly adequately – some residents attended the class simply to fill their evening – with two who could not read at all, setting simple alphabet and spelling tasks. The steelworks apprentice had learned the basics at Sunday school but had never attended a formal school. His father told Hope he and the boy's mother were determined their son would be better educated than they had been, which was not at all.

'If I weren't here, the little bugger – pardon my language – would take the coin and skip off to the Q,' he said. 'He's a clever lad and I've told him doors'll open for him if he gets educated, and they'll be better doors than the ones that lead into taverns.'

'And you, sir?' said Hope. 'Are you joining the class?'

'I'm afraid you'll get nowhere wi' me, love. Can't teach an old dog new tricks.'

'Perhaps you can observe, also?' she said, glancing at Angus Deveraux who grinned and sketched a salute in return.

'Shall I go to the back?'

'No, no, sit here by your boy.' She manoeuvred her bulk around the table to reach for the teaching equipment kept on a shelf, handing the father a board and slate pen. 'You might take these from me. It's a condition in this class of having a chair to sit upon.'

He laughed. 'I haven't a spare shilling on me.'

Angus Deveraux jumped to his feet and fished in his pockets. 'I'll stand you. Here's a two-bob bit. That will cover both of us.'

'Oh. Well. I don't… you can put it in the jar,' Hope said, turning away so Angus wouldn't see her blush. She should have argued that as he wasn't taking the class there was no need for him to pay, but he had a disconcerting effect on her, an ability to tie her tongue in knots. In another life, he might be leaving his calling card with her mother. She quashed the thought. It had no business sidling into her brain.

That life no longer existed.

Hope had acknowledged Amelia's entrance with a simple nod of welcome, afraid that if she revealed her joy at finally seeing her friend at the class Amelia would walk out as quietly as she had sidled in. She sat halfway down the table and folded her arms.

'Save the chair beside you,' said Hope. 'I'll take it.'

'Aye, all right then.' Amelia looked around the room. Her eyes lit up. 'Mr Deveraux! Is that you I spy on the floor back there?' She turned to Hope. 'I only told him about your class this afternoon. Keen, in't he?'

Angus didn't bother to contradict her but smiled at Hope. He smiled so charmingly. 'Miss Hope, I have been caught in a lie. It is my own interest that propels me here.'

She had no ready answer to that so busied herself with the sweet shop proprietor who wanted to practise her Copperplate, spelling and grammar for shop display signs and newspaper advertisements. 'I know I can pay others to do that,' the woman said, 'but I need to see it's right for mi'sen.'

Hope interrupted two of the house residents after seeing one point at her before whispering in the ear of the other. She took down a book of poetry by Elizabeth Barrett Browning and asked them to practise reading the first two verses of 'The Cry of the Children' so they might recite them to the class at the end of the lesson. She was learning to disregard the knowing smiles and the judge-mental looks, and had reconciled herself to the fact that she'd be a source of gossip whenever her back was turned. Nevertheless, this was her domain and she wouldn't have them spoil it.

'Let people talk,' Miss Barlow had advised, after finding Hope in tears in the store room one day. 'Some of them have nothing better to do.'

She was satisfied she'd given these women something better to do.

Late that night, when all the lights had been turned out and the only sounds were the snores and snuffles of the women in the dorm, Hope allowed herself to think about Angus Deveraux. He'd been the last to leave, lingering at the back of the room, bowing to Amelia as she exited. Amelia had turned to raise an eyebrow at Hope, which she ignored. He told Hope how much he had enjoyed her class and that he would have complimentary things to say about the new assistant warden to his grandfather. She'd laughed and they had shaken hands.

His eyes had not once fallen to her swollen belly but had remained fastened on hers. They were light green and gave his gaze an intensity that made her feel he could see through to the truth in her heart.

She groaned and carefully swung her legs out of bed, and sat on the edge, rubbing her knuckles up and down her breastbone. Heartburn, again.

–

Jane Millthorpe was, everybody acknowledged, one of the lucky ones. Recovered from smallpox, she was returned to the house early one morning in a weakened state and with the permanent marks of the disease covering her cheeks, chin and forehead. She refused to come down at breakfast time and Amelia took up a tray.

'Looks like her face has been shoved through a metal colander,' she said on her return to the kitchen.

'Oh, Amelia,' said Hope. She knew Amelia well enough by now to appreciate she had been shocked by the sight of Jane Millthorpe's face. This harshness was the result, and Hope resisted the temptation to tell Amelia she ought to be kinder.

She had already seen Jane's face for herself. Driven out of bed at dawn by discomfort in her back, she had been lighting the kitchen range to brew tea when she heard the commotion of the young woman's return to the house. She had gone to investigate, keeping her expression carefully neutral when she saw Jane's face. The girl's encounter with smallpox would be written all over her face for the rest of her life.

At breakfast time, Hope hadn't much appetite for her poached egg, while the coffee, brewed in the usual way, tasted strange on her tongue. The life within her was making its presence felt, each kick and roll pitching her off-balance, as if she was standing on the deck of a boat in choppy water rather than sitting on a kitchen chair. Miss Barlow had assured her the nausea would fade as her pregnancy progressed but she had been wrong. Hope set down her cup and hauled herself to her feet to get a drink of water. She was thirsty all the time now.

She flinched when Miss Barlow clapped her hands, the sound a pistol shot in her ears. 'All right, ladies. It's time for us all to get on with our day.'

Miss Barlow generally brought Friday morning break-fasting to an early and abrupt end so that she, Hope and Amelia – the warden, her deputy and the housekeeper – could have the kitchen to themselves for their weekly meeting. Later, Miss Barlow would closet herself in her quarters to write her end of week report. Amelia or one of the women would deliver the report to Mr Wallace, who was geographically the nearest trustee to the house.

Miss Barlow placed the notebook and pencil used for this meeting on the table and pushed them into the stripe of sunlight that fell across the surface. Hope would make the record. The window was open and the air was filled with the usual sounds of activity in the back lane and beyond. Hope reflected that she had come to think of this house as her home, the sights and smells and noises becoming as familiar as her own face. The smile she gave Miss Barlow, who nodded curtly in response, was full of gratitude. She had been here five months now – *our cuckoo in the nest*, teased Amelia – and the chances of discovery diminished with every day that passed.

What to do with Jane Millthorpe was the special item on the warden's agenda.

'She needs a period of convalescence,' said Miss Barlow, 'and we have an arrangement with a landlady in Cleethorpes who's offered accommodation in her guest-house for a reduced fee. A full week breathing in some fresh sea air should clear Miss Millthorpe's mind as well as restore her physical health.'

'Her parents want her to be returned home,' said Hope, 'after all that has happened here.'

Miss Barlow tapped her finger against pursed lips.

'That's up to Jane,' said Amelia. 'Anyhow, she's immune now.'

Miss Barlow nodded. 'She was adamant about making a new life in the town.'

'The town hasn't been kind to her,' said Hope, 'but she might return from her convalescence with her confidence restored.'

Miss Barlow gazed out of the window, then glanced conspiratorially at Hope. 'We'll send her. She can't make the journey alone, though. She'll want a companion.'

Amelia had been slouched in her chair. Now she sat up straight. 'I'll go.'

Miss Barlow shook her head. 'No, you're needed...'

Amelia interrupted her. 'Here it comes. You're sending Hope, aren't you?'

Hope knew what was coming, although Miss Barlow had inferred she would wait until after the baby was born. She bit her lip.

'No,' said Miss Barlow, patiently, ' 'course not. Look at the size of her. I'm going myself. I've some business to attend to.'

Amelia leaned forward. She was frowning mightily. 'Where? Where's this *business*?'

'Does it matter where?'

'You're going to Grimsby, aren't you?' Amelia shook her head. 'You're going home. It's not even your home, is it? You hardly ever set foot in the place. I should be going, not you.'

'I'm going to appoint Hope acting warden while I'm away,' said Miss Barlow, still in a reasonable tone, 'and you will be needed here, to help her.'

'But she's about ready to drop!'

Miss Barlow shook her head. 'We've got a midwife on call and she'll contact the doctor if it comes to that.' She turned to Hope. 'Which it won't, I'm sure. I'll come straight back...'

'From your gallivanting,' said Amelia, tartly.

'I wouldn't call it gallivanting.' Miss Barlow's brow darkened. 'I'll come straight back if summat happens. This is the plan, Amelia, and you being narky about it won't make a speck of difference.'

Acting warden. The idea of it thrilled Hope, and daunted her too. It was all very well being Miss Barlow's deputy. As acting warden, she would be the gatekeeper, required to make decisions about the women and girls who came and went, and managing the house's overall budget. Perhaps she would be blessed with a quiet week.

But there never had been a quiet week in all the time she had been at the house.

'I don't know what you're smirking about.'

She realised Amelia was addressing her. 'I'm not. It was a silly thought that made me smile. I admit, I'm flattered Miss Barlow considers me capable of holding the fort.'

Amelia dismissed her with a curl of her lip and swung back to her sister. 'You're going to see Auntie Gertie and I want to know why.'

Hope had never before seen Miss Barlow looked flustered. 'I shouldn't have said I had business. Wrong choice of words.'

'When have you ever said owt you don't mean?'

'I'm making a courtesy call. Now that's the end of that.' She held up her hand when Amelia opened her mouth to speak. 'No. I don't want to hear it, girl. We've got a lot to get through this morning.'

At the end of the meeting, it was abundantly clear that Amelia wanted to say more to her sister. Hope excused herself, asking Miss Barlow if she'd be permitted to take a short nap. 'I didn't have a restful night,' she explained.

She lay on top of the white candlewick, thinking that she wouldn't sleep despite the quietness of the dorm. She could hear, distantly, water running in the scullery, then the door of the water closest being opened and closed, and, in the far distance, the plangent call of a church bell. Then she was being shaken awake, by Amelia.

'You've been asleep for hours,' she said. 'Hetty practically had me guarding the door so you wouldn't be disturbed.'

'Thank you.' She sat up, groggily.

'Here,' said Amelia. 'I've brought you some water.'

Hope took the glass and looked at Amelia warily.

'Oh,' said Amelia, 'I'm all right. I have to say I feel doubly insulted but that makes no odds, does it?'

'Doubly?' Hope coughed and swallowed some more water. 'Thank you for this.'

'Well, I'm not good enough to chaperone Miss Pock-mark or to run this place, am I?'

Hope sighed. 'But would you even want to have Miss Barlow's job? All you ever do is complain about the house and how much you want to get away from it.'

'Allus the voice o' reason.' Amelia shrugged. 'It won't be long before I'll be leaving this place for good. I'll come and visit, to see you, if you're still here. But I've had my fill of Hetty telling me what to do.'

'Well, I hope to be here. I hope to build a life here.'

'Hope by name and nature. Mrs Gunson got it right,' said Amelia. 'I get why you can't go home but don't tell me you don't miss your old life. I'd give owt to be waited on hand and foot. I bet you never had to lift a finger, did you?'

She thought about the live-in maid who was always up before her, however early she rose, cleaning the grates, making the beds, getting into the corners and up to the coving with an ostrich feather duster, polishing the brass and bronze and silver, sweeping and scrubbing the hearths. The maid had been shy with the master and mistress of the house but chatty otherwise. Sweet Sarah. How she had taken her for granted.

'Help me up?'

Amelia took her hands and pulled her to her feet. 'Flippin' eck. I reckon you're carrying a sack of potatoes in there.'

'I wouldn't be surprised.' Hope rested her hands on top of the mound of her belly. 'Is it very warm in here or is it me?'

She went to the window and looked down on the square. Amelia came to stand beside her and slipped her arm around Hope's hips.

'Linus is coming up on Sunday to take me to the boating lake. D'you fancy coming along? A ride on the 'bus might just shake that bairn out of thee. Hopefully not onto the feet of the other passengers, eh?'

Hope laughed, her melancholy evaporating like smoke into the sky. 'Amelia, you say the most terrible things.'

'Made you laugh, though, din't I?'

'You did.'

'Well, now you're in a better mood I've got a favour to ask.'

'Ask away.'

'Well, the thing is, I was thinking, while the cat's away...'

Hope's heart sank as Amelia outlined what she intended to do in her sister's absence, not because she was dismayed – and she was – but because her answer would have to be a firm and unequivocal *No*.

Chapter 13

Mr Wallace had got wind of the trip to Cleethorpes and turned up that afternoon. He was cradling a carpet bag in his arms. 'For your expedition,' he said to Hetty.

He proffered the bag and, surprised, she took it. The leather handles were softened from years of use. The bag was patterned with rose blooms in pink and blue and red, faded but still pretty.

'Shall we go into the parlour?' Hetty said.

'Oh no, no thank you,' said Mr Wallace. 'I have to return to my office.' He touched the nap of the bag with his fingertips then withdrew his hand. 'This belonged to my late wife. It's rather shabby, but serviceable. I would be very glad to see it in use again. Look inside.'

'It's so kind of you,' said Hetty. 'I have a bag of my own but...'

'Of course, of course you do. I'm sorry.' He clapped his hands together and looked over her shoulder, although no one was there. 'It's a donation to the house, Miss Barlow, for use on this and future expeditions.'

'Then, thank you very much.'

He had asked her to look inside. She opened the bag. Sitting snug inside was another, smaller carpet bag. This one looked newly purchased.

'For your companion,' he said.

'Mr Wallace, this is very thoughtful.' She was touched. 'I wonder what I will find inside, if I open this second bag?'

Mr Wallace laughed and struck his forehead with the heel of his hand. 'Why didn't I think of that? I might have put a still smaller bag inside this one.'

Hetty smiled. 'And on and on, until the tiniest can carry only a sewing thimble. Not very practical.'

'Indeed not.'

Although he had declined her invitation to go into the parlour, he seemed reluctant to take his leave. Perhaps, it occurred to her, he was merely waiting for her to open the front door.

Hetty did, and stepped into the square of sunshine that appeared on the tile. The air was warm on her face and she tilted her chin towards the sky. 'We're having such a good run of weather this spring,' she said. 'I think I appreciate this all the more for the chilly winter we endured.'

He came to stand beside her on the threshold. 'It's been most clement. I am sure our poor girl will enjoy her convalescence at the seaside.'

'Have you ever visited Cleethorpes?'

'Why yes, I have. The walk along the pier is most invigorating. One might travel to Bridlington or Great Yarmouth, but Cleethorpes is the closest. Sheffield-on-sea, they're calling it now. A home away from home.'

Hetty laughed. 'But with less of the factory smoke, I hope.'

She would not tell Mr Wallace that she knew Cleethorpes well, had been taken to play on the wide golden sands of the tributary as a child. Her parents would have taken Amelia there too, after Hetty had left Grimsby behind her. She'd returned only three times, first for her

163

father's funeral soon after Amelia had learned to walk, then only last year her mother's, and finally to collect Amelia from the care of their aunt. It was then she had learned the details of her mother's will. Now she would be making her fourth visit to the cottage, and this would be the most difficult yet. Gertie could destroy Hettie's carefully constructed life. She hated the old woman for it.

'I wonder,' said Mr Wallace. 'Have you given our Mrs Calver a tour of the house yet?'

There was potential danger from that quarter, too. Hetty feigned ignorance, and frowned. 'Mrs...?'

'You met her in my office. You must remember. The widow of a recently deceased trustee. A former matron, like yourself. I imagined you might become friends, having so much in common.'

Hetty smiled. 'You sound like Mrs Shaw.'

He laughed. 'Oh dear, do I?' He coughed into his closed fist. 'It's only that I fear you must be lonely, being relatively new to the town. Mrs Calver has a lot to commend her and she is very interested in the work of the house. Her late husband was a trustee.'

'Yes, you told me that.'

It occurred to her that Mr Wallace had designs on the widow and was looking for an excuse to mention her name, rather than trying, clumsily, to engineer a friendship between the two women.

'I'll find the time from somewhere.' She turned her face back to the sun. Hopefully, that would be the end of it. She had no intention of acting as match-maker for the pair of them.

'Well,' said Mr Wallace, after a few moments of companionable silence. 'I'll leave you. Good day. Safe journey.'

'Good day, Mr Wallace.'

She watched him walk away until he reached the corner, and waited until he stopped and turned and raised his hat, before stepping back inside the house and closing the door.

-

Young Mr Deveraux drove Hetty and Jane Millthorpe to the station. He installed them in the waiting room at the back of the platform, much to Hetty's chagrin. She was uncomfortable surrounded by much more finely dressed passengers travelling first or second class. She ought to have been standing on the platform with the third-class passengers.

Angus Deveraux found them seats together on a varnished bench with individual seats and arm rests decorated with minute carvings of demonic-looking gargoyles that only served to remind her she'd be in the belly of a coal-guzzling monster soon enough.

'I'll be two ticks,' he said, and went to organise their tickets.

Hetty smoothed her hands down the grey dress she was wearing over a navy-blue underskirt. The correct attire for train travel ruled out white entirely. Too much grit and dust. Jane Millthorpe wore a maroon-coloured linen dress, borrowed from the donated clothes box, and an old-style black felt hat. Hetty wore a straw bonnet with a simple pale blue band that Hope had kindly said matched her eyes.

It was only when Mr Deveraux returned and led them towards the great black engine and the carriages slung to it, shielding them with his tall frame against the shoving and pushing and throwing about of bags and trunks, that she realised he had purchased second-class tickets. Angus laughed when he saw the expression on her face.

'Don't worry,' he said, pushing their bags under the seat. 'I'm not wasting house funds. Good seats, eh? My treat. Bon voyage!'

And he was gone.

She sat in the window on the comfortably upholstered seat, facing Jane Millthorpe. The carriage quickly filled. The girl was smiling broadly.

'What is it?' said Hetty.

'I've never been on a train before.'

'I have, love, but it gives me the shivers,' said Hetty. 'We weren't meant to travel faster than a horse can carry us.'

'Oh no. Do you want to face for'ards instead of back-wards?'

Hetty glanced at the other passengers and leaned forward to whisper: 'I don't know whether we go on past here or back to Cleethorpes.'

A whistle sounded loudly, startling them both, and the train began to chug slowly out of the station, emerging from under the iron and glass canopy and into the open air like a great metal beast out of its cave. Sluggish to start, it would soon be tearing through the countryside. She didn't think she'd ever get used to it.

And she was facing backwards.

The cadaverous gentleman sitting beside her companion tapped his cane on the wooden flooring of the carriage. 'We're away,' he said.

During the journey, Jane Millthorpe seemed enthralled by the unravelling landscape, so much so that the hand she usually kept lifted to conceal her face was instead clutching the window sash. The wings of her bonnet provided protection against prying eyes – she had complained of the looks of pity she received from everybody, that only served to emphasise her lost looks – and Hetty realised that was why she had chosen it.

Hetty obligingly admired the arches of a great stone viaduct in the distance. She acknowledged the graceful beauty of horses cropping in a field, and assured Jane she had glimpsed the barge rising in the black water of a canal lock. After each sight, she returned to her observation of the floor of the carriage.

The station at Cleethorpes was located not in the centre of the town but alongside the promenade, with a view of the giant cross beams of the pier that extended over the sands and disappeared into the sea. Alighting the train, Hetty took from her pocket the piece of paper with the address of the guesthouse on it. She found a porter who directed them to walk along the promenade until they reached the public gardens. They would see that on the far side stood a long, straight terrace of three-storey houses with bays on the first two floors. The guesthouse she was looking for was painted pink with white trim. It didn't look like much from the front, but there was a patio garden for the use of guests at the back of the house, a vegetable garden and apple and plum trees. It was a lovely place to have breakfast on a sunny morning.

Hetty hadn't been expecting this level of detail.

'The landlady's my sister,' the porter said. 'Stay here a few days and tha'll know everybody's business, and everybody'll know tha's.'

Let's hope not.

Before setting off on what the porter had promised would be no more than a twenty-minute walk to the guesthouse, the two women leaned against a low wall that separated the promenade from the beach and breathed in the salty air. As a child, Hetty had walked barefoot on the tightly packed sand for what seemed like miles to reach the place where the water lapped the land. On that boundary, she would dig her toes into the sand, and try to prevent the tiny grains from washing away beneath her.

She had built her life, and Amelia's, on similarly unsteady foundations. *So let's just hope I don't lose my balance.*

She turned to Jane. 'We should find our accommodation.'

The landlady was a pleasant woman who dispensed with the niceties efficiently, sending a young boy ahead with their bags, showing them where the dining room was and pointing out the location of the shared WC on the first landing. Breakfast was served at eight o'clock and dinner at six in the evening, these meals being free of charge for ladies from the House of Help. She showed them into a small sitting room at the back of the house. A man seated in an armchair by the fireplace, reading a newspaper, looked up and nodded a greeting. The landlady explained that books could be borrowed out but the chess and backgammon boards, the playing cards and newspapers must not be removed from the sitting room. If there was nobody about and assistance was required, the ladies should ring the bell on the table by the front door and someone would come.

The landlady didn't look at Jane after her initial greeting or make any comment about circumstances of the girl's convalescence. Hetty thanked her on behalf of the trustees.

It was a relief to reach their room. The view was of the back garden. When Hetty looked directly down she could see wrought iron tables and chairs clustered on a patio. A garden stretched down to a tall hedge. She surveyed the room. A soft round bolster had been provided that would go lengthways on the mattress, under the covers of the double bed, separating it into two. Pegged rugs covered most of the floorboards. There was a dressing table and chair against the opposite wall alongside a tall wardrobe. In the window, two armchairs flanked a low table that held posters and leaflets detailing local attractions, and a bowl of sweets.

Jane Millthorpe picked one out, unwrapped it and popped it into her mouth. She sat on the edge of the bed and stroked the velvety throw that covered the bottom half of it.

'I suppose this'll have to do,' she said, before bursting into laughter.

Hetty smiled.

The charms of the seaside were already working their magic.

-

She spent a fitful night, anxious about what lay ahead, acutely aware of another person's body in close proximity to hers, on the other side of the bolster, of being in a room where the shadows were unfamiliar and her ears attuned to the faintest sound. Finally, she dozed and the next morning decided the scuttering sounds of mice in the walls had been a dream.

After a breakfast of kippers, fried bread and tomatoes, and strong, milky coffee, the two women strolled along the iron pier, stopping to watch fishing boats sail in and out of the mouth of the Humber river. Hetty told Jane she would be visiting the port of Grimsby, a short distance upriver, probably the day after tomorrow, and she should amuse herself for the day. She might consider spending her time reading in the sitting room and not stray too far from the guesthouse. Hetty would be back in time for the evening meal. She didn't say she might be back much sooner than that, depending on how she was received.

She was prepared to tell the girl she was dealing with a private matter but Jane didn't ask.

–

The day came around. Hetty stood on the steps of the guesthouse, watching grey clouds scud across the sky. She pondered for a few moments then went back inside and took an umbrella from the stand in the porch. It was an hour's walk up the estuary to Grimsby but she came upon a bus stop on the edge of Cleethorpes and, at the last moment, decided to cut the journey short. There were others at the stopping post, and she joined them, looking up to count the breaks in the cloud where the cobalt sky revealed itself like broken jewels, pretending to herself that the distraction would calm her mind.

Perhaps it might have been better to walk after all.

But it wasn't long before she heard the clop of horses' hooves and commands of the driver that signified the arrival of the omnibus. There were plenty of seats inside and Hetty took one at the back, in the corner, her eyes skimming over the passengers. Almost two decades had passed since she had left her home town but she was primed to encounter a face from the past. She wondered whether she'd be recognised, and thought not. Hard times had prematurely greyed her hair, had drawn lines at the corners of her mouth and hollowed out her cheeks. Had she once been as pretty as Amelia, looked as fresh, as wide-eyed in love? It was difficult to imagine now.

Satisfyingly, she recognised nobody and settled back for the ride.

Her mother's house sat the end of a lane dominated by fishermen's cottages. It had been old when she'd purchased it, built from rough-hewn local stone and flat-fronted, with four wooden-framed sash windows facing the lane and a chimney pot at each side of the roof. Hetty had always imagined it looked like the sort of house a small child might draw. Nothing so simple went on inside.

Her beloved father had died suddenly in a mining accident not long after Amelia was born and her mother decided a fresh start was required in a different neighbourhood. She purchased the cottage with the compensation money from the coal company and set up as a seamstress, making extra on the side from the shell collages she made and sold to tourists. When she slipped on fish guts in the lane and broke her leg, Hetty's aunt had moved in and never left. As a child, Hetty had always been slightly afraid of her late father's sister, wary for a reason she couldn't explain. Her aunt was a spinster who earned a living by dressing ladies' hair and also by another means Hetty had discovered on her mother's death.

This woman had coaxed into full bloom the seeds of disharmony between Hetty and her mother. Hetty had gone, by then, and was attempting to build a new life. She'd received a letter, written in her mother's hand, explaining it might be best for all concerned if she stayed away, for good. She recognised her aunt's voice in the sloping text.

Hetty opened the garden gate. She was not returning home. This was not, and never had been, her home, but it had been Amelia's.

Her stomach lurched when she caught a flash of movement in a downstairs window. The net was lifted and an arthritic hand paused in the act of placing a vase of flowers on the sill, a blue vase filled with yellow blooms. Her aunt's face appeared behind the petals, her eyes widening in surprise. She put down the flowers, dropped the net and Hetty walked up the path and waited for her to open the door.

Chapter 14

A weight lifted from Amelia's shoulders on her sister's departure for Cleethorpes. She discovered she could breathe easier in a house that did not bend to the will of her older sister. Unfortunately, it was as clear as crystal that the acting warden had been infected by Hetty's controlling nature.

Hope had asked for a bit of time to consider the favour Amelia had asked of her and then proceeded to avoid her as much as possible, and to change the subject whenever Amelia circled near it. Finally, Amelia suggested they take one of their evening walks. It had been a while, she reminded Hope. There were plenty of places she could rest if she started flagging, and the air would do her good. 'The air?' said Hope, sceptically. 'All right, then,' Amelia replied. 'Come for the exercise.'

She coaxed Hope from the house in the early evening of Hetty's third day in Cleethorpes. Hope leaned heavily on her arm as they strolled up to the high street. They stopped to sit on a bench where the high street intersected with Church Street and Fargate, and observed the transition of the town from day to night. Shop proprietors came out onto the pavements to roll in their awnings and lights began to appear in the windows of coffee houses, taverns and hotels. People on foot and on horses crisscrossed the junction, all with somewhere to be. The wheels of barrows, wagons cabs and carriages clattered over the cobbles.

It was a balmy evening and Hope expressed the wish that the summer would be just as lovely. She stroked her enormous belly, absently, and Amelia wondered how long it would be before that chapter of Hope's life ended. Surely days, rather than weeks. Amelia wanted a large brood, four or five or even six, to make up for her own lonely childhood. She'd raised this with Linus and he had declared he'd be right as rain with it. He agreed with Amelia that he, too, could never imagine giving up a child, not in a month of Sundays.

'Can I tell you something?' said Hope.

Amelia smirked. 'You're a Russian princess.' She loved making Hope laugh. Her face lit up, all her woes temporarily forgotten.

'Not quite.'

'Go on, then.' She nudged Hope's arm.

'You're the only person I can tell.'

Amelia laughed. 'Then why are you keeping me waitin'?'

Hope's chin trembled. 'It's my birthday today.'

'Oh, Hope.' She wanted to say something comforting but couldn't find the words. 'Happy birthday.'

Hope laughed shakily. 'I'm twenty.'

'Seven months older than me,' said Amelia. 'I'm a Christmas baby.'

'That makes me your senior,' said Hope.

'Doesn't mean you can boss me about, though. I have enough of that with the other one.'

'I wonder how they're getting on in Cleethorpes? Have you ever been?'

'A few times,' said Amelia, shortly. 'It's allus windy and everything is covered in seagull shite.'

'Amelia!'

'Oh, I'm joking. It's not that bad really. Have you ever swum in the sea?' She nudged Hope again. 'Emma?'

Instead of repeating her plea to desist from using her name, as Amelia was anticipating, Hope nodded wistfully. 'Yes, I remember swimming at Bournemouth. We hired a hut where we changed into our bathing suits. My mother complained about the sand getting everywhere. She said we took half the beach home with us.'

Amelia reached down to a clump of dandelions growing against the leg of the bench they sat on. She plucked one and presented it to Hope. 'A flower for your birthday.'

Hope took it and pushed it into the top buttonhole of her blouse, where it hung limply.

'Not like the pricy gifts you're used to, I'll bet,' said Amelia.

Hope smiled. 'But worth just as much to me.'

'Daft apeth. What did your parents give you last year, when you turned nineteen?'

Hope's cheeks coloured.

'Come on,' said Amelia, 'I bet it was summat better than a scruffy weed.'

'They gave me a family heirloom,' said Hope. 'A pair of diamond earrings. They were my mother's and before that my grandmother's.'

'Oh my.' Something occurred to her. 'Were you wearing them when…'

Hope looked away, fiddling with her earlobe.

Amelia decided it was time to change the topic.

'You know that Linus is coming up on the train tomorrow,' Amelia said. Hope was already beginning to shake her head. 'Will you give us her room for a few hours in the afternoon?'

Hope sighed. 'I am sorry, Amelia…'

'There you go again,' she tried for a breezy tone, 'allus apologising.'

'…but I can't allow it. I have thought about it, but… I'm sorry. The answer has to be no.'

She knew that the sympathy in Hope's voice was real. It didn't help.

'I don't see why,' said Amelia, trying to keep her voice level. 'All I want is some private time with my fiancé. We won't… you know. And Hetty'll never find out.'

'But if she does,' said Hope, 'her trust in me will be destroyed. I have thought about it, and I do think that one of the reasons she gave me her quarters was because she wanted to avoid this very thing, and not because I'm acting warden.'

All of Amelia's earlier compassion towards Hope evaporated in an instant.

'Hetty gave you her bed so you'd have somewhere private when the baby comes. You can't very well have it in the dorm!' She got up, walked a few steps then returned to stand over Hope. 'All you're bothered about is savin' your own skin. I just want some privacy. I can't get that in the dorm, or anywhere else in that house without somebody comes knocking or barging in. We can't…' she rubbed her forehead, searching for the right words, 'we can't be affectionate in public, not properly.'

'That's what I'm worried about,' said Hope quietly.

'So holier than thou but look at the state of you!'

As soon as it was out she regretted it. She clamped her lips together.

'That was uncalled-for,' said Hope.

'Aye.' She sat beside Hope and took her hand. It was cold. 'But put yoursen in my shoes. I love Linus. He loves me. A bit of private time together...' she trailed off.

She wanted to feel his arms around her, to have her face smothered in kisses without fear of interruption. She wanted to lie with her head on his chest and listen to the beat of his heart, to stretch out on the bed beside him and imagine their married life. She wanted to murmur words of love and hear them in return.

'I promise you,' she forced a laugh, 'I won't even be taking off my boots.'

Hope looked crestfallen. 'If you would like to stay in your sister's quarters while she's in Cleethorpes then I will move back into the dorm, at least until the baby arrives.'

Amelia put her hand against her heart. She might burst with joy. Good old Hope.

'But I can't allow you to entertain Linus in Miss Barlow's bedroom.'

She dropped Hope's hand. 'So that's it then?'

'You'll just have to be patient. I'm sorry. I don't know what else to say.'

She made one last attempt. 'But I promised Linus.' Now he would think her a child who had been well and truly put in her place.

'I'm sorry,' said Hope.

'Not as sorry as I am. You keep that bed. I'll just have to find another.'

Amelia rose early the next morning to supervise the weekly top-to-toe clean of the house, sweeping, dusting and polishing alongside three residents, all new arrivals she had little to say to, while Clara got on with the day-to-day chores that included emptying the chamber pots, lighting the range and sorting the laundry.

She waited until all the women had left the dorm before washing, brushing and braiding her hair and changing into her summer dress, a pale blue skirt and bodice in lightweight cotton. She had replaced the artificial daisy on her bonnet with silk ribbons to freshen it up. She checked her reflection in the wall mirror in the hallway, turning this way and that, and, satisfied with the result, went to sit in the parlour to await Linus's arrival. She would tell him she was sick of the house, sick of being mithered by the residents, and preferred to go on a jaunt.

She was barely on speaking terms with Hope. At breakfast time, Hope had given her a book to read. It was called *A Child's Garden of Verses* and would help Amelia with her reading, said Hope. She had accepted it with a stiff *thank you.*

Now, she looked up from the book to see the appointed time for Linus's arrival had come and gone. She pushed aside the disquieting thought that it had been a long while since his last visit, and that their latest arrangement had failed because of his work, and that she always seemed to be waiting, waiting, waiting.

She knew what her sister would have to say about it. He'd become bored. He'd found another love closer to home. He would continue to write letters with excuse after excuse until finally the penny dropped. She had been discarded.

She battled on with the book of children's verses for another half an hour then tossed the book aside and strode out of the room. She could hear voices and laughter coming from the kitchen. Perhaps he had let himself in and gone there to work his charms on Cook and be given something to eat. She poked her head around the kitchen door to find Cook and the scullery maid peeling potatoes. Amelia greeted them and ducked back out of the room. Cook called after her: 'You've had a letter. It's on the hall table.'

She hurried down the hall and picked up the white rectangle, which had been left on the table gummed side up with no return address written on it, entertaining the wild hope that the letter might be from her aunt. She hadn't heard from the old woman since Hetty took her away. Perhaps her aunt had reconciled with Hetty and was inviting Amelia to visit. Or she was advising her to never darken her door again. Either would suffice, provided this letter was not from Linus. She still clung to the hope his train had been delayed.

But she could not put off looking at the envelope any longer. And she knew any letter from her aunt would not arrive so quickly. Hetty had been gone for only four days. She turned the letter over. Her name and address were written in Linus's extravagant and unmistakeable hand, every pen stroke a dagger piercing her heart, telling her he wasn't coming today. Perhaps the last time she had seen him was the last time she'd ever see him. She tried to remember his words of farewell – had there been any clue in them, any indication of his change of heart? – and could not.

She glanced at the door to Hetty's quarters, now temporarily Hope's domain. She would not go running to her. Amelia's reading skills had improved no end at the Thursday night class. She was more than capable of tackling this letter alone.

She could hear the patter of rain against the front door, putting an end to her idea of going into the town and finding a bench to sit on, where she could read the letter in peace. She stood, tapping the envelope against her chin. She would go to the top of the house.

The foot of the attic stairs was bathed in light from the second-storey window in the gable end of the house. She sat on the worn carpet on the bottom stair and opened the envelope, drawing out the letter slowly. Her eyes dropped to his signature at the bottom. He had drawn two tiny heart shapes beside his name, as usual. Relief flooded her chest. Her eyes flicked back to the top of the sheet. *My dearest darling*, he had written, *I yearn to see your face again*. She struggled with the word *yearn* and was pleased with herself when she got the meaning, not to mention the sentiment it expressed.

> *I am sorry to say I'm required to spend a week in Nottingham to develop new business. Please forgive me. I hope that when we next meet I will be collecting you at the station to bring you to my parents' house. They are desperate to meet the girl who has stolen my heart. I am forever and ever yours, Linus.*

Short but undeniably sweet.

-

She had changed back into her work pinafore and was helping the scullery maid clean the kitchen range – one of those filthy jobs that invariably induced a sense of deep satisfaction when the metal gleamed again – when Clara came to tell her there was somebody for her at the door.

Amelia wiped her hands on her dirt-streaked apron and swiped perspiration from her brow. No doubt another girl seeking salvation stood on the doorstep.

'Where's Hope then?'

'It's for you,' said Clara. She was grinning.

'Who is it?' She spoke sharply. She ought to be out with Linus today and wasn't in the mood to be teased. And who would call on her, except for Linus?

She flew from the kitchen.

The door was open and he stood inside the threshold, facing the square. Outside, rain fell steadily and the bowler he held in his hand dripped water onto the rug. Her heart swelled to see the familiar set of his shoulders but she stopped halfway down the hall. She must look a sight. Could she creep upstairs and change back into her dress? No, he was already turning, merriment creasing the corners of his eyes.

'Have I called at an inconvenient t—'

She threw herself into his arms, then remembered and stepped back. 'I'm getting muck all over you!'

He pulled her back into his arms and nuzzled her neck, sending thrills coursing through her body. 'I'm partial to a bit of muck,' he said.

Amelia laughed. 'I got your letter. It came this morning.'

He released his hold on her so he could look into her eyes. 'I had more important business than tramping around Nottingham. You see, there's this girl.' He took her hands in his and a peculiar feeling, not unlike fear, stirred in her stomach. 'I had to come and see her to ask a very important question.'

He let go of her hands, which she put over her mouth to contain the cry of excitement building in her chest, and dug in his pocket. 'Must be in here somewhere,' he muttered.

Amelia stood back and folded her arms. 'I swear, if you're playing a joke on me, Linus Harmon, I'll give you such a clout.'

He winked at her, at the same time producing a narrow gold band that he held up for her to inspect.

'Will you marry me, Miss Barlow?'

He took her right hand. *The wrong hand*, she thought, but allowed him to put the ring on her finger. It was a perfect fit.

'Wear it on this hand for now,' he said, 'until the day we wed. And when I'm absent it will remind you of me. It binds you to me.'

'I think about you all the time, anyway,' she blurted.

He brought her hand to his chest. She could feel his heart pounding. 'But you haven't given me your answer.'

She stood on tiptoes to whisper in his ear. 'Yes, you barmpot. Yes, I'll marry you.'

–

Linus let out a low whistle when she entered the parlour in her blue cotton. She had run back into the kitchen to show off the ring on her finger and beg Cook to make sandwiches and a pot of tea she could share with Linus in the parlour. Cook had agreed readily enough and told Amelia she was happy for her. Clara had hugged her, but then wagged a finger in her face and told her it was bad luck to wear the ring on her finger – even the wrong finger – ahead of the wedding day, and when was that? Had Linus given a date? Amelia had laughed. Nothing could ruin her mood. Nothing at all.

Well, perhaps one thing.

When she entered the parlour, Linus was sitting in one of the armchairs leafing through the book she had been reading earlier. He dropped the book onto the hearth and told her how lovely she looked. She knelt at his feet, unlaced his boots and eased them off.

'I should like to lie down beside you,' he said. 'There must be no end of beds in this house.'

'Well, we can't,' she said flatly.

She got up to sit in the armchair opposite his and stuck out her lower lip.

'Your sister returned early from her travels.'

'No. It's the other one.' She sighed. 'Hope. She's so self-righteous I could lamp her.'

Linus laughed. 'Poor Hope.'

Amelia shook her head. 'Nowt poor about that one, believe me. And you're supposed to be on my side.'

'I wasn't aware there *were* sides.' He shrugged. 'I thought Hope was your friend.'

'She is.' Amelia paused. She wanted to share Hope's secret so badly and now she could. 'There should be no secrets between a husband and wife, should there?'

'Of course not.' His eyes narrowed. 'What do you have to tell me?'

'Oh, it's not about me.'

Could she put aside the fact that this was not her secret to share? Confiding in Linus would strengthen their bond. It would demonstrate her complete and absolute trust in him. She had the self-awareness to know she was kidding herself. She could justify it all she liked. What she really wanted to do was thrill him with the truth.

'It's summat about Hope,' she said.

'Hope?'

'Aye. Her real name is Emma. She never lost her memory, and she's rich as Croesus.'

She watched his eyes widen and his jaw hinge open. Unease stirred in her gut. With those few words, she'd transformed Hope's secret into something else. Now it was gossip.

Chapter 15

Gertie Barlow was a tiny, bird-like creature, her face as wrinkled as a walnut, the white frizz on her head pulled back into a messy knot. Not the best advertisement for a dresser of ladies' hair, thought Hetty, but an unkempt look – a *witchy* look – was probably appreciated by her other clients.

'Weren't expecting to see you again.' This was her greeting. It had been eight months since her sister-in-law's funeral.

Hetty smiled thinly. 'I was in your neck of the woods.'

'A bit of notice would have been appreciated.'

'Why?' said Hetty. 'Would you have got the flags out for me?'

Her eyes fell on the crocheted black shawl that hung loosely on Gertie's shoulders. It was probably the same shawl she had used to shroud her head – for dramatic effect – when she and her cronies gathered in the back room to conjure the spirit of Hetty's recently departed mother.

She'd had the gall to conduct this seance at the wake, and had encouraged a terrified Amelia to attend. When Hetty broke it up, three of the women who had been sitting around the table in the darkened room had demanded their money back. They weren't mourners, but had come in the hopes of communicating with their own dead.

A horrified disgust had propelled Hetty to act. She could not believe her aunt would ply her trade on the day her mother had been put in the ground, that she had no qualms about taking coin from gullible customers on such a day. Hetty had screamed at them all to get out. Gertie had remained seated at the cloth-covered table, her features flickering in the candlelight. She calmly accused Hetty of dishonesty, of demanding an end to the seance not because she thought it was nonsense but because she was afraid to communicate with her estranged mother, whose spirit Gertie claimed still lingered on the earthly plane. *You need to hear, girl, what your mother has to say to you.*

Hetty had slapped her, lashing out in the belief Gertie was about to reveal a truth that had remained hidden for more than eighteen years.

Amelia had been cowering in the corner, her arms over her head. What must she have endured, left to the devices of this mad witch? Hetty had pulled Amelia to her feet and took her up to her bedroom, cursing Gertie and cursing herself. The last time she had seen her aunt had been a week later when Hetty returned unannounced to take Amelia away. Gertie had sneered at her, at Amelia too, who stumbled out of the house mutely, white-faced with grief. 'You'll be back, tail between your legs.' Hetty had ignored her. 'Where will you go with her in tow?'

'Why not ask your spirits, Gert?' This had been Hetty's parting shot before she reached for the handle and pulled the door closed on a face she had hoped never to see again.

Now, the old woman turned and walked into the house. After a moment's hesitation, Hetty stepped over the threshold.

She followed Gertie into the kitchen where the air was thick and cloying. A fire blazed in the blackened grate and steam rose from the spout of the kettle on the range. On the blue check cloth that covered the kitchen table sat a cracked-glaze teapot alongside a packet filled with muddy-looking crumbs. A tin box decorated with a cheery Christmas scene – children sledging down the side of a snow-covered hill, couples skating on a frozen pond – might contain biscuits or tarot cards or dead frogs, for all Hetty knew.

Gertie sat at one end of the table and Hetty at the other.

'I won't offer you a cup of tea,' said Gertie.

Hetty snorted. 'Start as we mean to go on, eh?'

'Oh no.' Her aunt's eyes widened in mock-innocence. 'You misunderstand me. This is a special mushroom brew, for the guests I'm expecting. It has properties that aid the spiritual experience. It helps my clients to become more receptive.'

'You drug them,' said Hetty.

'Hush, now. The spirits are all around us. Let's not agitate them.'

The back of Hetty's neck prickled. Acutely aware that the kitchen door was standing open behind her, she looked over her shoulder. Her intellect told her that her aunt spouted rubbish but her body, the animal part of her, was on high alert.

'Don't worry,' said Gertie. 'My guests won't be arriving until long after you've gone, and I can hold the spirits at bay. I find that séances held late at night seem to be the most effective.'

'It's a lot easier to frighten people in the dark,' said Hetty. 'It's no use trying to convince me you're in touch with some spirit world.'

The old woman waved a dismissive hand. 'This is like listening to your mother.' She glanced at the ceiling – 'Sorry, love,' – then back at Hetty. 'She never really understood it. Even when I laid healing hands on her, I could tell she was only humouring me.' Gertie leaned forward, her eyes shining. 'She sees the truth of it now.'

Hetty felt the hairs on her arms rise. 'You don't scare me.'

'I'm not trying to.'

'I'm not here to talk about my mother.'

'I know.' Gertie fiddled with her shawl, twisting her thin and bent fingers in the holes in the wool. She's nervous, thought Hetty, I'm making her nervous. Good. 'You're not here for your own sake, either, are you.'

'That's right.' Hetty took a deep breath. 'I want to ask you if we can put our differences to one side. I'm not putting a claim on you.' There was no point beating about the bush. 'I'm asking whether you'd consider leaving the house to Amelia.'

'You can't wait to put me in the ground, can you?'

Hetty held her tongue.

'You could beg me…'

'All right, I'm begging you.'

'…but it won't do any good. Amelia's, what, nineteen?' The look she gave Hetty was sly. 'A dangerous age for young women, especially ones that're too eager to open their legs.'

Hetty gazed at her steadily. The old cow.

'Your mother left this house to me and when I depart for the astral plane this house is going to my church. How else can we cleanse this family of your sin?'

Hetty flushed. 'We dealt with that, at the time. I agreed to go. It's not fair to—'

'Amelia should be grateful to me, if she ever hopes to ascend.' Gertie's eyes were small black holes in her head. 'There's no hope for *you*.' She continued in a breathless staccato. 'I did more for your mother, and that girl, than you ever did. All you bring is pain. You killed your father.'

'He died in a mining accident.'

'There are no accidents. There's only what we manifest and you piled shame onto my brother's shoulders and he broke under it.'

The old crone was now moving her hands through the air above her. She allowed her eyes to roll back into her head. Hetty sighed. *Here it comes.*

'Your aura chills me to the bone. I can see it. It's yellow, like phlegm. I can smell it. It's foul, like scum on a pond.' Her chest heaved. She hiccupped and dropped her head onto her chest. 'It makes me sick.'

She began to mumble incoherently.

Hetty waited for the show to be over. Gertie Barlow could probably teach that young actress Anneliese Titterton a thing or two. Presently, her aunt looked up and blinked several times. She looked about her as if she was surprised to find herself in her own kitchen. Then she gave Hetty an enquiring look.

'A solid performance, Auntie Gertie.'

Hetty took a deep breath and released it slowly, reminding herself of the reason for her visit. She was the warden of the House of Help and not to be trifled with. Telling herself that did no good. In this house, she was once again the frightened girl packing her bag to leave for good.

'Please,' she said, 'don't cut Amelia out because of your low opinion of me. It's only right that she inherits this house. My mother would want this.'

'*You* don't know what she wanted.' Gertie pointed a finger at her. '*You* weren't here.'

'I couldn't stand to come back, after.'

'You agreed to it, though, didn't you? To the lie?'

'I did as I was told, to save a scandal. I was distraught.' Hetty was proud of the clear-eyed look she gave her aunt. 'I thought I was in love, and that he was in love with me. I wasn't the only girl he took advantage of. You read the newspapers. At least our family wasn't named.'

'Don't give me that.' Gertie's lip curled in distaste. 'He was old enough to be your father. A man of the cloth, too. Ruined. None of the elders in my church would allow themselves to be tempted by a jezebel like you.'

'There's no call for that. I came here to try and have a civil conversation.'

Gertie cackled. She was enjoying herself.

'My mother...'

'Don't talk to me about your dear mother. You had nothing to do with her for nigh on twenty years.'

Hetty pushed back her chair, her body trembling with fury. She got to her feet and came around to where her aunt sat, planting her hands on the table and putting her face within inches of the old woman's. Gratifyingly, she shrank back.

'You were always so damned worried about what your precious church would say if the truth came out. What happened to forgiving and forgetting?' She stood upright. 'You're nothing but a filthy hypocrite.'

Gertie smiled, as if they were exchanging pleasantries. 'It doesn't take much for the mask to slip,' she said. 'Strike me, if you want to, go on.'

Hetty laughed and went to the door. 'I'll do better than that, Gertie. If I die first, I'll come back and haunt you.

I'll turn up at one of your little seances and tell them all what a nasty and bitter old crone you are.'

'No, you won't.' Gertie nodded at the floor. 'You're going to the other place. Only moral creatures can ascend to a higher level of being, so I'll be safe from you.'

Hetty shook her head. She would make one final attempt. 'I didn't come here to insult you, although God knows you're an easy enough target. I came to ask you to consider Amelia. You must have some feeling for her. She's a good girl.'

'You can't take credit for that.'

'I don't.'

'You'll lose her if the truth comes out.'

'You lied to her too, Gertie, ever since she was old enough to understand. You and my mother.'

They looked at each other from opposite sides of the room, the hatred between them as palpable as the sheen of sweat on her aunt's brow.

'Are you proud of yourself,' Gertie said, 'for coming here and frightening a weak old lady?'

Hetty stared at her, incredulous. 'I've heard it all now.'

'You want to be careful, coming back here. You've no friends here.'

'Now who's being threatening?'

Her aunt pointed to the door. 'Go on, get out.'

'I'll go,' said Hetty, 'but I'm glad I came here today, if only to remind myself that I did the right thing, taking Amelia away from you.'

She turned her back on her aunt and left the room, aware the old woman was following a few paces behind. She opened the front door and stepped outside, leaving the door open behind her. She didn't look back, although she felt the old woman's hateful glare.

She ought to have known her aunt would not let her have the last word.

Gertie's parting shot, delivered from the doorstep, rang in her ears.

'Do you know what I'll do if she turns up? I'll tell that girl the truth.'

Hope kept walking. The skin on the back of her neck prickled as she opened and softly closed the garden gate behind her. She would walk home, along the estuary, so that by the time she reached the guesthouse she might have regained her composure.

The old woman was shrieking now.

'I'll tell her the truth, d'you hear me? I'll tell her you're not her sister. I'll tell her you're her mother! Her mother! Do you hear me? Harlot!'

The threat was a dagger in her chest. Hetty gasped, and almost faltered, but somehow managed to keep a steady pace to the end of the lane. When she turned the corner and knew she was lost from view, she stopped and put her hands to her face. She had failed here today. Now she would have to cling to the hope that Linus Harmon was as good as his word, that he would marry Amelia, and that Amelia would stay away from this hateful place, so that Hetty would not lose her to the truth.

Chapter 16

'It's a trade-off, see.'

The girl sitting between Hope and Amelia on the bench in the graveyard of St Peter's Church see-sawed her hands in the air.

'More money if I take the ladies' maid job, but it's live-in, it's in the middle of nowhere, and I'd be at her beck and call all hours of the day and night. She seems an all right sort, but that's not guaranteed.'

Hope nodded encouragingly. 'Go on.'

'Well, I'd be a lot poorer at the cutlery works, on account of paying for lodgings and feeding myself, but my nights and Saturday afternoons and all of blessed Sunday would be mine. I'd have more freedom, see? But I'd not be living in a fancy house.'

The girl, named Nancy, had travelled on foot from Stocksbridge and had come to the house for one night to break the journey to a large country estate south of Chesterfield. When Hope and Amelia had risen from the kitchen table after tea, to embark on their evening walk, Nancy had asked whether she might join them. Hope had suspected she was wrestling with a dilemma. It transpired Nancy had picked up the local newspaper and seen an advertisement for factory work for young women, here in the middle of town, no experience necessary, and good prospects for hard workers.

'Answer me quick,' said Amelia. 'If I were to toss a coin and heads was the big house in the country and tails was the factory just over yonder, which side would you want it to land on?'

'Tails.'

'There you go then!'

Hope frowned. 'This needs serious thought. It's not a game.'

Amelia rolled her eyes. 'First instincts count for a lot, in my book.' She reached over the girl to pat Hope's belly. 'Heads a girl, tails a boy. What do you choose? Look sharp now!'

Hope batted her away. 'It doesn't matter,' she said, 'provided it's a healthy child.'

'With the usual number of fingers and toes,' Nancy chimed in. 'My sister's a slave to five boys, poor soul. Keeps hoping for a girl that'll help her round the house.'

Amelia tipped her head to one side and raised an eyebrow. 'Come on, Hope. Heads a girl, tails a boy.'

Hope blew out her lips. 'Oh, all right then. Heads.'

'Ha. You can call her after me, if you like,' said Amelia.

'I won't be calling her anything, will I?' Hope smiled to soften her harshly spoken words. Amelia's flippant remark had wounded her. She rubbed her eyes wearily. It wasn't even that. She was used to Amelia's ways by now, and found her more amusing than not, even when thoughtless or caustic comments were directed at her. There was no malice intended. No, it was fear of what lay ahead that sharpened Hope's tongue. The baby inside her would have to come out. The prospect was terrifying. How ridiculous she would sound, expressing that thought aloud.

She shifted in her seat to try to ease the ache in her back, and the heaviness that had settled in her limbs.

She flexed her fingers. They were swollen and white and reminded her of the puffball mushrooms she'd forage from the forest as a child, washing them clean of dirt at the standpipe and presenting them to Cook who would slice them up for breakfast. She loved mushrooms. When all this was over, she'd go foraging again, for mushrooms and wild garlic, and fry them up for the residents of the house. She'd pick apples and pears and plums and make giant crumbles. Rhubarb too. Was there anything finer than dipping a raw rhubarb stick into a bowl of sugar?

A young woman strolled past, pushing a perambulator with a large black hood that concealed the baby inside. She smiled and nodded to Hope as she went by. 'Only way to get him off to the land of Nod,' she said. 'You've got it all to come.'

Hope smiled back politely. The wife of the owner of a forge, or the nanny if she employed one, would be pushing her child's pram. Mrs Gunson had reluctantly given her a small amount of information about the couple. They owned a large townhouse – Mrs Gunson refused to say where it was located – and were in their mid-life and still devoted to one another. He'd been a farmer's son with big dreams about life in the steel industry, and she had been born higher up the social strata, betrothed to a wealthy gentleman she did not love. They had battled the odds to be together. It all sounded incredibly romantic. Mrs Gunson wouldn't tell Hope their names. She could meet the couple if she insisted upon it, but it was suggested that she might prefer not to. Hope had signed an agreement, witnessed by Mrs Shaw and Mr Wallace, agreeing to relinquish all claims on the child. 'Put this entire episode behind you,' Mrs Shaw had advised briskly. 'A clean break is often kindest.'

Hope flattened her hands against her stomach. It was as hard as stone. A dull throbbing had started, low down. The baby she was carrying was an *episode* in her life, and not the story of it. It was only in the early hours when sleep eluded her that she had any doubt she had made the right decision. She was Hope now, Miss Hope of the House of Help, and the mystery of her ongoing amnesia came up less and less frequently. Even Amelia had given up teasing her with her true name when they were alone. She hadn't been addressed as *Emma* for a long time. Perhaps that would be a good name for her baby. Then she remembered anew she wouldn't be naming the child.

Her neck was stiff. She tilted her head back as far as it would go, gazing up at the canopy spread above their heads by the oaks on the edge of the graveyard of St Peter's. The leaves rustled in the breeze, whispering their secrets to one another.

'Good evening, ladies.'

She recognised the voice immediately and jerked her head down to find Angus Deveraux standing before her. He was finely dressed in tailcoat and topper, a white cravat at his throat, his green eyes full of mirth. He introduced the young lady whose gloved hand rested in the crook of his elbow. Hope didn't catch her name – she was preoccupied with trying to maintain a smile that very quickly made her jaw ache – only that she was the daughter of a friend of the Deveraux family, new to the town. Angus was taking her to the Theatre Royal to see a production of *The Red Lamp*.

'It's a most powerful drama,' the woman said, shyly.

Hope ignored Amelia's snort. 'I have heard of it,' she said.

'What's it about?' said Amelia.

Angus answered. 'A Russian princess tries to save her erstwhile brother from the baying mob. It's a comedy.'

Hope laughed. 'You ought to pen the review for the newspaper.'

'I would if they would have me!' said Angus. 'I should love to do nothing but enjoy free visits to the theatre with the only obligation being the requirement to write a review.'

The woman on his arm looked into the distance. 'We ought to be going or we'll miss curtain up,' she said.

Angus tipped his hat. 'Ladies.' He held Hope's eyes for a moment. 'I wish you well.'

'Who,' said Nancy, after they'd watched the couple stroll away, 'was *that*?'

Amelia laughed. 'That's Angus Deveraux. He likes our Hope here, but…' Her shrug said it all. 'Anyhow, she's not half as pretty as thee.'

It hadn't occurred to Hope, although it ought to have, that Angus would be stepping out with young ladies. He was a handsome man with a wealthy background, a catch. And here Hope sat, her dress stretched across her enormous belly. She had seen the eyes of the woman on his arm flit from her belly to the bare fingers of her left hand and back again.

Hope could have been the woman on Angus Deveraux's arm. She had had the life mapped out for her snatched away. What would replace it?

She did not want to raise her cousin's child, and how could she? Where would she go? An unmarried mother with a bastard in tow. Unthinkable.

Perhaps, once she'd given the baby up, she'd remain a spinster for the rest of her life, like Miss Barlow, and find happiness in devoting herself to the good work of the house. More immediately, she should curtail any further conversation that centred on Angus Deveraux's wit and charm.

'What you might do,' she said to Nancy, 'is find out how you go about securing the factory work. It's not a given, whereas the other job is yours for the taking.'

'The advertisement says to turn up at six o'clock tomorrow morning, those that want training. They'll take twenty girls.'

Amelia laughed. 'Sounds like it was meant to be.'

'In that case,' said Hope. 'You could go along, see if it suits and if it doesn't, continue your journey. We can take you for another night or two while you find accommodation.'

'You might be kippin' on the kitchen floor, mind,' said Amelia.

The girl nodded vigorously in agreement. 'Yes, that'd be grand.'

Hope was too uncomfortable to remain seated any longer – more than that, she felt a compulsion to *move*. 'I think I'll go back now,' she said.

When she stood, the back of her skirt clung wetly to her skin. She looked for a damp patch on the bench but it was dry as dust. Underneath her petticoat, liquid trickled down her thighs, the tickle of it making her shudder. She gasped when a painful spasm rippled across her lower back.

'Hope?' Amelia's concerned face filled her vision.

'I need to get back to the house,' she said. Her throat felt as if it was stuffed with sheep's wool. 'I think I've had an accident.'

'An accident? What's that mean? Hope, you're white as a sheet. You're scaring me.'

She opened her mouth to reassure Amelia, but another bolt of pain shot through her body and she stumbled, leaning over the bench to grip the back of it. The wood was rough against her palms, reassuringly solid. Her heart was galloping, the blood pulsing in her ears.

'Jumping Jehosephat. She's not wet herself,' said Nancy. She took Hope's elbow and indicated that Amelia should support her on the other side. 'Her waters have broken. Come on, love. You need to find somewhere more comfortable to do this than a bench in the street with everyone gawping at you.'

–

After a wretched night followed by a full day spent tangled in the covers on Miss Barlow's bed, Hope reflected grimly on the girl's words. She had thought the baby's arrival was imminent when the others set a fast pace back to the house. She was certain that at some point both her feet left the ground. Yet here she remained, in purgatory.

It was impossible not to think of the stories she'd been told around the kitchen table. There were those who seemed to think she wanted to hear about giving birth in all its grisly horror. One woman had dared to say she'd had an easy time of it – she'd got up for work one morning after a good night's sleep and the child had popped out like a cork from a bottle – but her experience was derided by the others. Hope was told, with relish, this was the exception that proved the rule. And it was this particular woman's sixth child. The first was always the worst, and took the longest to arrive.

She was so relieved when Miss Barlow appeared on the evening of that long day, just returned from Cleethorpes, that she burst into tears. Amelia hovered over her sister's shoulder, an anxious look on her face. Miss Barlow placed a cool hand on Hope's brow and spoke in quiet tones to the midwife, and then told Hope that there was no cause for alarm, the labour was progressing normally, if slowly. This wasn't uncommon with a first child. The midwife declined the offer of a meal and said she'd walk home, get a few hours' sleep and return early the next morning. 'Might be out by then, love,' she said cheerfully to Hope as she took her leave.

Between clenched teeth, Hope apologised for taking Miss Barlow's bed.

Amelia didn't give her sister a chance to reply. 'You could hardly do this in a dorm full of women!' she cried. Hope was barely aware of her being shooed out of the room by her sister.

She tossed and turned in between bouts of agony that she thought would squeeze the life out of her. When the midwife returned before dawn, Hope threw across the room the flannel Miss Barlow had laid on her brow and screamed for a doctor.

'I'm dying,' she said. 'My heart can't take it.'

The midwife laughed. 'You're not dying, love.'

'You'll forget this,' said Miss Barlow, 'as soon as the baby's out.'

What did she know about giving birth? Hope cursed Miss Barlow, cursed the midwife, and cursed all men for the thing they had between their legs. The two women took her under the arms and hauled her up onto the pillows and told her that it was time and she should push as hard as she liked. 'Put that fury to good use, girl.'

She did.

Chapter 17

Emma Hyde was ten years old, sitting on her bed, legs stretched out, grumpily watching her mother sort through the clothes in her wardrobe. Mama had already filled a box with old toys. The one-eyed rag doll stuffed under Emma's arm had barely escaped banishment. One by one, Mama was removing the clothes Emma had outgrown to donate to a second-hand clothes shop. The plainer things would be sent to the orphanage.

She thought Mama looked very beautiful in the early morning light that streamed through the window. Rose Hyde was elegant. She spelled the word in her head. She was good at spellings. Elegant, and compassionate. She could spell that word too. Emma knew that donating her clothes was a *good deed* but it still made her sad to see her favourite red boots transferred from the floor of the wardrobe into the trunk at the foot of the bed. She could no longer squeeze her feet into them, but that wasn't the point.

'I want to keep those,' she said.

Instead of answering, Mama took out a dress and held it up to the light critically.

'This is looking rather worn,' she said.

Emma loved that dress. It was her favourite colour, green, with a flouncy skirt and black buttons, and a soft black velvet bow beneath a round white lace collar. She wailed.

'That still fits me!'

'No, I noticed the other day that it's sitting above the knee, which won't do at all. You've sprouted up again, my darling.' She folded the dress into the trunk and smiled at Emma. 'Give me the baby.'

'What?' Emma looked down. Instead of a rag doll with one black button eye, she was holding in her arms a sleeping new-born wrapped in a thin cloth.

'Give him to me, Emma. Please do as you are told.'

Ice-cold terror filled her veins, making her teeth chatter. The baby was freezing too, his lips turning blue. She began to scream.

'My darling, there's really no need for that,' said Mama calmly. She reached out and plucked the baby from Emma's arms. She laid him on top of the dress in the trunk and lowered the lid. When she looked at Emma her eyes were sad. 'You can't keep him, my love. We're donating him to the orphanage.'

Emma screamed and screamed.

'*Hope*! Wake up.'

She came to in a tangle of sheets, gulping for air. Amelia stood over her, holding a breakfast tray.

'You were tossing and turning like I don't know what,' she said. 'Bad dream? Here, take this.' She thrust out the tray. 'Hetty says you have to eat summat.'

Hope wriggled into a sitting position, wincing in discomfort. The midwife had told her she might be sore for a few days then all would be well. Gradually, her heart resumed its normal beat. She peered into the bassinet as she took the tray from Amelia. Swaddled tightly, her son was sleeping soundly. His long black lashes lay against cheeks that were perfectly smooth and round. His nose was a button she wanted to spend all her days kissing.

She turned her attention to the contents of the tray. A plate of buttered crumpets sat beside a large mug of tea. The burnt smell of the toasted edges reached her nostrils. It was delicious. She realised she was ravenous.

'Thank you,' she said. 'Yes, that was a horrible dream.' She began to describe it but the words stuck in her throat. 'Never mind.'

Amelia laughed. 'Good. There's nowt more boring than hearing about other people's dreams.'

The clean nightgown Hope had changed into during the night was stuck to her body, the material stiff over her nipples where milk had leaked and dried. When the baby had been born, and his startlingly loud cries filled the room, Miss Barlow and the midwife had helped her to encourage him to feed. Hope had been exhausted and cross but as soon as she felt those tiny, hard gums latch on, her stomach had tightened and a warmth, a wonderful warmth, spread to every part of her. It lingered still, a new-found emotion she knew would never leave her.

After he had finished feeding, Miss Barlow had tucked him into the bassinet and Hope had slept.

She shuddered. Her child wasn't going to an orphanage. He would be raised as she had been, watched over by doting parents in a household that would never feel anything but secure and loving.

When he woke and began to wail, she loosened the ribbons of her gown and took a large bite from one of the crumpets before setting the tray aside.

She spoke through a mouthful of food. 'Can you pass him to me?'

Amelia carefully lifted the baby from the bassinet. 'Hetty said to eat when you can, because this one,' she gently laid Hope's son in her arms, 'won't give you a minute to yoursen. I don't know what makes her the expert, though.'

Hope gazed down at her son, knowing she would never tire of drinking in every perfect detail. He was so innocent, so helpless, and she was in complete thrall to this tiny scrap. She bent to kiss the whorl of dark hair on the top of his head. She would kill for him. She would die for him. How could she ever give him up?

'I can't get over it,' said Amelia.

'What?'

She pointed at Hope. 'Thee.' She pointed at the baby. 'This.'

Hope laughed. 'The signs were there for all to see,' she said. She picked up the half-eaten crumpet and crammed the rest into her mouth.

'Was it terrible?' said Amelia. She sat on the edge of the mattress. 'The whole house could hear the racket you were making.'

She held up one finger, chewed and swallowed. 'No,' she said. 'It wasn't terrible.' She positioned the baby more securely on her breast, self-conscious under Amelia's fascinated gaze. 'This is reward enough, just this moment.'

'Would you do it again?'

'Never.'

They burst out laughing. 'Oh no,' wailed Amelia, 'and I want to have five or six with Linus. How do women do it?'

Hope remembered Miss Barlow's words.

'We forget,' she said.

'Well, you'd have to.'

She drained the cup of strong, sweet tea Amelia had made, aware of her friend's eyes examining her face. It was a similar look to the curious one she had given Hope on her first morning at the house, when she had sat, terror-struck, at the kitchen table, and been given a cup of tea, a piece of toast and a new name.

'Want another cup, love?' said Amelia.

'No, thank you.'

'How will you be able to do it?'

Hope knew what she was talking about. In a few days, her son's new parents would be coming to collect him. She rested her head back on the pillow and stared at the ceiling. 'Simply by doing it,' she said. 'What choice do I have?'

–

Miss Barlow came in later that morning and shook Hope awake to tell her water had been heated in the copper for her bath. Hope quickly braided and pinned up her hair, kissed the baby on his sweet-smelling forehead – he smelled like butter and almonds – and padded down the hall, eyes still half-closed, to the water closet. The tin bath had been placed on the linoleum in the space between the varnished flanks of the commode and the matching stand on which sat a wash basin, jug and soap, and a towel. Hope saw that her day dress, and underclothes including a corset, stockings and a drawstring chemise, were folded on the closed lid of the commode.

Her toiletry bag containing tooth powder, brush, hair-brush and flannel sat on the floor by the bath.

It seemed she'd had all the bed rest she was going to get.

The bath was half-full of lukewarm water. She pulled the nightgown over her head, took the bar of soap and climbed into it, lowering herself gently down. She sat for a few moments, her eyes closed, enjoying the warm silkiness of the water against her bare skin. The soap was a plain block of carbolic. She sniffed it, wrinkling her nose. She could no longer remember the smell of the jasmine-scented soap her mother loved.

Her previous life seemed so distant now, as if it had belonged to someone else. She rubbed the soap over her limbs, her armpits, the sore parts between her legs, splashed water over herself and climbed out of the bath. She dried herself vigorously with the towel, leaving it draped over the edge of the basin. On her first morning at the house, Miss Barlow had brought her into this room and had her bend her head over the basin so she could scrub the dried blood out of her hair. Then she had been instructed to return to the dorm to make her bed. Even the girl she had been then seemed a stranger to her now, smaller, mouse-like.

Once dressed, she opened the door of the water closet and stepped into the hall. Mrs Gunson was standing by the door to the parlour, talking to a girl wearing a servant's uniform covered in mud and grass as if she had spent the night sleeping in a field. The girl glanced at Hope and away again, her tear-streaked face set in grim lines.

'Hope!' Mrs Gunson came forward to embrace her. 'You're on your feet already. How marvellous.' She seemed uncertain what to say next. Hope supposed that congratulating her on the birth of a baby that was to be taken away from her in a matter of days would be inappropriate.

Instead, Mrs Gunson took the girl's arm and moved her forward to face Hope. 'This young lady was sitting on the steps outside when I arrived. Have you a bed?'

'I can check with Miss Barlow.' Hope smiled at the girl. 'Come into the kitchen. I'll make you a cup of tea. Do you have a name?'

Chapter 18

Amelia handed her basket and her list to the grocer's boy and promised to return in two shakes of a lamb's tail. 'I'll be back right after the ball drops outside Brown's,' she called as she hurried out of the store.

In the high street, she waited for a covered wagon steered by a weary looking man and pulled by a dusty Shire to clop by, before crossing towards the impressive five-storey edifice at number thirty-nine which housed John Walsh's baby linen and ladies' outfitting store.

She glanced at the tiny garments on display behind the plate glass and strode on. The baby was already buried under an avalanche of long white gowns and knitted or crocheted white caps, mittens and bootees. Cook had bought him a broderie anglaise embroidered jacket that must have cost her a month's wages. He had also been gifted a cream-coloured silk bonnet by the house trustees that had been put to one side as it kept slipping over his eyes.

Amelia reached Market Place and stopped outside the shop door of Brown's jewellers, where the time ball hung. She had witnessed this ball drop many times and remained fascinated by it. The last time she had stopped to observe this unique attraction, along with others who had been passing by, the jeweller had come out of his shop and explained in heavily accented English that the time ball was connected through a wire link to Greenwich and faithfully dropped at one o'clock every day to an accuracy of one-sixtieth of a second.

If anyone cared to step inside he would sell them a time piece that was equally accurate.

The others drifted away but Amelia stayed and asked him where he was from. He'd told her he had fled Poland two decades earlier and was a revolutionary. She hadn't known whether to believe him or not.

In addition to the time ball, there was something else on display at this particular jewellery shop that Amelia coveted. She peered in the window. It sat there still, beside a gemstone-encrusted pendant. A simple, unadorned silver locket on a thin silver chain. She stepped inside the shop before her nerve deserted her and gazed about her self-consciously. The jeweller – the same man she had engaged in conversation – greeted her cordially, his bald pate gleaming and his eyes lively behind wire-rimmed spectacles. This man would know just by looking at her that everything in his shop was beyond her means.

'Good day to you, miss,' he said.

'You have a small silver locket, in the window,' said Amelia. 'I noticed it the other day.'

'You noticed it the other day?' He nodded enthusiastically. 'I remember you, miss. You asked me where I had come to this town from, but I don't think you believed my answer. It's a wise girl who mistrusts the stories people tell her.'

While he was speaking, he was unlocking the display cabinet and lifting out the locket. 'This one?' Amelia nodded. He draped it on a small black velvet cushion and laid it on the counter.

'How much?'

'How much? A fine piece like this, I'll sell it to you for eight shillings.'

Amelia tried not to let her disappointment show. 'That's reight expensive for such a little thing.'

A handsome woman emerged from a curtained alcove. She gave Amelia a friendly nod. 'Isn't the price on that ten shillings, my dear?'

The jeweller peered at her. 'That one is ten shillings?'

Amelia couldn't help smiling, despite her dismay. Eight shillings was beyond her, let alone ten. But the jeweller repeated back every question he was asked and that was amusing.

All she wanted to do now was leave as gracefully as possible a shop she should never have entered in the first place. She made a show of sorting through the coins in her purse. 'Oh dear, I've not brought enough. I'll come back, though. Another day.' She felt a blush warm her cheeks. 'I need to get back to work now. I love coming here to see your time ball.' She needed to stop herself babbling like a brook in full flow. 'Sithee later.'

'Just a moment.' The woman came around the counter. She must be the jeweller's wife. She wore a fashionable dress with a high bustle. Amelia straightened the sleeves of her jacket. It needed a wash. 'Where you do work, my dear?'

She coloured slightly. 'At the House of Help in Paradise Square. I'm the housekeeper.'

'Ah!' The woman clapped her hands. 'I know it. In fact, we are donating a brooch to raffle off at the bazaar. Aren't we, Harris?'

'We are donating a brooch?'

'Yes, dear.' She smiled at Amelia. 'I so admire the work you do there. It must be difficult. But I hear the warden is formidable.'

Amelia laughed. 'You can say that again. She's my sister.'

'Hmm. I think, my dear, we could offer a discount?'

'Could we offer a discount?' Mr Brown repeated. 'Let's see.' He took off his spectacles, polished them on a piece of cloth and wrapped them back over his ears. 'How much do you have on you, miss?'

Amelia tipped coins onto the glass counter, and subtracted the grocery money. 'A crown and a two-bob bit.'

The woman put her hand on the jeweller's arm. 'I think that might be the perfect price for the young lady, don't you?'

–

When she was far enough away from the shop, Amelia stopped to examine the beribboned box containing her locket. She had explained it was for someone else, and the jeweller had insisted on gift wrapping it. She was so flustered she had forgotten to pause to watch the time ball drop. It was time for her to finish her errands, that was for sure.

Back at the house, Hope was in the kitchen, banking up the fire in the range.

'Where is everybody?' said Amelia, putting her basket on the table. The gift box was concealed beneath a packet of flour and a bag of onions.

'Here and there,' said Hope. She looked exhausted, her cheeks hollowed out and her hair loose as a madwoman's.

But her eyes twinkled when she took an envelope from her pocket. 'You've had a letter from your one true love.'

'Stop it,' said Amelia, beaming with pleasure. 'Give it here.'

'Do you want me to read it to you? The baby is sleeping.' She yawned and added, 'for now.'

Amelia's gut tightened. What if Linus made mention of Hope, or Emma, in his letter? She should never have confided in him. She felt herself colour slightly. 'No, it's all right. I'm more than capable, and that's thanks to you, love.'

Her mind raced. Should she come clean now before Hope inevitably discovered what she had done? She would give the excuse that there should be no secrets between a husband and wife. She had been obliged to tell him. Hadn't she?

'You're miles away,' said Hope.

'Am I?' Amelia rubbed her forehead. 'Oh. I went into town and got thee summat.'

She fished in the basket and took out the gift box, then hesitated. What if Hope thought it was a cheap trinket? She was used to much finer things in her past life. She would have picked out the jewelled pendant, Amelia was certain. 'It's nothing fancy.'

'One moment,' said Hope. She wiped her hands on a damp cloth and took the box from Amelia. 'Thank you so much!'

'You've not seen what it is yet.'

Hope turned the box over in her hands. 'Well, I know it isn't baby clothes. Two days old and he's already the best dressed boy in town.'

Amelia held her breath as Hope unwrapped the box and lifted the lid. It was so small, worthless really. A waste of money, even if she had got it cheap. She shouldn't have bothered.

'It's lovely,' said Hope. She held it up, setting the locket swinging gently on the end of the chain. She looked at Amelia with tears in her eyes. 'How incredibly generous of you.'

Amelia shrugged to hide her delight. 'It's nowt, really. I was thinkin' you could put a lock of his hair in it. Summat to keep.'

Hope's face crumpled. She dropped into a chair, clutching the locket in her fist.

'Oh no,' said Amelia. She put her arm around Hope's shoulders. 'I've upset you. I'm sorry.'

'No, no.' Hope's mouth trembled. 'It really is so thoughtful of you. And that is a wonderful idea. Help me put it on?'

Amelia was fastening the clasp when her sister entered the room.

'There you are,' said Hetty. 'He's awake and hungry.'

Hope sprang to her feet and gave Amelia a quick hug on her way out of the room. 'You are the best friend to me, Amelia.'

Amelia was touched. 'Daft apeth,' she said.

Hetty waited until Hope had gone. 'What was all that about, then?'

'Nowt much.' Amelia shrugged. 'Shall I mash us some tea?'

Hetty shook her head. 'I've an errand to run and then a meeting with Mrs Gunson about—'

Amelia interrupted her. 'You'll have to tell me how it went with Auntie Gertie sooner or later, or I'm telling thee, I'm hoppin' on a train.'

Her sister sat down heavily and drummed her fingers on the table. 'There's nowt to tell. I've washed my hands of her and so should you.'

'Did you tell her I'm getting wed? Did she give you owt?' She was thinking about the locket that had belonged to their mother, and the tapestry she would hang in the home she made with Linus.

'I got nowt but a flea in my ear,' said Hetty. 'She's leaving the house to that cult she worships. There's no inheritance, for either of us.'

'Then I'll try,' said Amelia. 'I grew up with her. She must have some feeling towards me.'

'Please,' said Hetty and, to Amelia's surprise, began to cry. 'There's nowt for you there. I can't keep telling thee. She's poison, that woman. I'm begging you to stay away from her.'

Amelia touched her shoulder awkwardly. 'All right, then.' She had never seen Hetty weep before. It frightened her. 'Come here.' Hetty stood and they embraced. 'No need for the waterworks, eh?'

'I'm tired, that's all.' Hetty went to the door then returned and took Amelia's hands in hers. 'I want to give you and Linus my blessing.'

'Well, that's going in my next letter to him, and no mistake.'

Hetty laughed and wiped her eyes and sniffed mightily. 'So, that's that. And what's this?' She picked up the envelope Amelia had left on the table. The subject was clearly closed.

'From Linus,' Amelia said. 'Hetty...'

'Hmm?'

'If there's nothing needs doing right away, I'm going to take this upstairs to read.' She would go to the classroom, where there were spelling books donated by the private boys' school in the square, in the event she couldn't decipher Linus's words.

Hetty nodded. 'Yes, all right. There is summat else I want to say.'

'Oh aye?'

'I know that Hope is very good at keeping herself occupied with the business of the house. I don't know what we'd do without her. But she's going to need a friend, once the baby is gone.'

'I know,' said Amelia. 'Don't fret. I'll look after her.'

What would her sister do if she learned the truth? Amelia had been fascinated to learn Hope's true identity, but that knowledge was increasingly a burden. She did not yet know that the contents of the letter she held in her hand would soon relieve her of it.

–

Linus began by explaining that *due to unforeseen circumstances* he would not be visiting the following Sunday, and might be absent for several weeks.

> *Until we meet again, I hold you in my heart as I hope I am held in yours.*

Amelia sat in a chair by the window, the letter held loosely in her hand. Another excuse. Not even an excuse, as he hadn't done her the courtesy of giving a reason. She wondered whether Hetty had been right about him all along. It was ironic her sister seemed to be warming to Linus just as he was cooling off.

There was more – he'd covered three sheets in his elaborate lettering – but he'd already disappointed her.

What was the point in reading on? No doubt, he'd go on to shower her with compliments, to ask if she was still wearing his ring, and on and on. Thank goodness Hope was not reading this letter to her. The humiliation would be too great.

Amelia lifted the pages onto her lap. She didn't want to face anybody. She might as well finish reading.

My darling, some good news.

Amelia frowned. He had visited a spa town called Bath and got into a conversation with a police constable, who took him to his local hostelry for a meal. Amelia wished she read well enough to be able to skim all this detail, instead of having to focus on every word. When would he get to his *good news*? The patrons of this hostelry were having a conversation about a young lady belonging to a wealthy family who had gone missing near the end of the previous year.

You will have already guessed the name, my dear. Emma Hyde.

Amelia's hand flew to her mouth. She crumpled the pages in her fist and closed her eyes. 'No, no, no.'

She could picture Linus, waiting to throw in his morsel of gossip. He knew where the missing girl was. He knew she was expecting a child. She was up in Sheffield, living in a house of help for women, under an assumed name. *I can give you the name*, he would declare, *and the address.*

Amelia smoothed out the paper. Her heart was tripping in her chest.

I am sorry I haven't had the opportunity to discuss this with you, my darling, but I believe that poor couple deserve to know where their only child is. The good news – our good news – is that a reward has been offered. It will set us up nicely. I am sure your friend will thank us, in the end. Surely, a reunion would be better than the lie she is living.

Amelia's stomach churned as she read on to the very end. She ripped the letter into pieces. She would throw it on the fire in the kitchen range on her way out. Linus didn't say whether he'd been in touch with the Hydes, or even given dates for the period of time he was in the spa town. Hope would never forgive her. Amelia had ruined the only real friendship she'd ever had. She wanted to wail at the injustice of it, but knew she had only herself to blame. She closed her fist over the shreds of the letter. She had to prevent Linus from revealing Hope's secret, if it wasn't already too late.

Amelia prayed she could get to him first.

Chapter 19

The dormitory was quiet, all five beds made up neatly, each small bureau tidied. Hetty stood in the doorway and mentally traversed the room, tallying up.

The bed at the end, nearest the window, was Amelia's, next to it Hope's – temporarily occupied by Hetty. The third bed in the row belonged to a young woman delivered yesterday evening by a police constable. He'd chased her through the town after she'd stolen a gentleman's purse and had decided the House of Help was a better option 'for the poor young lass' than a cell and the summary courts.

Ordinarily, Hetty would have her deputy interview the girl but Hope was busy trying to pacify the baby. His piercing cries echoed around the house as Hetty led the girl into the kitchen and directed her to sit. She dropped into a chair, pushed her hand through messy red curls and surveyed the room before turning friendly eyes on Hetty. She had told the constable she was living on the streets but there was nothing of the grubbiness of the gutter about her. Her mouth curved easily into a lopsided grin and her voice dropped an octave when she playfully asked Hetty if she was running a baby farm on the quiet. Hetty could see very well how she might have charmed the police constable into bringing her to the house rather than locking her up.

She gave her name as Nan Turpin, her age as twenty-six – to Hetty's surprise; she looked younger – and claimed to have no people. She'd been tasked with helping the laundry woman operate the mangle and hang clothes to dry, and before long peals of laughter filtered up from the scullery. The house had hooked a lively one there. Perhaps she could be landed in the training school.

Hetty continued her mental appraisal.

Opposite Nan Turpin's bed were two others. These were taken by a mother, her twelve-year old twin daughters and her older child, a sullen girl of fifteen. Ordinarily, a family would go to the workhouse but a new agent, a young and enthusiastic woman named Alice Leigh, had successfully pleaded their case. The father had disappeared, leaving a trail of debt in his wake, and their family home repossessed. Suitable lodgings would be found for them as quickly as possible but for now they were homeless with no extended family to call on.

The workhouse was the only other option open to them, and if the woman had been blessed with sons instead of daughters that's where they'd be sent.

Hetty had already checked the bedrooms on the floors above, and the attic beds. When Mr Wallace had visited earlier that day she'd warned him they were bursting at the seams and he had hinted that the trustees were looking for larger premises in another part of the town. He must have seen the expression on Hetty's face, for he assured her that the warden – and her staff – would be transferred to the new place. They had passed a pleasant half hour chatting about Cleethorpes and the grand bazaar being held a few days hence that would, said Mr Wallace, transform the fortunes of the house.

She swept her gaze over the ground floor dormitory a final time and was about to leave the room when something caught her eye. There was a scrap of half-curled paper on the pillow of Amelia's bed, the white on white almost invisible. As Hetty got closer she saw there was writing on it, in pencil, words spelled out in blocky capitals. She picked it up.

I HAVE GONE TO VISIT LINUS IN TAMWORTH. PLEASE DON'T WORRY.

Amelia's signature was scrawled beneath it.

Hetty dropped to her knees and wrenched open the drawer of Amelia's bureau. She found the stack of letters from Linus tucked into a set of undergarments and drew them out, a grim set to her mouth. The foolish child. Hetty scanned the postmarks on the envelopes. The latest had been delivered to the house several days ago. Where was the letter Amelia had received today? What were its contents? She shoved the rest back in the drawer and closed it. She had no intention of snooping at their correspondence, though she was surprised how extensive it was. These were love letters and not meant for her. She had written and received love letters, once upon a time, and destroyed them all when she was betrayed, a betrayal that now seemed inevitable. The problem was that Amelia had no experience. She didn't understand what men were like. She'd only get her fingers burned, running off like this. Worse, she had written *Please don't worry*, a plea that only served to do the opposite.

Running up the stairs to the classroom, Hetty rued the day that hawker had shown up on the doorstep. If only

Amelia had not come downstairs at that precise moment. Hetty had suspected he was no good. She ought to have snuffed out that spark of attraction. Her disapproval had only fanned the flames. Some of the dismay she was feeling had to do with the fact that Amelia had not addressed her note to anybody, or more specifically had not addressed it to Hetty. She had believed they were growing closer, that Amelia had finally accepted her, as a sister, which was all she could hope for, and as somebody she could trust. The note was a dash of cold water in Hetty's face.

She searched the classroom, opening books and shaking the spines, getting down on her hands and knees to look under the chairs, scattering the carefully stacked writing boards. No letter.

On the ground floor, the door to Hetty's quarters, the room that had once been the house's main parlour and ante-chamber, was closed. She rapped on it, impatient, and entered without waiting for a reply. Hope sat at the desk, going through house correspondence. She put her finger to her lips and pointed to the baby. He was fast on, making those sleeping baby snuffling sounds in the bassinet by the bed.

Hetty laid the fragment of paper on the desk in front of her. If anyone knew what Amelia was up to, it would be Hope. She spoke quietly, watching Hope's face carefully. 'What do you make of this?'

The corners of Hope's mouth turned down and she shook her head. 'I don't know. She hasn't told me anything. Are you sure she's gone?'

'Yes, I've just done the rounds of the house. She's nowhere to be found.'

A thin wail filled the room.

'He can't be hungry again,' said Hope. 'I feel like I'm feeding him constantly.'

It was on the tip of Hetty's tongue to say that things would settle down and he would find a routine both baby and mother could tolerate. Of course, that would never happen. She picked the baby up and passed him to Hope, who set about feeding him. Hetty waited.

'Perhaps,' said Hope, 'Linus has put off a trip to town. He's done this before. Amelia might have decided to take matters into her own hands. You know how impetuous she is.' Hope shrugged. 'She's gone to see him. I've no doubt it's as simple as that.'

'Well, she's left us in the lurch, chasing after this man. I don't understand how she could afford...' Hetty stopped. A terrible thought had occurred to her. She pulled open the bottom drawer of the desk where the house expense money was kept, a small clay pot containing crowns and shillings totalling some five pounds. The pot was there, the money gone. She groaned.

'What is it?' said Hope.

'The money we keep here,' said Hetty. She felt, for the first time in a long time, that she might weep. 'For emergencies. I've dipped into it when a train fare has been needed quickly. Amelia knew about it, and she knows it's not mine. It belongs to the house.'

Hope's eyes widened in understanding.

If only Amelia had simply run away. Now she was a thief to boot.

She closed the drawer. 'Foolish girl.'

'What shall we do?' said Hope.

Hetty went to the window and lifted the net. There was a queue outside the butcher's shop, two or three women standing in the shadow of the awning and the rest basking in the sunshine. There were men outside the Q, resting their tankards on the window ledge. Two gentlemen in toppers, tailcoats and striped trousers emerged from the solicitor's office and strolled down towards New Queen's Street. She wondered how far Amelia had got, whether she could intercept her at Victoria station, whether there would be any point. It would take twenty minutes to reach the giant Wicker Arches, the viaduct that had been built to feed into the rail station. Amelia would then have to wait for a train to take her south. Hetty didn't think there were any direct services to Tamworth. Even if Hetty found her waiting on the platform, she couldn't physically prevent the girl from stepping onto a train. She certainly wasn't going to create a scene for all to enjoy.

'Miss Barlow? What do you think we should do?'

She turned to look at Hope. 'Nothing.' She turned back to the view of the square. The boots of passers-by kicked up dust from the cobbles. A downpour was needed, to clear the air. 'We'll wait and see.' It was unthinkable that she'd lose Amelia again, so soon after claiming her back.

'Aye.' Hetty said. 'She's taken off in a temper. She probably came to her senses on her way to the station and is on her way back now. I don't think there's any need to tell anybody, not just yet.'

Hope murmured her assent.

Hetty was about to turn away from the window when she saw a man striding up the square, apparently making a beeline for the house, a woman following a couple of steps behind. He wore a dirt-streaked denim vest over a collarless shirt that must have once been white, and heavy trousers over scuffed workboats. A navvy or a miner. He was clean-shaven, with a mop of dirty blonde hair, and carried his cap in his hand. The woman's head was covered by a scarf and she was nodding at words he threw back to her, words that were indistinct. He began to climb the steps to the front door and stopped to look behind him. This time Hetty heard his words. 'Hurry it up, woman. I've not got all bleedin' day.'

'Looks like we've got visitors,' said Hetty.

'Do you know them?'

'No. I hope he doesn't think he's leaving that poor woman here.' Hetty grimaced. 'We're full to the gunnels.'

She turned to leave the room but Hope got up and handed the baby to Hetty. 'I'll go and see if I can help them,' she said. 'You're upset. Stay here a little while.'

'Aye, all right.' Hetty went back to the window, gently stroking the baby's back. He nuzzled his face into her neck. It was a delicious feeling. Amelia used to press her button nose into Hetty's cheek, shower tiny kisses like the touch of butterfly wings onto her skin. She remembered that as if it was yesterday. By contrast, leaving Amelia behind to be raised by Hetty's parents as a new addition to their family, well, that was a blur. She was numb to the details of it. How much of her banishment, she wondered now, had been driven by Gertie dripping poison into her mother's ear, telling her father she had to go, to avoid the truth coming out?

She heard the door open and Hope greet the couple, and was confident she'd keep them on the doorstep until they had stated their business with the house. Hetty had taught her that.

There was murmured conversation, between the two women, then the man spoke, overriding them both. Within seconds, he was shouting, his words now clear. 'We've come for what's rightfully ours!'

Hetty put the baby in his bassinet, ignoring his wails, tucked him in firmly, and hurried from the room. 'What's going on here? I won't have raised voices in my house.'

He came over the threshold and approached her belligerently. Hetty stood her ground.

'Where is she?' he said.

She turned to Hope. 'Who's he talking about?'

'Tilly,' said Hope quietly. 'This is her stepfather.'

'You're here to enquire about Matilda Townsend?' said Hetty.

The woman in the headscarf wrung her hands. 'She's my daughter. Do you remember me?'

Hetty did. The girl had been brought in when her mother remarried and took on another brood of children. Tilly was the woman's eldest. There had been no room for her in the new family.

The man put his arm out and shoved the woman behind his broad back. She began to sob. 'Quiet theesen. Tilly wrote to her,' he jerked his thumb over his shoulder, 'saying she'd got this good position. Full of it, she was. I never thought she was up to much but she fell on her feet, din't she?'

'That's our mission,' said Hetty mildly. 'We're here to help the girls sent to us.' She put her head to one side, trying to make eye contact with the girl's mother, who stood behind him with her eyes downcast, the fingers of one hand tucked into the man's belt, as if she needed to hold him back. Might as well try to restrain a rabid dog, Hetty thought. 'You were right about Tilly,' she said. 'She's a good worker.'

'Aye, but the thing is,' the man spread out his hands, appeasingly, 'the daft cow forgot to give us the address she's living at. Her own parents. We've had to come all the way here to get it.' His voice rose. 'I can tell thee, I've got enough on my plate without having to chase after one of hers.' He jerked his thumb at his wife. 'She din't want to come. Had to drag her here.'

Tilly's mother tugged at him. 'Don't get all riled up. You'll get in bother again.'

'Shut up, woman.' He looked from Hope to Hetty and back, and tried for a reasonable tone. 'She owes us. She should be sending her wages home, like a good girl.'

Hope spoke up before Hetty could open her mouth. 'Does she owe *you*? Aren't you the reason her mother brought her here? Too many mouths to feed, wasn't it?'

Hetty put a warning hand on Hope's arm but she shook it off. 'Tilly can please herself what she does with her wages. She's obviously wise to you.'

Tilly's stepfather clenched his fists. 'Who the fucken hell are you? You can't talk to me like that. She'll do as I say or she'll feel the back o' my hand!'

'Please, miss.' His wife peered from behind him. 'This isn't your business.'

Hetty folded her arms. 'You made it our business, Mrs…?'

The man scoffed. 'You don't need my name.'

'I will, for my report,' she said calmly.

'You blasted women…' He reared forward, his fists clenched. 'Where's yer gaffer?'

Hetty shrugged. 'You're looking at her.'

'No, I want the man in charge o' you lot.'

'You'll be left wanting, then.'

'Miss Barlow, shall I fetch the constable?' said Hope.

'You've not heard the last o' this.' He pushed his wife towards the door. She stumbled and almost fell. He gripped the woman's upper arm and leaned down to put his face close to Hope's. Hetty was impressed to see she didn't flinch. 'Tha'd better watch theesen.'

Hope drew herself up, glancing quickly at the door behind which the baby was now screaming lustily. 'Tilly will always have our protection.' She looked at Hetty, pointedly, and repeated her question. 'Shall I fetch the constable, Miss Barlow?'

Hetty nodded towards the door, which stood open on its hinges. 'No. They're leaving. Aren't you?'

Tilly's mother mumbled an apology and her husband turned on her, bundling her outside, hissing in her ear, telling her that coin would have to be found from some-where, and it would be up to her now to earn it. From the doorstep, Hetty watched him drag his wife through the square. She closed and – after a moment's thought – bolted the door. When she turned around, Hope had gone.

Hetty found her in the kitchen, rocking the baby against her shoulder, telling Cook the tale in a high-pitched voice, twin spots of colour on her cheeks. Hetty filled the kettle with water and Cook listened, continuing to work with her hands in a bowl, shaping sausage meat into patties and laying them in neat rows on a baking tray. This seemed to gradually have a soporific effect on Hope. From the scullery came the sound of laundry being washed in the dolly and indistinct chatter.

Finally, Hope sighed. 'It's a shame we can't help that poor woman. She should come here.'

'It's up to her,' said Hetty. 'She has children to look after. You did well there, Hope, standing up to that gorm-less wassock.' She smiled when Hope clapped her hand over her mouth to stifle a laugh. 'We'll have to warn Tilly, though.'

'Our lass is shaping up to be a fine deputy warden,' said Cook, slapping another patty on the tray.

Hope moved the baby from her shoulder to cradle him in her lap. 'I could see he was all bluster,' she said. 'I've suffered much worse at the hands of a man.' She bent her head to kiss the baby's downy cheek and spoke in a whisper. 'You'll never know him, I swear it.'

'What?' Hetty felt as if the breath had been knocked from her body. She looked at Cook, who had stopped in the act of shaping a patty and was staring at Hope, a puzzled frown on her face. 'What's that you're saying?'

'I didn't mean...' Hope seemed as stunned as she was. 'I don't know...'

'Are you remembering something, love?' said Cook.

'This man,' said Hetty. 'Did he bring you here? Is he the father of your child?'

Perhaps the altercation had shaken loose some long-buried recollection. The doctor had said the restoration of Hope's memory might happen all of a sudden. *I've suffered much more at the hands of a man.* Perhaps the baby Hope cradled was the result of an assault against her.

Hope looked stricken. She shook her head. 'No, no. I'm only thinking back to the night I arrived here. You told me, Miss Barlow, that I'd been attacked. That's what I'm talking about.' She lifted the baby to her shoulder, and kissed his cheek before raising her head and smiling, too brightly. 'I'm sorry to have confused you. I am sorry.'

'Hope, give over.' Hetty spoke gently. 'You're not in any bother. There's no need to be apologising.' The sound of the doorknocker interrupted her. She ignored it, determined to hold Hope's eye. *You'll never know him. I swear it.* Hope was already pregnant when she fetched up on the doorstep of the House of Help, some three or four months gone though nobody – not even Hope herself – knew it. The baby she cradled was not the result of that night's attack. She was talking about – had let slip – something else, something more. And she was denying the truth of it. Had her amnesia been a fabrication, all along?

'If there's something you need to get off your chest,' Hetty said, 'then we can find somewhere quiet to talk.'

Hope bit her lip and returned her gaze to the baby. The sustained rattle of the doorknocker filled the house. Clara came in from the scullery. She looked at the three women curiously. 'Shall I go?' she said.

'No, I'll deal with it,' said Hetty. 'Looks like trouble has returned.' She smiled at Hope. 'Stay put, love. This time he's getting a proper earful.'

She put Hope's revelation to one side, as far as she was able, as she unbolted the door, and opened it a crack, just wide enough to see who stood outside. *Tall* was the first word that came to mind about the man who waited on the top step. She saw he was wearing the blue cape of a police officer. Perhaps the earlier altercation had been reported by someone in the square. He was young, clean-shaven and moustachioed, and looked familiar. Hetty thought he had probably delivered a girl or two to the house.

'Could have used you five minutes since,' she said cheerfully, throwing the door wide.

'Good afternoon, Miss Barlow,' he said, his voice solemn as an undertaker's. 'Can we come in?'

Below him, waiting on the pavement, stood a finely dressed couple in travelling clothes. They reminded Hetty of the ladies and gentlemen she had seen being helped into first class on the train to Cleethorpes. The pair of them were peering up at the house anxiously. Her first thought was that this must have something to do with Amelia.

'Aye, come in, come in,' she said.

The couple ascended the steps. The woman's large eyes and rounded cheeks were lifted in a nervous smile. Her strawberry-blonde hair was held in a neat chignon under a plain felt hat that, despite the lack of decoration, somehow contrived to look as expensive as the unadorned blue cape she wore.

The man holding her elbow wore an equally plain but costly looking shoulder-to-floor duster over his suit and a topper that he removed as he stepped over the threshold. His eyes were dark with suppressed fury and Hetty was suddenly glad of the police presence. She stood back to allow them in, clocking the carriage and four handsome black horses on the cobbles outside. The driver sat on the box, eating a sandwich and observing the goings-on in the square.

In the hallway, the man took in his surroundings. Then his eyes settled on Hetty. He was obviously struggling with his emotions, his expression wavering between anger, confusion and – she was sure she was not mistaken – anticipation. Had this to do with her own deception? Were these people here to challenge her credentials? It seemed implausible. It must have to do with Amelia.

Neither of them had spoken a word. Hetty gave the constable an enquiring look.

'Miss Barlow, this is Mr and Mrs Robin Hyde.' He turned to the couple. 'Miss Barlow is the house warden. She is in charge of all the girls and women while they reside here.'

She had been right about the constable. He would know her name only if he'd had dealings with the house. 'How do you do,' she said.

'As well as can be expected,' said Mr Hyde in a brisk tone. His wife smiled weakly.

'Mr and Mrs Hyde set out two days ago, in great urgency, from the town of Bath.'

She knew of Bath. It was almost two hundred miles south of Sheffield. A long distance to cover in two days. They each held out a hand and she shook them in turn. Both were wearing soft kid gloves.

'Miss Barlow,' said Mr Hyde. 'We are pleased to meet you and hope you will forgive our unanticipated arrival,' he said. 'All will become clear, we pray.' His wife put her fingers on her lips. Her hand was shaking. 'We are here to collect our daughter from you.'

Hetty sighed. Another one. This couple didn't look like they needed a share of their child's wages. 'You believe your daughter is here, Mr Hyde?'

It seemed as unlikely as pigs sprouting wings.

'We've been assured she is.' The man turned for confirmation to the police constable, whose nod and grimace had more sympathy than confirmation in it.

'Mr and Mrs Hyde received correspondence,' he said, 'in relation to their missing daughter. It pointed to this house. I've advised them not to set too much store by the letter. It could well be a piece of mischief.'

'I understand,' said Hetty. 'What's her name?'

The woman answered, her voice as brittle as cracknel. 'My daughter's name is Emma. Emma Hyde. Miss Emma Clare Hyde.'

'Then,' said Hetty gently, 'I'm sorry to disappoint you. We don't have anyone here by that name.'

'Emma Clare Hyde,' the woman repeated.

Mr Hyde put a hand on his wife's arm, to still her. 'Can you check, please? She went missing in November last year. We had no reason to believe she'd run away. We were giving up hope. The letter...' he gulped. 'She's nineteen years old.'

Mrs Hyde turned her head so that her face was hidden in the folds of her husband's coat. She began to sob. 'She's twenty now. My darling girl has just turned twenty.'

'Come and sit,' said Hetty, guiding them towards the parlour. 'I'll go and fetch the ledger. I keep a record of all our girls and women, including the date they arrived at the house, where they went when they left and any other salient details. If Emma was here, she'll be there.'

'Thank you,' said Mr Hyde.

Hetty paused, her hand on the door handle to the parlour. 'I should tell you that once I've written a name in the ledger I rarely forget it. Emma Clare Hyde isn't ringing any bells, I'm sorry to say.'

'Well, you see,' said the constable. 'Mr and Mrs Hyde may have forgotten, in their understandable distress, and exhaustion from their long journey, but here, at the house, she goes under a different name. At least, according to the letter her parents received. Of course, we may be barking up the wrong tree.'

Hetty smiled patiently. 'And what would that name be?'

'We're given to understand,' said the constable, 'that she's been calling herself Hope.'

PART THREE

Chapter 20

Hope was filled with a strange sense of relief. She had known there would come a time when her deception fell apart. She'd untethered herself from that enormous weight with a few whispered words. *You'll never know him, I swear it.* She was more determined than ever to keep that promise.

She smiled at Cook who was staring at her.

'I'll go and explain,' Hope said.

'Aye, you better had.' She nodded at the baby. 'Shall I take him for thee?'

'No.' Hope held him tightly. 'Thank you.'

As she climbed the few steps from the kitchen to the main hallway of the house, she heard Miss Barlow's voice utter her name, questioningly. Disbelievingly. *Hope?*

She knew before she set eyes on them, knew in an instant, to the depths of her soul, and stopped in the dimness of the back of the hall, all thoughts of appeasing Miss Barlow vanquished. She looked down at the baby in her arms. A lock of dark hair had escaped from the cap he wore and she tucked it in, stroking his tiny forehead. His eyes opened, his face puckered and he turned his head towards her, searching for milk. She put the knuckle of her little finger in his open mouth. She couldn't move forward, so stuck was she in the quicksand of her terror.

How had they found her, and was her cousin with them, or close by? Her throat tightened with fear.

There was another emotion shaking her body. A white-hot rage. She could not bear to have this tiny creature in her arms looked upon as the mark of her shame.

She wanted to run from her parents. She wanted to throw herself into their embrace. If she moved, the maelstrom inside would tear her mind apart, rip all her senses to shreds.

'Emma?'

Her father's voice. He'd seen her, standing in the shadows.

'Emma, is that you, my darling girl?' Her mother.

No, I'm Hope now.

But the sound of her mother's voice released her body from its paralysis. As if she was a puppet on strings, at the mercy of an inexorable force, her feet moved her towards the group of people standing in the shaft of light cast from the open doorway. She stared numbly at what might be a tableau in oils, a painting worthy of Vermeer, of Rembrandt. The tall young constable in his uniform, an expression of curiosity on his face, beside him poor Miss Barlow, shock written across her features, and her mother, who had sunk to her knees, laughing and crying, brushstrokes of joy and relief. Her father stood a little apart, his hand clamped on her mother's shoulder, his magistrate's face painted in a carefully neutral expression.

His eyes were on the child in her arms.

The spell was broken by Miss Barlow, who moved forward and took the baby from Hope's arms. She said something Hope couldn't hear for the roaring in her ears. She bent to raise her mother to her feet, and they clung to each other. Then she was in her father's arms, deep sobs wracking her body, her mother clutching her hand, squeezing her bones as if she might disappear into thin air. The constable was speaking but nobody paid him any attention.

Eventually, Miss Barlow made her voice heard. 'You can't be standing here all day,' she said. 'Take your parents in the parlour, Hope.' She was trying for a cheerful tone but Hope could hear the pain, the deep hurt, that underlay her words. 'I'll fetch you all a cup of tea.'

'It's Emma,' said her father. 'Or, rather, Miss Hyde.'

She pulled away from him, horrified, intending to apologise to Miss Barlow, only to be enfolded back into her mother's arms.

'Oh, my darling, my darling. I can't believe the evidence of my own eyes.' She broke their embrace to put her hands against Hope's cheeks and shower her face with kisses. 'It's really you.' She was laughing now. 'It's really you. I told you, Robin, I told you we'd find her.'

The constable coughed. 'Shall we?' He indicated the door to the parlour and she took her mother's arm and led her inside. She guided her to the chaise longue and sat beside her, their hands entwined.

She searched her mother's face in wonder. 'I never thought to see you again.'

Her mother's eyes were feverish. 'This is where you've been living, all this time? Why, Emma? Why here? We've been beside ourselves. You have no idea. Everybody searching for you. Why did you run away?'

Her father unfastened his duster and handed it to the young constable, who looked surprised to receive it, cast about him and finally draped it over the back of a chair. Her father sat down heavily in a winged armchair.

'My dear,' he said. 'I think we know why Emma ran away, don't we? I think we've just seen why.'

Miss Barlow stood in the doorway, holding her son.

'Do you want to take him, Hope? I mean, Miss Hyde?'

She extricated herself from her mother's grip and went to Miss Barlow, who handed over the baby but refused to meet her eye. 'I'm Hope in this house. I'm so sorry. I'm so sorry I lied to you.'

Miss Barlow looked away, down the hall. 'Now is not the time, Miss Hyde. I'll bring you some tea.'

She walked away.

Hope turned to face the room. Her mother was looking at her imploringly. A frown creased her father's face. The constable broke the silence that followed.

'Miss Hyde, perhaps you can tell us what happened to you, how you came to be at the House of Help?'

Her father reached into a bag and took out the creased pages of a letter. He handed them to the constable, who got up from his seat and gave them to Hope.

Her father leaned forward, his elbows on his knees, his hands hanging between his legs. She had never before seen him look defeated. 'Is this the father?' he said.

Hope placed the baby against her shoulder and unfolded the letter. She recognised the handwriting. Linus Harmon had revealed her hiding place. Amelia had told him her secret. Her face burned. She had called on reserves of strength she hadn't know she possessed to finally speak the truth to her friend. Amelia's betrayal felt so casual, so cavalier.

Her father repeated the question, this time in a voice full of repressed anger. 'Is Linus Harmon the father?'

'No.'

'Are you sure? He wants his reward.' Her father looked at the empty grate, at the fire irons hanging from their metal brace. 'You can imagine the reward I would like to mete out to him.'

'Father, it's not him.'

The constable said: 'But you know this Linus Harmon?'

'Yes, he's engaged to be married to the housekeeper here.'

She quickly scanned the contents of the letter. Linus had informed her parents he knew where their daughter was, and had given the address where they would find her, and had reminded them of the generous reward they had offered. He had told them their daughter was carrying a child, but there was no mention of her cousin. Perhaps Amelia hadn't confided that detail. Hope found this difficult to believe. More likely, he hadn't thought it relevant, not for his purposes.

She was doubly betrayed, first by Amelia, then by Linus.

Her mother laid her head on Hope's other shoulder. 'I am grateful to this man, whoever he is, for returning our daughter to us.'

'She has a child,' said her father, quietly. 'What's to be done?'

There was a tap on the door and Miss Barlow entered with a tea tray. She placed it on the table and left the room without speaking or acknowledging anybody, as a servant would. Hope's face burned with shame.

'Can you tell us who is the father of this child?' said the constable.

She forced out the words. 'I can't.'

Her father said: 'You will, my girl.'

She had sworn to herself to never speak his name. The fear that lay always in the pit of her stomach rose up to clog her chest and choke her throat. He would be waiting for her return, and then what? She would not be able to look upon his sneering face without screaming.

Hope tightened her grip on her son, who began to wail.

'He needs feeding,' she said, and blushed. 'I'll have to take him into the other room.' She looked at the constable. 'If you'll allow it.'

'You're not under arrest, miss.'

Her mother lifted her head from Hope's shoulder and smoothed her hair away from her face. 'Would you let me...' her breath hitched in her chest. 'Would you let me hold him for just a moment?'

'Of course.' She passed him over. Her mother cradled him, made comforting noises, and his wails subsided.

Her father was staring in the distance, the fingers of one hand pulling at his goatee beard, a habit that meant he was deep in thought. She had always found it endearing, until now. Finally, he looked at her. 'Did you allow this to happen under our roof?' he said. 'And then continue to deceive us, for how many weeks and months?'

The baby began to wail again.

'Hush,' said her mother. 'Hush now.' Hope couldn't tell whether she was trying to placate the screaming infant or appealing to her husband. She rose to her feet and took the baby.

'I'm sorry. I must go. He's hungry.'

The constable followed her to the door. 'Mr and Mrs Hyde, I'll take my leave,' he said, 'and give your family some privacy.' He addressed her father. 'If there is action to be taken, charges to be laid, and so on, I'm sure you'll be in touch. Perhaps you might contact your local police force. I believe this is a matter out of the town's jurisdiction?'

Her father pounced on this. 'Our daughter was hidden away from us by the people in this house!'

'It appears she concealed her true self, certainly from the warden,' the constable said mildly. 'She isn't a child.'

Hope looked at him, surprised. She had never really considered it, but of course she was a grown adult, a woman, one who could, in the limited arena allowed her sex, make her own choices. She was being led by the nose, by her parents, when there was one thing – her child aside – that only she could decide upon.

–

When she returned from a blessedly peaceful interlude feeding her son, she saw their tea and the plate of biscuits Miss Barlow had provided remained untouched. Her father had moved over to sit beside her mother, who was dabbing at her swollen eyes with a handkerchief.

She could see the name *Emma* embroidered on the corner of the white linen. She had sewn it herself, clumsily, as a child, so that she could present embroidered handkerchiefs to her mother and father on a long-ago Christmas morning. She remembered the sharp sewing needle and the silver thimble, and her patient stabbing at the linen. *Mother* with rose petals sewn alongside, for her given name. A simple, child's effort at a red-breasted bird beneath *Father*.

How she had wounded them. How undeserving her parents were of the anguish she had inflicted. She sat in the armchair her father had vacated, facing them, holding her sleeping child in her arms like a shield to protect her.

'I'm sorry.'

'We're sorry too,' said her mother, 'sorry that you couldn't confide in us, that you had to run away, that you had to bear this all alone.'

They thought her a *runaway*. Better that than the truth. 'I have been well looked after,' she said. 'I have made some wonderful friends.' This brought to mind Amelia, her betrayal and her sudden departure. Hope would not think about that, not yet. Not now. 'I'm sorry to be a source of shame to you.'

'We'll repair the damage,' her father said. 'You'll come home with us. We'll devise a reason for your, ah, escapade.' He laughed, humourlessly. 'Perhaps we can tell people you ran away to join the circus.'

He looked at the baby, his lips pursed, the unspoken assumption being that living with a troupe of acrobats, freaks and captured monkeys was less scandalous than presenting an illegitimate child to the rest of the Hyde family and Bath society. It was, she supposed.

'A good friend of the house, a kindly friend of mine, has arranged for his adoption.' She gazed down at him. 'He's being collected in a few days' time.'

Her mother began to cry again, snuffling into Emma's handkerchief.

'Our family has been through so much since you ran away,' she said. 'So much heartbreak.'

Her father nodded grimly. 'You won't be aware, Emma, and I do regret to have to tell you this.' He took a deep breath. 'Your beloved cousin Matthew was killed in a highway accident. It happened only a week or so after you disappeared.'

'He was riding to see us,' said her mother, 'to offer words of consolation, and to promise he would devote himself to finding you, to returning you to us. His father told us this was the final act of a young man renowned for his many kindnesses.'

He was dead. The thought circled and circled and grew and grew until it engulfed her. Outwardly, she kept perfectly still. Her tormentor, her *rapist*, the man who had kept her in thrall to the deep fear that gnawed at her during her every waking moment, was dead. He was dead. He was dead. She hiccupped, and transformed the terrible urge to laugh in her mother's face – *his many kindnesses!* – into a sob. Her father gave a handkerchief and she hid her face in it. He was dead. Matthew was dead.

She wanted to tell Amelia. Thinking about her friend sobered her up.

'How terrible,' she said and blew her nose.

'We all loved him,' said her mother. 'There's been so much loss, so much sadness. It's overwhelming, having you returned to us. I never lost hope, you know.'

Hope. It was the name she'd been given, the name she'd adopted. But Hope would be lost, as soon as she stepped inside her father's carriage.

Her mother reached forward to grasp her wrist, her eyes shining with tears. 'We'll never let go of you, ever again.'

Chapter 21

Amelia's fingers clutched the rail on the exposed upper deck of the omnibus carrying her and a full complement of passengers from the rail station into Tamworth. With her other hand, she held the brim of her straw hat, although it was securely tied beneath her chin. The branches of the trees on the edge of the road moved restlessly in an early evening breeze that brought the scent of a ploughed field to her nostrils, at once sweet and earthy.

She hadn't eaten all day, hadn't been able to stomach food. Her guts were tied in knots.

Distant church spires pointed, as was their wont, towards the heavens and the swaying backsides of the horses hauling the bus along the narrow country lane were no different to the ones in town, and yet everything seemed alien, as it had when Hetty had first brought her to Sheffield. She was in a new place, for all its familiarities. And, exactly as it had been when her sister had uprooted her, she had no idea what she'd find at the end of her journey.

After she'd changed trains at Derby, she'd shown the piece of paper with Linus's address written on it to the woman sitting on the third-class bench beside her, and was given directions to the house. That woman now travelled on this same omnibus, but happily had taken a seat inside. Amelia didn't want to get into a conversation where she might be expected to state her business. It would be humiliating to discover she wasn't the only girl being courted by the handsome young hawker. Tamworth was a small place and a stranger's face stood out. She was conspicuous enough as it was.

The bus passed a tavern with a thatched roof and a low terrace of identical two-up two-down cottages. Beyond these buildings, a coalmine's slag made a fat black mound on the horizon. She'd learned from Linus that most of the town's residents were employed across the mines that surrounded the town. He'd not wanted a life spent hunched in underground tunnels, never able to get the grime out of his hair and skin, coughing his lungs up by the time he got to his forties. Linus had wanted to get about a bit, see something of the country. He'd told Amelia that if they hadn't met he'd already be steaming to America by now. How did she feel about emigrating, once they were wed? The prospect thrilled her.

An hour later, in the hazily blue-skied evening, she stood on the pavement opposite his parents' cottage. There were a dozen brick houses and stone cottages on the street, casting long and slanted shadows of different shapes and sizes on the ground. The cottage Linus lived in was not unlike the house she had grown up in with her mother and mad old Aunt Gertie. This similarity felt like a connection and it soothed her. Linus had once told her he was an only child, and she had replied eagerly that so was she, before she remembered. She might as well have been. Hetty had disappeared before Amelia could form memories of her.

Now that she had thought about her older sister, she could hear Hetty's no-nonsense voice in her head. *Well, you're here. What are you waiting for?* Amelia crossed the road and opened the gate onto worn stone paving slabs that curved towards the front door. On her left was a low drystone wall, the boundary between this cottage and the next. Small flowering plants were embedded in the crumbling soil on top of the wall, set amongst painted pebbles. It made for a pretty display. On her right was a well-kept garden containing a plum tree and a vegetable patch.

There was a tool shed behind and to the left of the tree, the door to it wedged open by a basket of logs, and she could see hammers and a razor-toothed saw hanging on the wall inside. Linus had told her his father was handy, that he could fix any broken thing given to him.

'Is anybody there?' she called.

There was no movement or sound from within. She turned towards the house. Linus's mother probably cultivated the vegetables and flowers and the climbing honeysuckle that partially obscured the ground and first floor windows on one side. She reached the front door and stood on the step – clean, newly whitewashed – knocked on the door, then stepped back onto the path, holding the brim of her hat with one hand and the valise she had taken from the house in the other.

She waited. If there was no reply she would have to find somewhere to stay for the night. She had passed a couple of inns on the walk from the omnibus. She hoped it wouldn't come to that. But what if she was just one of many girls who'd stood in this exact spot, and been sent away, humiliated? Another, equally unattractive, scenario had been playing in her mind. Linus had already contacted Hope's parents, collected the reward money, and disappeared to who knows where. To America, without her. She shivered. It was cold in the shadow of the house.

When the door creaked open, no more than a few inches, and a woman's face peeked out, Amelia pasted on her friendliest smile. The woman looked as old as Mrs Gunson, which surprised her and made her fearful she'd come to the wrong address. Fluffy white hair stuck out from under her cap and her beaky nose and eyes were red-rimmed. Amelia had her speech prepared.

''Ow do, I'm Amelia Barlow. You must be Linus's mother. I've heard so much about you.'

The woman stared at her blankly. It was obvious that she had no idea who *Amelia Barlow* was. Linus had been lying to her all along.

'Who?' she said, loudly.

Amelia took a step back. 'I'm sorry, I...' She didn't know how to complete the sentence.

'Who's there?' A tremulous male voice. The door was opened wide on its hinges and a thin, stooped man with a bushy white beard joined the woman in staring at Amelia.

She tried again. ''Ow do. Am I right in thinking this is where Linus Harmon lives?'

He nodded and smiled, before the corners of his mouth turned down. 'You must be Amelia,' he said.

Relief flooded through her. 'Aye, aye, I am. Linus has told you about me, then.'

'He certainly has.' He frowned mightily, shaking his head, and Amelia took a step back. Something was up. But then the man's brow cleared. 'It's a pleasure to meet you, young lady. You'd better come in.'

The woman moved aside to allow Amelia to cross the threshold.

'Excuse Molly here,' the man said. 'She's deaf as a post but won't accept it.'

'What's that, Bert? I hope you're not spouting your usual nonsense.'

'IT'S AMELIA.'

'Oh!' She wrung her hands. 'I should have known. You're Linus's fiancée.'

Linus's fiancée. She beamed with pleasure. 'I am. Is he at home?'

The man nodded. 'In here, in here.'

She was ushered into the front room, which was cosily cluttered. There was no sign of Linus. Amelia took in the knick-knacks that sat on doilies on end tables, the window ledge, shelves; every available surface had a paperweight or figurine or some other frippery covering it. She picked up a framed drawing of Linus and exclaimed in delight. It was a caricature executed in bold black lines that emphasised his wide smile and thick brows. He looked wolf-like and endearing all at once.

'This is lovely,' she said.

'A newspaperman drew that for him while he was on his travels a while back,' said the woman. 'I know we look old enough to be his grandparents. We were blessed to have him late in life.' She glanced up at the ceiling. 'He's not told you, has he?'

'Told me what?'

The woman ignored her. Perhaps she hadn't heard her. Instead, she turned to the man. 'Do you think it's safe?'

Amelia looked from one to the other. 'I've come a long way to see Linus. Will you tell me what's going on?'

–

She had flown up the stairs but now paused at the door of Linus's bedroom, and rested her palm against it, thinking.

Amelia had not been vaccinated, as an infant, against smallpox. Auntie Gertie had persuaded her mother that not only was it an unnecessary precaution, the medicine was a poison that would rot her brain. When she arrived in Sheffield, as the smallpox epidemic was reaching its peak, Hetty had insisted on Amelia getting protection from the disease. She was glad of it now.

She knew from Hope, who occasionally, to entertain the others, read aloud the debates that raged in the letters page of the local newspapers, that vaccination might not prevent her from catching smallpox entirely. But if she did, it would be probably only a minor case, perhaps even symptom-free, and she would likely make a full recovery. These days, most of the population was vaccinated in infancy and then again in early adulthood.

She realised now that she had never talked to Linus about it.

What crowded out all rational thought was her determination to see him. She had told his parents she was prepared to take the risk to spend a little bit of time in the same room as her fiancé. Once infected, he'd succumbed quickly, they said, and was now very poorly. The hospital wouldn't take him and when the doctor visited – only that morning – he said there was nothing to be done, except to wait it out. The epidemic raged in Sheffield, and a handful of cases had been reported in other towns, but not Tamworth. There was no isolation hospital he could be transferred to, and anyway his parents wouldn't allow it. He should remain at home, in his own bed, with his parents looking after him. He'd be more likely to recover, that way, said his mother.

On the other side of this door lay the man she was going to marry. She could hear him snoring, an endearing, vulnerable sound that drove her to twist the handle and slip into the darkened room. Quietly, hardly daring to breathe, she tiptoed to his bed and sat on the stool beside it. He lay on his side, one hand flung out to hang over the edge of the bed. She folded it back against his body.

His fingers were hot and rough.

Amelia waited for him to wake, shifting on the uncomfortable rickety wooden stool beside his bed, wishing she had brought up one of the embroidered cushions that were stacked on the settee in the front room. Linus turned onto his back, still snoring, and she studied his face. She had seen the aftermath of this disease on the skin of Jane Millthorpe. Now she was seeing it in all its glory, and was glad of the dimness of the room. His face and neck were shadowed with scores of pustules. They invaded the soft inside of his lips and the well of his ear. Fear crept up her spine. What might he look like, afterwards? Would his handsome face be destroyed? She would love him, just the same.

When his eyelids rose, a fraction, and he glanced sideways, she squeezed his fingers, not too hard. Afterwards, she would stand at his mother's kitchen sink and scrub and scrub at her hands with carbolic soap until the unblemished skin on them was raw.

He opened his eyes wider, and smiled at her.

'What are you grinning about?' she said. 'You look like you walked into a bee's nest. I hope the honey was worth it.'

He laughed, tried to speak but began to choke and turned his head away. The thick dark hair he was so proud of was a tangled mess on the pillow. She gently raked her fingers through it. There was a mug of water on the bedside table and when he turned back towards her she lifted his head so he could drink from it.

She tried not to look at his blistered mouth.

'See, this is what happens when you leave my side,' she said. 'Best not let that happen again.'

His voice was hoarse. 'How did you...' he stopped, and gestured to his neck. 'It hurts too much.'

He was shivering. Amelia tucked the sheets around his body. 'I can do the talking for both of us,' she said.

She slipped off her shoes. 'How about I lie down next to you? On top of the covers, I mean. It's been a long day.'

He smiled again, and nodded, and she lay down beside him. It was all she'd ever wanted to do.

She stared into his eyes, the only part of his face that the disease had left untouched. His eyes fastened on hers, greedily.

'Reight then, mister, so listen to this. I came here on two trains and an omnibus, no less, *and* had a good walk at the end of it. My feet are killing me.' She watched the smile spread across his damaged mouth. 'I got in a bit of a tizzy over your letter telling Hope's parents where she was hiding. I was thinking all sorts. Had you buggered off with the reward money, had you got another girl, even, and your letter to me was to keep me in my place, sitting and waiting. I couldn't do that.'

Linus's eyes widened and she put her finger to his lips, not quite touching his skin. 'I know, I know. Your mum and dad have reassured me on that score. And they say you told them about Hope and they thought it was the right thing to do. They would, wouldn't they, being parents?' She stroked a stray lock of his hair away from his forehead. 'I'm sure we'll be the same, with our children.'

'I wanted to give us a good start,' he whispered. 'I know your sister thinks I'm a cad. But it was all for you, Amelia, for you and me together.'

'You're a soppy sod, really, aren't you?'

'I'm glad you're here.' He began to cough, and retch, and turned over in the bed so he had his back to her. 'But I don't want you seeing me like this.'

Amelia pressed her body against his and put her arm over him. It was the best she could do. 'I wish these covers weren't in the way.'

He coughed again. 'I wish I could kiss you.'

'Best get yourself fit then, hadn't you?' She felt the touch of his fingers on the hand she had draped over his body, then his hand dropped away and he sighed. 'Are you tired, love? I'm going back down now, let you get your rest. I'm kipping here tonight.'

He lifted his chin and half-turned his head towards her. 'Oh aye?'

Amelia swatted him lightly on the arm. 'In the box room. Your dad's made up a cot bed for me.'

She snuggled into his back. She couldn't get close enough to him. 'I'll just stay with you for a bit longer. Get better, love. I can't do without you, you know.'

He lifted his hand again, knotted his fingers in hers and whispered something she didn't catch. She lifted her head slightly.

'What?'

'Hush now, love.' He relinquished his grip on her hand. His voice was faint, so faint. 'You'll be all right.'

Chapter 22

Late that night, Amelia lay wide awake under a musty-smelling blanket in the small upstairs room at the back of the house. It was unsettlingly quiet. At the house, there was always somebody clattering up or down the stairs, or banging for entry, not to mention the snores and snuffles from the transients with whom she shared the dorm. So many women, coming and going. Except for Hope, of course. Hope had slept in the bed alongside Amelia's for so long now that she couldn't imagine reaching out in the dark and not finding her.

Linus's actions – hers really, in telling him Hope's secret – had probably ruined their friendship. Amelia's main priority, once Linus had recovered, was to make things right with Hope. She owed her sister an apology too. Hetty would be furious, she realised uncomfortably, on several counts. Amelia had disappeared without a word, leaving only a hastily scrawled note. She had taken money from the house. She had left the house without a housekeeper, and Hetty would soon discover that she had colluded in Hope's lie, if she didn't already know.

She reached out an arm and turned down the lamp on the overturned crate Mr Harmon had hastily positioned by the side of the bed. The silence pressed deafeningly against her ears and when she turned on her side the darkness blinded her. She'd been selfish and cruel. She had treated Hope's great secret like tittle-tattle. She must make certain Linus didn't bear the shame of what she'd done.

She thought she would never sleep but must have dozed off at some point because when she opened her eyes the room had brightened in the morning light. The unease she had experienced during the night melted away. Linus *did* love her. He *was* going to marry her. Everything was going to be all right, just like he'd said.

The spare set of clothes she'd brought hung over the top rung of a small ladder in the corner of the room. When Amelia swung her feet out of bed, it was a paint-spattered dust sheet she stepped onto. Linus's father had begun to decorate the room, to make it ready for her stay, when Linus suddenly took ill. Here she was, anyway, and she didn't care that the room was unfinished. The fact his family had wanted to make her feel welcome was good enough for Amelia. When Linus had recovered, they would return together to Sheffield to make reparation and collect the rest of her possessions.

The simple fact of the matter was that Linus was here, and her life lay here with him.

She might visit with her sister from time to time, and all being well with Hope, perhaps joining in the Sunday afternoon tea party, turning up unannounced just like previous inmates of the house. Amelia smiled at the memory of Violet Hargreaves, her whinnying laugh and the jam on her teeth. How envious she'd been of her. Hope had been in the house just about a week then.

A cock was crowing, over and over, as Amelia buttoned up her blouse. She twisted the knob on the door of the room, which creaked when she cautiously opened it. There was the sound of coughing in the room across the hall, and whispered voices. She tiptoed towards the other room and opened the door that Linus lay behind, creeping inside.

All she could see of him in the dim light was a shapeless hump under the covers and the top of his head on the pillow. She perched on the edge of the mattress. When they were married, they'd share this bed until they found their own place. The room was sparsely decorated, functional, a man's room. It needed a woman's touch. She would fill it with flowers from the garden, install a dressing table and stool – perhaps Linus's father could make the furniture. Her father-in-law was a carpenter, with the same strong square hands as Linus.

She leaned over his inert form, and gently pulled the blanket from his head. Linus was sleeping, his eyelids fluttering and his breathing ragged. Perhaps he was dreaming of her. She leaned closer. His breath was sickly-sweet. She drew back, deciding against waking him. Sleep was restorative. A shaft of sunlight pierced the curtains and fell across his cheek, bringing the angry pustules that covered his skin into stark focus. She got up and closed the curtains more tightly to block out the light, and stood for a moment, at a loss. Then an idea occurred. She would go down and light a fire for the kettle, perhaps cut some bread to toast, make herself useful.

The tea was brewing when she heard his parents shuffling down the stairs. Amelia straightened up the cups and jug of milk she'd laid on the tablecloth, stirred the leaves in the pot, and checked the strainer, and prepared herself to wish them good morning. But their footsteps faded. There came the unmistakeable sound of the front door being opened and, a few seconds later, pulled shut. She wasn't sure what to do. Perhaps their morning routine involved taking a walk before breakfast. She hadn't heard either of them speak but it could be that Mr Harmon didn't want to be shouting at his deaf wife first thing in the morning.

She found them outside, closer than she'd imagined. They were sitting on a wooden bench under the honey-suckle, holding hands.

'Good morning,' she said. 'I hope you slept well. I did. Thank you for letting me stay.'

Mr Harmon got to his feet. 'Amelia, we wanted to ask you whether you'd mind walking over to the doctor's house. It's not far away. I'll give you directions. Can you go now?'

'Aye, of course, I can.' She was relieved to have something meaningful to do.

'Only, his mother can't seem to rouse him. He might just be in a deep sleep.'

Amelia breathed in sharply. 'I went in, and he was asleep then. Shall I go and have another look at him?'

'No, no, that'll be it. He's asleep and no point disturbing the poor lad. We'd like the doctor to look at him, that's all. As soon as he's able to.'

'I'll just get my bonnet.'

She ran inside. She'd left her straw bonnet in the front room but at first couldn't find it amid all the general clutter. She cast about her, and spotted it half-hidden by a dimpled cushion. Picking it up, she burst into tears completely unexpectedly and had to stand in the middle of the room for a minute to recover herself. Linus would be all right. He had to be. It was only that his parents were over-anxious, as all parents were. Jane Millthorpe had been *so terribly ill*, Mrs Gunson had told Amelia. *That one seemed at death's door*, Hetty had said. And Jane had survived, albeit disfigured.

She sniffed mightily, put on her hat and went back outside. Mr Harmon gave her the directions and off she went, anxiety gnawing at the pit of her stomach. Linus's parents were afraid; she could see it in their faces.

It was an overcast day. A bluebottle buzzed near her ear, making her flinch, and her nostrils were filled with the smell of silage from the fields. At the end of the terrace, she walked alongside a high stone wall overhung with fuchsia before turning left when she reached the road junction. The first house on this street was a beer-off. Further down, she passed a grocer's and wondered who would be checking the stores and ordering the staples at the house today.

Mr Harmon had told her to go straight over when she got to the crossroads. So far, the route was familiar. She had come upon the wide junction from the other direction where the omnibus had dropped her off. Was that only yesterday evening? She took the unfamiliar fork in the road. Mr Harmon said that after two hundred yards, she should walk down the lane on her right. On that lane, she'd pass a chandlery and a blacksmith's and in no time at all she would see the doctor's house, set back from the road.

'You can make the journey in half the time we could,' said Mr Harmon, by way of indicating he wanted her to hurry. 'If he's in and he agrees to come back with you, all the better.'

'I'll do my best,' said Amelia.

Outside the blacksmith's three young navvies lounged on the edge of a horses' trough, ribbing each other in loud voices. She averted her gaze and walked by them as quickly as possible. One of the men let out a long, low whistle which set the others laughing. This emboldened him to shout after her. 'Where's a pretty thing like you come from? Cat got your tongue?' Amelia ignored them and increased her pace. Finally, she reached the gravel drive that led to the doctor's house. Safely out of sight, she stopped, took the ring Linus had given her from her right hand, recalling Clara's superstitious warning, and slipped it onto the ring finger of her left hand. From now on, she would present herself as a married woman, until she was one. It was only a matter of time.

Linus would send those boys flying arse over tit if he ever got his hands on them.

–

Amelia hesitated at the ivy-framed door to the doctor's house. There was a small iron plaque, half-hidden in the foliage, that directed tradesmen to the back door, with a slim arrow pointing towards the flagstone path between the wall of the house and the hedge. At the end of the path was a small wooden gate. Did this rule apply to patients, too? Perhaps the front door was for distinguished visitors only.

But this was an emergency and Amelia couldn't be doing with the niceties. There was no knocker on the red-painted wood so she tapped on the door, reaching above a bronze oblong panel fixed to the centre of it. She waited, gazing at what looked like the butterfly-shaped end of a key protruding from the middle of the panel. Perhaps, at the doctor's house, patients were expected to let themselves in? She grasped the key, and turned it. The sound of tinkling bells came from within. She turned it again, entranced. Each twist of the key produced the same trill.

She was about to turn the key a third time when the door was wrenched open. A middle-aged woman in a mop cap and apron stood before her. She looked Amelia up and down.

'I heard it the first time,' she said. 'No need to keep ringing the thing.'

'Is the doctor in? I need him to come. Now.' She gulped. 'Please.'

'And who might you be?' The woman folded her arms over her abundant chest. 'You're not a patient of his.'

'It's for my fiancé. For Linus. Linus Harmon. The doctor saw him yesterday. He's worse today.' She didn't know if he was or not but it seemed wise to say so. 'He's got the smallpox.'

The woman reared back. 'Smallpox? Aye, I heard him talking about that. We don't have it in Tamworth. I reckon he brought that back from that filthy town.' She eyed Amelia suspiciously. 'Is that where you're from?'

'I've come down from Sheffield.'

'That's where I meant.'

'Please, ask him to come.' Amelia wrung her hands. 'It's urgent.'

The woman began to close the door, and Amelia pushed against it.

She made an exasperated sound. 'I'll fetch him. Wait here.'

The door closed in Amelia's face.

Only two or three minutes must have passed but it felt like an age: Amelia was reaching out to twist the key when the door opened and a tall man with bushy grey sideburns emerged. He was carrying his bag, and Amelia could have wept with relief.

'It's Linus,' she said. 'He's very poorly.'

'Yes, I saw young Mr Harmon yesterday.' He strode down the path, Amelia hurrying to keep pace. 'Come along, then.'

On the way back, she tried to explain that she thought Linus had been sleeping peacefully, that she was certain that was the case, but his parents had been anxious. The doctor nodded absently. He had a long stride and she could never seem to quite catch him up, always lagging a few steps behind.

He let himself in to the Harmons' cottage, bade Linus's parents good morning and immediately went upstairs with them following behind. Amelia had begun to climb the stairs after them when his bedroom door was softly closed. Unsure what to do, feeling absurdly like an intruder in the house, she stopped halfway up and sat on the almost-worn through runner. She began picking at a loose thread.

If only Hope, or even Hetty, was sitting beside her. She was a long way from home. But where was home? She supposed it was the House of Help. Although if she told somebody she was *going home* she would be talking about her mother's cottage on the estuary. She had been glad to escape the isolated existence she'd endured there. She would never have met Linus if she hadn't gone with Hetty. Without her mother to protect her, she'd have been subsumed into her aunt's church, sitting around a table in the dark, calling up the dead.

She shuddered and pulled the thread in the carpet until it came up against a tighter part of the weave. She dropped it and started on another. The grain of the pale wood beneath was becoming visible. She looked up at the bedroom door. There were no sounds from within, that she could discern. This wasn't *home* either, but one day it would be, as soon as Linus recovered.

A whispering started up, and quickly grew in volume. Rain, pattering against the window panes. An early summer downpour that would be over as quickly as it had arrived. From where she sat, she had a view of the open sash in the cluttered front room. She decided it would be better to go and close the window than continue to destroy the runner.

She was pushing the frame down when she heard feet on the stairs.

Amelia intercepted the doctor in the hall. He was already buttoning up his cloak. She'd thought him brusque, earlier, but now he gave her a kind smile, a sad smile.

'Is Linus any better?' she asked.

He shook his head, seemed to consider, then took her hands and guided her back into the front room, stopping near an armchair. 'His parents are remaining with him. I believe you were engaged to be married. I am sorry.'

'But is he over the worst of it, now?' A strange hollowness was spreading through her chest, her body telling her what her mind refused to comprehend.

'Will you sit?' the doctor said, indicating the armchair.

'No.' If she obeyed him, if she sat, she would be admitting defeat. She hugged herself tightly, suddenly cold enough to be shivering. Her voice sounded small in her ears, like a child's. 'Can I go up and see him?'

She looked up at him, and quickly away, not able to bear the grave look on his face. His words seemed to come from far away, so distant as to be insignificant. But hearing them, the hollowness inside her swallowed her up.

'If his parents will allow it, then yes. It might help you come to terms.'

Chapter 23

It was finally the day of the grand bazaar. The fundraiser for the House of Help For Friendless Girls was being held in the grounds of Tylecote, the property of Mr Dixon, a wealthy silversmith and Master Cutler of the town. 'This will mark the end of your involvement with that house, Emma,' her father had commented.

As soon as word got around – and it got around quickly – about Hope's true identity and the arrival of her parents in town, the Master Cutler had sent a message and subsequently a carriage to the King's Head Hotel where the Hydes had taken a room. They were now honoured guests of Mr and Mrs Dixon until such time as their daughter was judged fit enough to travel. A story had been duly devised. The poor young lady had run away from home after suffering a mental incapacity – a temporary condition, not likely to be repeated. God forbid, she thought grimly, it should wreck her chances of an advantageous match. The young lady had then developed amnesia, and was not able to remember even her own name. Her parents had, fortuitously, been alerted by a family friend who lived in Yorkshire to the *Missing Person* poster produced by the police. They drove to Sheffield post haste and their arrival at the House of Help had been an enormous shock for Miss Hyde, but, happily, the sight of her parents had immediately restored her memory.

There had been no pregnancy. There was no child.

This morning, Hope had been summoned to breakfast at the Dixons' residence.

She murmured her thanks when one of the two maids who were clearing the detritus of breakfast reached over her shoulder to remove her plate. Earlier, she had risen to pour more tea from the pot that sat on the sideboard, earning a sharp look from her father. The maid had taken the pot from her hands and she'd returned to her seat, chastened.

She'd eaten hardly anything. That morning, dressing for the bazaar, she had put on the same simple high-necked blouse and dark blue skirt she had worn when she attended her first Sunday afternoon tea party at the House of Help. It was too tight, a straitjacket, the corset digging into her ribs.

How she wished she was breakfasting at the house instead of here with the Dixons, who were strangers to her. At the house she would be surrounded by women, conversation would be flowing, Miss Barlow surveying it all from her little table in the corner. Sipping tea and replacing her china cup in its saucer, she tried to imagine the scene. Miss Barlow would be contemplating Amelia's absence as she compiled the grocery list. One of the noisier women would be dominating conversation at the table, while a quiet pair might be whispering to one another. Clara would be sitting in the armchair by the range, hand-feeding the baby. The thought of this made her chest tighten and her yearning to return to the house become almost unbearable. There was no substitute for mother's milk. She would give her child her breast all day long if she could, for the short time she had him. She shifted in her seat, earning a muttered *Stop fidgeting* from her mother, who sat beside her like her jailor. Before leaving the house, she had folded squares of cotton under her corset to try to prevent any leaks from showing up on her blouse, and for extra insurance was wearing a plaid shawl around her shoulders that she could pull across her chest if necessary.

Now her whole body was tingling with the need to return to the baby. She had made a mistake in trying to imagine the cosy kitchen scene at the house. She must return to the present moment. Here she sat at a round mahogany table covered by a white cloth embroidered with sprigs of yellow flowers and banded by yellow ribbon. Instead of leaning on a ladder-back chair, her back rested against plump yellow cushioning on a delicately carved rosewood chair. A silver bowl stood in the middle of the table, crammed with yellow roses.

She wondered whether the lady of the house employed a different colour scheme for every season. Yellow for summer, obviously. Perhaps red for autumn, blue for winter and green for spring. No, that wasn't right. Winter ought to be green, so the centrepiece might be sprigs of holly and ivy. What then, for spring, if winter took green? Blue for the sky. The flower? She sighed. Forget-me-not.

She paid attention to Mrs Dixon, pretending interest in the two ladies' conversation about the weather. They had enjoyed a clement spring but, according to the forecast in today's newspaper, the summer months would begin with unseasonably strong gusts of wind and rain, due in overnight.

'If it rains sooner,' said Mrs Dixon, 'there are plenty of shelters for our visitors. We certainly don't want people tramping about inside the house.'

'Do stop slouching, Emma,' said her mother.

She obediently sat up straight.

Her father and Mr Dixon had been conversing about the silversmith business throughout breakfast. She supposed it was a safe topic. Most of the items on the breakfast table were Dixon-produced, from the sugar scuttle to the large silver tureen that had been delivered full of sausages, bacon and ham. Earlier, she had exclaimed over the clouded green glass of an oval bon-bon dish set on a silver tripod that sat on the mantelpiece. A fancy spoon Mrs Dixon described as a bon-bon helper rested against the edge of the bowl.

'If you return for supper, Emma, I shall have that bowl you admired filled with sweets,' said Mrs Dixon.

'That's very kind,' she said, 'but I ought to return to the house after I've finished helping at the bazaar. I will have been away for a very great part of the day by then.'

'I'm sure the warden and the inmates of that house can do without you, Emma,' said her father, in the new, impatient tone he had adopted with her. 'I imagine they managed perfectly adequately before you came along.'

'If Emma is required at the house,' said Mrs Dixon, smiling kindly at her, 'then we shouldn't monopolise her time.'

She folded her hands in her lap, aware of her father's watchful gaze. It heated her face more effectively than would a blazing fire in the hearth. He would assume she was blushing because the conversation was skirting around the great shame she had brought to her family, but her distress had more to do with the alteration in their relationship.

She was no longer his innocent child. He looked at her now with disappointment, and judgement. Those awful sentiments might be tattooed across his face, they were so plain to see. His own daughter was no better than the harlots dragged before him in the magistrates' court. To her father, she was a fallen woman and would always remain so. He would never believe the truth, would instead accuse her of speaking ill of the dead, of slandering a highly respected man who was no longer here to defend himself. Even if he could allow himself to believe her, he would think her cowardly, culpable in her own misfortune. Nothing she said, no appeal she could make would change the low regard in which he now held her.

Her breathing quickened and she was afraid she might break down in tears in front of them all. Miss Barlow had warned her that her emotions might see-saw in the days following the birth, but Hope had imagined she would be able to maintain control of herself. In truth, she was as helpless as the baby.

She bit back a shriek when she felt the light touch of her mother's hand on her arm. 'My darling, you look tired. Would you like to be excused?'

'I have an idea,' said Mr Dixon, rising from his chair and clapping his hands together heartily. 'Why don't we all go out and see our wonderful bazaar being brought to life? I imagine it's safe to do so.' He winked at Hope. 'Most of the heavy work should have been completed by now.'

In the vestibule of the house, the manservant and ladies' maid brought out their hats, coats and jackets. Hope declined the offer of a fitted jacket. 'My shawl will suffice,' she said. She needed to breathe fresh air. Even the small delay of finding and buttoning up a jacket would be unbearable.

The door was opened for them and they trooped outside. Nearby, the wrought iron gates to the house, fitted into the high stone wall that encircled the extensive grounds, stood open. She watched two workers, their boots crunching on the gravel drive, carry a desk and two stools to the pavement immediately outside the gates. It would be Hope's job to take tickets and check season passes alongside another volunteer from the House of Help between the hours of noon and one o'clock. After that, she would be serving tea and sandwiches in the refreshment tent. She'd also been given the task of making sure the various entertainers stuck to the time slots they had been allotted on the stage that had been constructed near the refreshment tent.

'I should like to see the stage,' she said.

'Right this way,' said Mr Dixon. He waved both arms at her parents, who were lagging behind. 'Roll up, roll up! You know,' he reflected, 'I think I missed my calling. I could be master of ceremonies in a circus. Or a lion tamer. What do you think?'

'I think,' said Mrs Dixon, 'that being Master Cutler provides quite enough excitement.'

'Perhaps you've passed the point where you could conceivably run away to the circus,' said Hope.

He laughed. 'Miss Hyde, is that a friendly way of telling me *I'm* too old to run away and have an adventure?'

Her mother smiled tightly, but her father turned on his heel and stalked off.

Mr Dixon looked abashed – 'Oh dear,' he muttered – and Mrs Dixon took her mother's arm. 'Shall we go and find the stage?' she said. 'Come along, Emma.'

Finishing touches were being made to the wooden structure. Three men wrestled with a canvas canopy, with a fourth supervising, his voice carrying on the light breeze. A woman Hope recognised as one of her fellow volunteer committee members stood before an easel, consulting a piece of paper she held and chalking the acts and the times they were due to appear onto the board. A broad-shouldered man bent over the steps to the stage, wielding a hammer, his back to them. When he straightened and turned, laying down the hammer and pushing his hands into his lower back, Hope realised who it was and smiled in delight.

He was dressed like a working man but there was no question this was Angus Deveraux, sleeves rolled up to his biceps, trousers and waistcoat covered in dust and woodchips. He bounded over, a wide grin on his face, took off his cloth cap, releasing a thatch of dark hair, and bowed to Hope. He showed her the palms of his hands, which were covered in scratches. The thumb on his left hand was swollen and discoloured. Hope drew in a breath.

'Yes, my carpentry skills leave a lot to be desired,' he said. 'All in a good cause though, eh? How are you, Miss Hope? I'm afraid I've had to play truant from your night classes latterly.' She wondered whether this had to do with the girl who had been on his arm the evening Hope went into labour. 'I'm sure you haven't noticed my absence.' He turned to the others. 'Our lovely Hope is a wonderful...'

She didn't get to hear what she was wonderful at. Her father, who had strolled over to investigate, interrupted.

'I'll thank you to address the young lady as Miss Emma Hyde,' he said.

Confusion flitted across Angus's face, then his brow cleared. 'Goodness me,' he said. 'I do apologise.' He turned to Hope. 'Your true identity has been discovered at last. How marvellous. And these are your parents, of course.' He turned to her father. 'I'm sorry, I wasn't made aware. Not,' he added hastily, 'that there's any reason I should have been notified.'

He looked helplessly at Hope.

Mrs Dixon cleared her throat. 'Come, Mr Dixon. We're needed elsewhere.'

'Are we? Oh, yes. Excuse us, please. Always a pleasure to see you, Angus.'

'The feeling's mutual, sir.'

Her father waited until the Dixons were out of earshot. 'How are you acquainted with our daughter?' he said. His voice was cold enough to raise goose-bumps on Hope's arms.

'I have an association with the House of Help,' said Angus. 'My grandfather is a trustee and I help where I can,' he glanced at Hope, clearly weighing up how much he should divulge. 'I met Miss Hyde soon after her arrival at the house. I took the young lady and her chaperone to an interview with a police officer, and it appears their investigations have borne fruit. Hope, you must be thrilled.'

'Miss Hyde,' said her father. His voice was tight with anger.

'Yes, of course. Again, my sincere apologies.' He turned to Hope. 'I'm very glad to see you reunited with your parents,' he smiled broadly, 'and your memory restored?'

Her father stepped forward, between her and Angus. 'Miss Hyde has been through a great deal of trauma. You seem to have a disregard for that.'

'I only meant...'

'Are you the father of her child?'

Angus's jaw dropped open. Hope put her hands to her face. 'Father!'

Her mother tugged on his sleeve. 'Rob, you cannot go around accusing every young man who has an association with our daughter. Mr...'

'Angus Deveraux,' he said, grimacing sympathetically at Hope.

'Mr Deveraux, I apologise. My husband is… we are both in a state of distress, as I'm sure you can imagine. We've suffered a tremendous shock.'

The fury on her father's face terrified Hope but there was anger in her voice when she stepped out of his shadow. 'Angus has been very kind to me. I consider him a friend.'

'After the mess you got yourself into! No man,' her father said, 'should have any kind of *association* with my daughter. The sooner we get out of this town the better.'

He stalked away. Her mother took her arm and smiled politely at Angus as if they were acquaintances meeting on a promenade through the park. 'Good day to you, Mr Deveraux.'

Angus nodded formally, his face set – 'Good day to you, madam.' – but when Hope turned back to glance over her shoulder as her mother steered her away, he grinned at her and sketched a salute.

Chapter 24

The third-class compartment reeked of tobacco smoke, stale sweat and hot metal. Crammed between a matron wearing more layers than an onion and a scrawny man with a nasty habit of lifting his chin to scratch at the stubbled skin of his throat, Amelia picked crumbs from the cake that had been forced upon her by the woman sitting opposite. So close were they that their knees were touching. This woman, who had been disappointed in her hope to engage Amelia in conversation in payment for the cake, held a sleeping child on her shoulder while another wriggled on the soot-stained floor, playing with the straps of Amelia's bag with his filthy paws.

The woman wagged her finger in Amelia's face. 'Waste not, want not.'

Amelia frowned, then realised she hadn't eaten any of the cake the woman had given her. She was merely slowly destroying it.

'Here,' she said to the boy at her feet, who, with a quick glance at his mother, took it from her. The woman made clucking sounds of disapproval and Amelia looked away, staring out of the window above the door to the compartment. The pale blue of the sky was intermittently obscured by billowing clouds of grey smoke as the train clattered on. There was nothing to see, nothing she wanted to see, except for Linus's smiling face.

She closed her eyes. The stuffiness of the compartment made her long for the salty, fishy smell of the estuary. She wanted to feel the freshness of the sea breeze on her face. She opened her eyes again, nauseous from the motion of the train. No, not the sea. She wanted to lie in a darkened bedroom, scented by a blazing fire, aware of the weight of Linus's body beside her. She wanted Hope to tell her what to do, because she had a decision to make when this overcrowded train reached its destination. There were two tracks to choose from, for her onward journey. She could take either, or neither. The rhythm of the train kept time with her listless mantra. Either-or-neither. Either-or-neither. Either-or-neither.

But really, what did any of it matter?

She had asked Linus what she should do, when his parents had allowed her into his room and had left her there, alone. His eyes were closed and his hair had been combed, although one unruly curl stuck up beside his ear, and a rush of love for him made her smile and forget the terrible truth, for a moment. He might have been sleeping peacefully. She waited until she heard the door snick closed behind her then sat on the little stool beside the head of the bed. Yes, sleeping so deeply that the covers remained undisturbed by the rise and fall of his chest. Sleeping, but when she dared to reach out and tuck in that stray lock of hair his skin was as cold as the grave.

She had laid her head on his unmoving chest. 'What will I do?' she had whispered. What had he said to her, the day before? *You'll be all right.* How was she to go on, with that as consolation?

As she rested her cheek on the cold block of his body, a thought slid into her mind, a worm of an idea that made her shudder in fear and set her heart pounding in excitement. There might be a way – there *was* a way – she could hear his voice again, perhaps even feel his touch? What was it Aunt Gertie had said about her mother? About her passing into a place between this realm and the next, where the living could more easily communicate with the dead?

As the train rattled on, a shiver rippled across Amelia's shoulders. She looked around the compartment, at the mother sitting opposite, the child dozing with his cheek pressed against her shoulder, at the elderly man placidly puffing on his pipe. He looked back at her, his eyes sharp in a network of wrinkles, and she blushed. Had he read her mind?

And what would Hetty have to say? She'd taken Amelia from that house when she learned what mad Aunt Gert was dabbling in, that she was getting Amelia involved in it too. *No good comes of that nonsense.*

Amelia shifted on the wooden bench. The rhythm of the train was changing, slowing. Either-or-neither. Either or neither. Either… or… neither. Either.

She had a decision to make.

Chapter 25

Hetty strolled between the tents and stalls. She had no use for a piece of artisan jewellery, wicker table or original watercolour painting of a local scene, but was at the bazaar to show her face for a reasonable amount of time, as requested by the trustees. She'd explained that she hadn't had time to buy an admission ticket – it went without saying that she didn't hold a season ticket – but Mr Wallace had turned up that morning, having purchased the two-shilling ticket for her. He insisted they travel together in his curricle and drove too quickly through the town and out to Ranmoor so as not to miss the opening ceremony by the Mayor of Sheffield. Alderman Clegg was expected to say many complimentary things about the House of Help.

'We'll have cleared our debt before you know it, Miss Barlow,' he called to her as they whisked along, turning to look at her for what felt like an inordinately long time. She'd nodded briskly, resisting the urge to tell him to watch the road, not her.

Her fear of imminent death on the route out of town had briefly eclipsed her fretting about Amelia and her anxiety over Hope's situation. Now, she had time to ponder and decided it was far better to be always rushed off her feet, dealing with one house crisis or another, than be granted the supposed luxury of having time on her hands. Amelia had run off. Hope had made a fool of her. Hetty was failing as an ersatz sister and warden. She would have to do some thinking, whether she liked it or not.

A makeshift stage had been built on some flat ground at the edge of a large pond. The stage was presently occupied by a group of fiddlers whose tunes had set a gaggle of geese honking. The musicians seemed to be enjoying the general hilarity this provoked as much as the audience. Hetty walked along the jetty, gazing down at the treacherously inviting lily pads that spread over the surface of the murky water, all pretence in their seeming solidity. She reached the end of the jetty, turned around and returned to solid ground. She found a chair near a bed of roses, deciding she would while away a few minutes listening to the music, now that the geese had waddled away.

She wanted nothing more than to return to the house but was trapped out here in the middle of nowhere. On arrival at the bazaar, Mr Wallace had suggested that, if the two of them became separated, they should meet by the iron gates at three o'clock. In no time at all, he had been monopolised by a group of ladies who descended like butterflies upon him, and Hetty had taken the opportunity to wander off.

She asked the time of the gentleman sitting on the chair beside hers. There was an hour to go until the appointed time. A whole hour.

'Good afternoon, Miss Barlow.'

Hetty looked behind her, and up. Mr Hyde towered above her, made even taller by his black topper.

She was surprised he had made himself known to her. As far as this gentleman was concerned, Hetty was of the servant class, and a woman to boot, so doubly inferior. It was true that a bazaar allowed the classes to mingle freely.

She had witnessed Mrs Shaw and her daughter serve tea and cake to their own maid, fussing over her, making it an amusing spectacle, tolerated with a polite smile by the maid who had that job to do the other three hundred and sixty-four days of the year. Hetty couldn't blame Mrs Shaw. For ladies of the higher classes, organising and running a bazaar offered a certain kind of freedom. They were permitted to step outside their sphere for the sake of a good cause, taking on roles that would never be viewed as employment, and therefore were not beneath their social standing. No, she was surprised to be attended on by Mr Hyde because the man disliked her. He could not comprehend that she had believed Hope's story of amnesia and had taken Hetty to one side to quiz her about the identity of the child's father.

'She has been under this roof all these months,' he'd said, '*your* roof, and you did not suspect she was lying to you all along, and she has not revealed the father's name to you. It's preposterous.'

Hetty had told him about the state his daughter had arrived in, how she had obviously been mistreated and what strength it must have taken for her to conceal whatever had happened to her, and he had given up his interrogation. There were certain things, she supposed, that a gentleman couldn't bring himself to think about.

Perhaps Amelia knew who the father was; she had been in on the lie. But Amelia wasn't here to ask.

'Are you enjoying the bazaar?' said Mr Hyde.

'I am,' she said. 'I'm thinking of getting my fortune told.' She pointed. 'The tent's just over there.'

'An exceptionally good idea. Perhaps a means of avoiding receiving any further nasty surprises?'

'How is Mrs Hyde?'

'Coping as best she can.'

Hetty forced a tight smile. 'And how are you coping, Mr Hyde?'

'I'm very well indeed, and looking forward to returning home with my two ladies as soon as we possibly can.'

'I'll miss her,' said Hetty, the words escaping, unbidden, from a deep well of hurt and sorrow she could no longer conceal from herself. She folded her lips against the lump that rose in her throat.

'Yes, I gather you allocated her a role in the house,' said Mr Hyde. 'A job.'

He spoke the word as if it was a stone he would like to drop to the bottom of a very deep well.

'She enjoys it,' said Hetty, 'and she's good with the residents of the house.'

He laughed, a short bark like the report of a gun. 'You transformed her into a common jailor.'

'I don't operate a jail, Mr Hyde.' She was on firmer ground now. Any danger of breaking down in front of this man had passed. 'The house is a haven for friendless girls, as your daughter gave every appearance of being, and destitute women. None of them are kept against their will.'

'But some of them *are* criminally-minded.' He flapped a hand, as if bored of the conversation. 'It is of no consequence. Your Mr Wallace has explained the intricacies of the endeavour. My wife and I have agreed to make a substantial donation, one that will solve your financial woes.'

And ensure our silence.

It occurred to Hetty that she might never speak to Hope again, at least not in any meaningful way. The girl's time was being managed. She had left the house early that morning, before Hetty rose, collected by the Master Cutler's driver and taken for breakfast with her parents at his residence. The child was being looked after by Clara until Hope returned in the evening, when no doubt she'd retire straight to Hetty's bed. She would want to spend as much time as possible with her son. He was being collected by his adoptive parents the day after tomorrow, and Hope would depart with her parents the same morning.

Tomorrow, Mrs Hyde would call early to collect her daughter and take her to a haberdashery, an establishment in town recommended by the wife of the Master Cutler, to find a suitable outfit in which she would return home. Mrs Hyde had been horrified to learn that her daughter was clothed in donated garments. *You should have seen what she was wearing when she turned up on the doorstep*, Hetty thought grimly.

Now, she nodded her thanks to Mr Hyde. 'The house is grateful to you.'

He smiled thinly and pointed in the direction of the refreshment tent. 'My daughter,' he said, 'has prevailed on me to invite you over for a cup of tea. Of course, if you're enjoying the entertainment,' – he looked towards the stage where the fiddlers were trooping off and members of a local amateur dramatics group preparing to go on – 'I would hate to drag you away.'

She thought about refusing – after all, that was what this man wanted her to do – but Hope appeared at the entrance to the tent and raised a hesitant hand in greeting. 'I'll come,' she said, waving back at Hope, who disappeared inside.

Mr Hyde lifted the canvas for Hetty to enter. It was warm inside the refreshment tent, the combined odour of cigar smoke, ladies' pomades and the raw wood of the boarded floor tickling her nostrils. Conversation buzzed in the air like a thousand bees. Mr Hyde excused himself and went in search of his wife, promising he would return in a few moments only.

Hope was holding a large kettle that she put down on a nearby table and turned to Hetty. They looked at one another, Hetty horribly aware of those *few moments* promised by Mr Hyde passing away. There was so much to say that there was no place to start. Wearing her hair in a neat chignon, a small bonnet perched on her head, and what must be some of her mother's jewellery around her neck, the girl before her looked as ladylike as her parents could wish. Hetty couldn't help feeling she was looking at a stranger.

'You've done a good job,' she said, finally, 'with the bazaar. There must be hundreds here.'

'We'll certainly raise enough money, and along with…'

'The kind donation from your parents.'

'Yes.'

In a sudden movement, Hope took both of Hetty's hands in hers, and the words tumbled out. 'I haven't properly apologised to you, or given you any kind of reasonable explanation, and you have been so kind to me, and I wish—'

Hetty looked away to hide the distress in her eyes, her blurred vision taking in the bonnets and hats of the ladies and gentlemen seated at the benches that filled the tent. There was Mrs Calver, the former matron, handsomely dressed in pale grey, a froth of blue feathers cascading from her wide-brimmed hat. She raised a hand in greeting and

Hetty returned the gesture, praying the woman wouldn't come over. She was relieved when Mrs Calver resumed her conversation with the woman she was sitting beside.

Words continued to tumble from Hope's mouth. '—I wish I had confided in you. And the thought of leaving, especially now, with my father so…'

Hetty interrupted her gently. 'Miss Hyde…'

'Oh, please don't call me that… I wish you would call me…' she stopped.

Hetty put on a quizzical expression. 'What? Hope? Emma? Isn't that too familiar, coming from the likes of me?'

'Let me…'

Her parents appeared at her shoulder. Mrs Hyde took her daughter's hand and peered into her face.

'How are you feeling, my darling? Are you tired?'

'Mother, I'm perfectly well.'

'I was just congratulating Miss Hyde,' said Hetty, 'on the wonderful work she has done to help make this event so successful. She's a credit to you both.'

Mr Hyde's mouth twisted but he didn't speak.

'There's a juggler outside the tent,' said Mrs Hyde, too brightly. 'Shall we go and take a look?'

–

Mr Wallace was already waiting at the gates for Hetty, although she had arrived ten minutes before the appointed time. He handed her a small package wrapped in newspaper. Hetty took it and looked at him enquiringly.

'It's for you,' said Mr Wallace. 'A gift. It's a delightful little thing that I couldn't resist purchasing. Open it, open it.'

'For me?' said Hetty, peeling back the wrapping. 'That's very kind of you.'

Mr Wallace rubbed his hands together nervously. 'My daughter had me buying up every piece I could carry from the arts and crafts stalls,' he said. 'I think it's because she made most of them. Of course, it's really for the house. I thought it was apt. You'll have heard Paradise Square referred to as pot square?'

'Aye, I have.' She smiled. 'I've never known why.'

'Well, there used to be an earthenware and pottery market on the cobbles, every Saturday. It's the reason there's a chinaware shop at number seventeen.'

Hetty examined the small, glazed vase in her hand. Five pale yellow spouts rose from a rounded base, each decorated with a delicate illustration of a climbing vine. It was flat on one side, designed to be placed against a wall.

'Your daughter is very talented.'

'Oh, this isn't her work,' said Mr Wallace. He coloured slightly. 'It's a quintel vase.'

'It's lovely,' said Hetty. 'Thank you, Mr Wallace. On behalf of the house.'

The return journey to Paradise Square was more leisurely than the outward trip had been. On the cobbles in front of the house, Mr Wallace thanked Hetty for accompanying him.

'I think it was a success,' he said.

'Without a doubt,' said Hetty. 'No, stay where you are. I can get myself down. Thank you again for the vase.'

'I haven't forgotten, you know, about our trip to the botanical gardens,' he said.

She looked at him, confused.

'You remember, Miss Barlow. An expedition, a fine day out for the ladies of the house. We must get it organised.'

'Will you be coming too?' She'd assumed he'd have better things to do.

'I wouldn't miss it.' He beamed at her and raised a hand in farewell.

Hetty waved him off and hurried inside. She had more pressing concerns on her mind than expeditions to goggle at exotic ferns. Nothing had been said about the replacement of her deputy once Hope – Emma Hyde – had gone. She hadn't told the trustees about the disappearance of the housekeeper. A scandal involving a resident turned employee might yet come to light, although Mr Hyde seemed to be succeeding in his aim of sweeping the whole affair under the carpet.

She had been in post for less than a year. If the trustees decided she wasn't running the house to the required standards she would not blame them.

She opened the door to her quarters and tiptoed over to the bassinet. It was empty. She left the room and walked through the house to the kitchen, passing two residents on their way out. Both were carrying baskets.

'Where are you off to, ladies?'

The older of the two women answered. 'All over the place. The grocers, the butchers, the chandlery. Cook gave us a list.'

Hetty nodded absently – 'Off you go then.' – and they went on their way.

In the kitchen, Clara was at the table, holding Hope's sleeping baby in her arms. Nan Turpin sat beside her, her fingers curled around a mug of tea. She was regaling both women with some tale and broke off when Hetty entered the room, straightening her back and offering a wide smile to the warden.

Hetty frowned. 'Have you finished the laundry already?'

Cook answered for the girl. 'She needed a rest.'

Nan pressed a hand against her forehead. 'I felt faint.' She took a deep breath and smiled bravely. It seemed she had a smile to suit every occasion. 'I'm much better now.'

'Nan here has been telling us she's related to Dick Turpin,' said Cook. She laughed. 'The highwayman, if you can believe it. Reckons he's her – wait a minute, let me get this right – great-great-great-great-grandfather.'

'How do you know this?' Hetty said. 'I thought you had no people.'

'Well, not *now* of course,' Nan said, and sighed. '*Now* I'm all alone, fending for myself.'

'Here,' said Cook, handing the girl a cheese scone from the freshly baked batch that had just come out of the oven. 'You need to put some flesh on those bones.'

Nan Turpin smiled warmly. 'You are a saint. Have you butter?'

Hetty's mouth dropped open when Cook gave the girl a maternal pat on the shoulder and scurried off to the pantry. She snapped it shut. 'We need to set about getting you some proper domestic training,' she said, 'and in the meantime you can continue to work here. There's no time to sit about reading books about highwaymen and making up stories, as entertaining as they are.'

The girl tilted her head contritely. 'Yes, Miss Barlow.'

Clara lifted the baby onto her shoulder and patted his back. 'I believe you, Nan,' she said.

Hetty turned to her. 'And I'm quite sure you haven't got time to sit about holding the baby.'

Clara pouted. 'Hope asked me to look after him.'

Hetty raised her eyebrows.

'To be fair, he's only just fell asleep,' said Cook, who had returned with the butter dish.

'Give him here,' said Hetty.

Clara relinquished the baby reluctantly and Hetty took him back to her quarters, where Hope's things were strewn around. Hetty would, she considered, remain in the dorm if it meant keeping hold of her deputy. She sat down heavily in the chair at her desk and took out a fresh sheet of writing paper, then leaned back and pinched the bridge of her nose. The tone of this letter must be conciliatory. She picked up her pen.

To my dear sister, Amelia.

Chapter 26

The following morning, Hope breakfasted in the kitchen of the House of Help, taking a seat beside a new arrival, a forlorn young woman who flinched when a mug of tea was set before her.

'Won't be serving on you like this every day, so don't get used to it,' said a woman sitting at the far end of the table, loudly enough to stop the general chatter and clatter of cutlery, but only for a moment.

Two of the younger women resumed the conversation they'd been having, heads together conspiratorially. An older woman got to her feet, complaining about the fine drizzle that was falling. 'I'll be soaked by the time I get to work.' Another woman nodded sagely. 'Aye, it's that rain that drenches you through.'

A pixie-faced young woman with thick blonde hair caught Hope's eye. 'I'd rather have the stuff that dries you.'

Hope smiled back absently, her attention focused on the girl beside her. When she gently introduced herself to the new arrival – 'I'm Hope. What's your name?' – she was aware of Miss Barlow lifting her head from the book she was leafing through at her little table in the corner of the room. Their eyes met.

' 'Ow do. I'm Maisie.'

Clara the maid made a noisy entrance, barging the door open with her hip, carrying a scuttle full of coal.

'You lot still here? It's gone eight, you know.'

'Has it?' Hope got to her feet hurriedly.

'Leapin' up to give me a hand with the chores, Hope? Whoops, sorry, I mean, Emma? Um, Miss Hyde?' Clara's cheeks flushed. 'Hark at me. What a daft question.' She apologised again. 'Sorry.'

The woman who had introduced herself as Maisie looked at Hope curiously.

'I'm still Hope here,' she said firmly. 'I would help, Clara, I'd be happy to, but I must go and change. My parents are collecting me later this morning.' She hesitated. 'I'm going home today.'

'Oh, aye.' Clara looked crestfallen. 'And what about...'

'Yes.' She steeled herself to speak the words in as ordinary a tone as possible. 'His parents are due to arrive at any moment.'

Miss Barlow closed her book with a snap. She scraped back her chair and left the room, muttering *excuse me* to Clara, who quickly moved out of her way and gave Hope a look that was far more eloquent than words.

She took the cue. 'I'll be back in a short while,' she said to Maisie. She stood and embraced Clara awkwardly, over the coal scuttle. The maid's eyes were wet when she stepped back.

'I'll come and visit,' said Hope, knowing that this was as unlikely as snow in summer.

Clara swiped her hand across her eyes. 'Just make sure you do.'

The corridor was empty. Hope trotted up the steps and down the hall to Miss Barlow's quarters. She found the warden leaning back in the chair at her desk, arms folded, staring out of the window. The baby slept peacefully in his bassinet. Hope averted her eyes from the bag at the foot of the bed, the bag that contained his clothes and the toys that had been gifted to him, including the cloth bunny and wooden teething ring that Clara, always on the go, had somehow found the time to make.

She massaged her temples. She was leaving behind people she had grown to love, who loved her back. More than that, she was leaving behind an entire identity. Would the shoes of Emma Clare Hyde still fit when she stepped back into them?

She scooped up the baby and sat on the edge of the bed, stroking his downy cheek, drinking him in as she had on the day he was born and every precious day since. She breathed in the sweet nutty smell of the crown of his head, examined his tiny fingernails, and wondered if she would always carry these memories, or if they would fade and disappear. And which would be worst? To remember him, knowing she would never see his face again, or for the fierce love she felt towards him to diminish. She could not imagine that happening. This child had her heart, her whole heart, and always would.

She couldn't trust herself to speak and, finally, Miss Barlow broke the silence. She spoke gently, almost in a whisper.

'Here they come.'

Both women stood, Hope's heart beginning to pound. She bent her head to kiss the baby and he stirred, turning his head towards her body, his mouth, a perfect tiny rosebud, puckering. Would he know her if they ever met again, from her scent, like an animal? Would he say, ah, so this is my mother. And would she know he was her son, recognise something primal? There was no point speculating. She was going far away. They would never meet again.

The door knocker sounded, and her heart beat correspondingly faster and harder.

'They're a lovely couple, by all accounts,' said Miss Barlow. 'He'll have a fine life.'

She nodded.

'I'll take him then.'

Hope allowed the warden to take her son from her arms. She sat back down on the edge of the bed, and a shudder rippled through her body. She turned away when Miss Barlow reached for his bag. She couldn't watch them leave the room, and studied instead the weave on the counterpane. She heard the door open and close, and voices in the hall, a man's and Miss Barlow's, and then a woman's exclamation of delight.

It was done. So quickly done.

Hope studied the panels of the closed door. Behind them, her child's new mother would be tucking him into the pram that had appeared in the porch a few days earlier and perched there like a malevolent black crow, waiting to take him away. She turned slightly, so that the view from the window would be completely obscured, afraid her eyes might betray her, might dart towards the light, and see the pram being lifted down onto the pavement and wheeled away. There was muted conversation on the doorstep. She couldn't hear what was being said.

Hope stood up and went to the door, pressing the palm of her hand and then her forehead against it. She knew she was doing the right thing, that there were no circumstances in which she might keep her son that weren't detrimental to them both. It didn't make his departure from her life any easier to bear.

–

When Miss Barlow returned, Hope was occupying herself by laying out on the bed her outfit for the journey home.

Her mother had chosen a white silk dress, for purity, she supposed. It came with a tall, fitted collar with a froth of white lace under the chin. The tight-fitting bodice that extended to her hips was, like the collar, boned. The long sleeves had mother-of-pearl buttons and, when fastened, were like a second skin. The skirt was as frothy as the collar, tiered and bustled, and designed to be pinned up on one side to show off an inch or two of petticoats. A short jacket, white with pale blue trim – *The perfect summer colour!* Her mother had exclaimed – completed the outfit. Her boots were of the finest kid. She heard Cook's voice in her head – *I could feed you all for a year with the money they cost.* Amelia would admire the boots and try them on for size. These thoughts brought a sad smile to her face.

She lifted the hat her mother had selected for her from its box and laid it next to the gloves. It was the new fashion, narrower and taller than the previous fashion, black, but adorned with a blue ribbon that matched the trim on the jacket.

Her baby had been gifted a cardigan with the cuffs and collar stitched in the same exact shade of blue. She hadn't told her mother that when she had selected the colour. It had felt like a small victory, at the time.

Miss Barlow came to stand beside her and looked over the outfit.

'Very smart,' she said.

'Hmm. I promised I would speak to Maisie before I changed.'

'Aye, she's a shy little lass.' Miss Barlow picked up the white gloves and examined the embroidery before replacing them on the bed. 'Come all the way from London for an apprenticeship but was left at the station. We'll get to the bottom of it.'

'She reminds me of Tilly,' said Hope. She went the door. 'I won't be long.'

'Wait.' Miss Barlow clasped her hands together. Her voice was uncharacteristically hoarse. 'I need to say summat to you, before you leave.'

Hope waited on the threshold of the room. 'What is it?'

She had never seen such an apprehensive expression on Miss Barlow's face before.

'Take this in the spirit it's intended, and we'll say no more about it.'

She nodded, wondering what was coming. 'Of course.'

'Even if your arms are empty, you will always be a mother.' Miss Barlow's eyes filled with tears. 'Even if nobody else ever knows it, you'll carry that knowledge in the deepest and most secret part of your heart. Don't dwell on how your motherhood came about. You are a mother and your son will have a fine life.'

Hope rushed across the room and embraced the warden, who patted her on the back.

'That's really all I wanted to say, love.'

–

Maisie was waiting for her in the kitchen, which was otherwise empty, although Hope could hear the scullery maid banging about in the next room. They talked about Maisie's arrival the night before. She had come to the town by train, having been promised a job at a milliner's and waited all day and most of the evening on the platform. She had shown a porter the letter confirming the position but it was late by then, and he'd delivered her to the House of Help. She didn't have a penny to her name. All her money had gone on the train fare.

Hope assured the girl that she was in a place where she would be treated kindly and somebody – not Hope, as she was leaving today, but probably the warden, Miss Barlow, or perhaps one of the agents for the house, who were all lovely ladies – well, the point was that somebody would take her to the address on the letter and the situation would be resolved. She would not be abandoned.

One of the residents appeared, yawning mightily. 'Mornin', Hope,' she said.

'I didn't see you at breakfast.'

'Night shift.' She used her forearm to swipe hair from her brow. 'I din't get in until five so I've had a kip. Cook said I could knock summat up if I tidied up after meself and didn't make a habit of it. I'll not be doing that, though, will I?'

'What do you mean?' said Hope.

'Din't Miss Barlow tell you? I've got lodgings sorted out. I'm off after breakfast.' She smiled at Maisie. 'Hope here'll look after you, love. Don't you worry yoursen.'

Hope didn't bother to correct her. She smiled and pushed back her chair. 'Well, I'll say goodbye then.'

Back in the warden's quarters, she took off her house dress and underclothes – quickly pulling on her newly purchased chemise shift and stockings in case Miss Barlow should return from wherever she had gone – and folded the borrowed clothes neatly on the seat of the armchair next to the bed. She laid her new clothes on top of these so she could strip the bed. She bundled up the sheets and pillowslips, tied a knot in the top, and left the bundle at the foot of the bed for Clara to collect later. Then she stood in the centre of the room for a moment, hugging her elbows. It took a moment for her to realise what was missing from the room, what it was that had nagged at her ever since she entered.

The bassinet had gone.

Tears sprang to her eyes and she pressed her fingertips to her lips to prevent the sob that was building in her chest from escaping. When she could be certain she would not lose control, she sat at the dressing table and picked up the hair brush. It was time to prepare for her departure. She had arrived at the House of Help with nothing and would be taking nothing with her except for the silver locket she wore against her skin, and the tiny curl of hair within. Home seemed like a distant dream, and one she was not sure she wanted to revisit. A terrible thing had happened to Emma Hyde there.

The best thing to do would be to focus on the job at hand. She brushed, plaited and pinned up her hair, then put on her new boots before tying and tightening her corset and stockings. Two petticoats went over her head. She tied the bustle cage around her waist, and then arranged over it another petticoat and, finally, the skirt. She pulled on her gloves before putting on the bodice and fastening the buttons from hips to the hook and eye at the throat, and up the sleeves.

Her locket was concealed under the bodice and the chemise beneath, snug against her skin. It would remain her secret.

According to the clock on the wall, forty minutes had elapsed by the time she finished dressing. It was almost ten o'clock, which was the time her parents were due to collect her. She wondered, again, where Miss Barlow had got to. She could not contemplate leaving without saying goodbye. She had already resolved to write to her when she returned home, to thank her for her kindness. She returned to sit at the dressing table and surveyed herself critically. On the surface, she was the perfect young lady again. The bits of lace around the rim of the high collar scratched at the underside of her chin. The house dress she'd been wearing had a simple collarless shirt, the top button of which she'd usually kept unfastened. This outfit was undeniably more flattering but it imprisoned her. She touched the high, boned collar with her gloved fingertips. It was a manacle around her throat.

Finally, she put on her hat, lifted her chin away from the irritating lace and looked sideways at herself in the mirror.

Emma Hyde stared back.

Chapter 27

'We imagined you would be ready to leave,' her father said dryly. 'I've allowed four days for the journey and simply cannot spare any more time than that touring around the English countryside, as pretty as it is.'

Her mother smiled. 'We're due at the Whittakers in Derby this evening, my darling. You remember them. We holidayed there when you turned ten years old. Mrs Whittaker had a special cake baked for you with your age piped on top. You must remember it.'

Standing before Hope, she held out her hand. 'Come.'

Hope didn't take her mother's hand but remained where she sat, on the edge of the parlour's chaise longue. She held herself very still.

Her mother ignored the rebuff and chattered on. 'We weren't able to visit any of our friends and acquaintances in our hurry to get here, my dear. That tavern we stayed at on the edge of Birmingham – I forget the name, but it was rather dubious, wasn't it, darling?'

'It was best to remain amongst strangers until we knew what we'd find here,' said her father. 'How could we explain ourselves while we were en route? It's going to be devilishly difficult hiding the truth from Whittaker and even from that dyspeptic old fool Ponsonby when we get to his place. Yesterday's breakfast was a disaster, and as for that fool of a boy – Deveraux, was it? – and his over-familiarity with our daughter. Well.' He shook his head.

'Hush, now,' said her mother. 'I'm looking forward to the stops we'll make on our way home, and showing off my beautiful daughter.'

With a view to marrying her off? Neither of her parents had spoken directly about the baby, although she supposed they knew that he had been collected that morning. It helped harden her resolve to believe that they were uncaring. But deep in her heart she knew there had been no scenario where she might have returned home with a child. She would be ostracised by society. Her father would be a laughing stock, her mother pitied. Their silence was their way of attempting to put behind them the shame of it. Their beloved daughter – their only child – had taken up with a man, had got herself pregnant and had run away.

They would not be interested in the truth about what had happened to Emma Hyde, the degradation and humiliation she had suffered, only in how they might limit the damage. There, that was better. Now her resolve was strengthened.

Her mother sat beside her. 'Emma will be dressed in ten minutes if I assist.' She turned to Hope. 'Why don't we redecorate your bedroom, darling? You can choose new furnishings that befit a young lady.' She stroked Hope's cheek. 'You've grown up so much. My little girl no longer exists.'

To hide the tremor in her hands, she clasped them together and rested them on the apron of the simple blue-checked dress she wore. She had hurriedly changed out of her travelling clothes, galvanised by the sound of the door knocker, picking frantically at the buttons and ribbons that held her outfit together while Clara showed her parents into the parlour. Her head was bare, her hair still plaited and pinned up, although a few tendrils had escaped.

She looked at her father, who was standing at the mantelpiece in his long duster, staring at the scuffed boots she wore. She took a deep breath and spoke before her nerve could desert her. 'I've reached a decision I hope you will honour. I won't be travelling with you today.'

Her mother murmured something. It sounded like *Oh darling, no*, and clutched at Hope's skirt as if she was afraid she might suddenly vaporise into thin air. Hope gathered all the courage she had and held her father's gaze. His lips were folded into a bloodless line and he was fixing Hope with the razor-sharp expression she imagined he used on those who came before him in the magistrates' court. When he spoke, it was in a slow and measured voice, a voice that was accustomed to being heeded.

'It is a daughter's duty to obey her father until such time as she has a husband to instruct her.' He laughed mirthlessly. 'Do you have yet another revelation for us? Are we to expect your husband to walk through this door at any moment?'

'No,' said Hope, deciding to take his question seriously. 'I am not married. I have one wish only, and that is to remain here, at the House of Help. I believe I... I *know* I have found my rightful place here, however strange that might sound. I feel I am wanted and...'

Her parents spoke at the same time.

'You *are* wanted, my darling, at home, where you belong!'

'Has that damnable woman poisoned you against us?'

Hope shook her head. 'Miss Barlow doesn't know anything about this. I made up my mind, I mean to say, I

297

decided I should seek your blessing to remain, only a few moments ago.'

'And what makes you think,' her father said, 'that these people want you here?'

Hope smiled, glad that her lips trembled only a little. 'Because this is where I belong.'

'Preposterous!' He took a couple of strides towards her and for a moment Hope was terrified that he was going to drag her to her feet and out of the house, and throw her into the carriage that waited outside. He had never laid a finger on her, but there would be nobody to prevent him from manhandling her now. He was her father.

Her mother stood, and, to Hope's astonishment, blocked his way. 'Stop it, Rob. Listen to me. Emma left us once before, or have you forgotten? I could not bear to live if she ran away again. My heart would not stand it. At least if she remains here, we will know her whereabouts. The trustees are good people.'

Our people, is what she meant.

Her father wrenched off his hat and flung it onto the carpet, an act so ridiculously childish that Hope had to quell an impulse to laugh. She knew if she started it would end in hysterical weeping. He paced to the window and glared outside.

'We are leaving now, young lady, and you are coming with us, even if it is in that rag you're wearing.'

Hope remained seated. Her mother sat beside her.

'Your father hasn't seen you,' she said, 'in your lovely new outfit.' She laughed nervously. 'Are we to take it home with us, and leave you behind?'

Hope unclasped her hands. They were hot and slick with perspiration. Her mother took her hand. Her touch was cool and soothing.

298

'You could donate the dress to the house,' said Hope.

Her father spluttered. 'They'd have no use for such fine clothes here!'

He mother laughed again, gently. 'Our daughter is being mischievous. I have a better idea. We'll hang it in your wardrobe and you can wear it when you return to us.'

Hope examined her mother's face. Was she genuinely supporting her daughter, or patronising her, humouring her as if she was a small child having a tantrum? 'I intend to stay here, with or without your blessing. I'm a grown woman.'

She ignored her father's snort of derision.

'Husband.'

'Yes?'

'You know where your daughter gets her headstrong nature from. Don't even try and deny it. Why don't we allow Emma to remain here for a period of time, say, a month, or even two?'

'To what purpose?'

Hope hardly dared believe the tide was turning in her favour. 'To help with the good, honest work of the house,' she said.

He looked at her curiously, as if he had never seen her before.

'Charitable work,' Hope added. 'Of course, I won't take a wage.'

'We'll send an allowance,' her mother said.

Her father stood facing her. Framed by the light from the window, his face was shadowed and she could not read his expression. Hope held her breath, afraid that any disturbance in the air would destroy the fragile truce her mother was brokering.

Finally, he spoke.

'You won't live here,' he said, 'amongst all these fallen women. I won't have that. You'll stay at the Master Cutler's residence. I'll speak with Mr Dixon. Arrangements shall be made for a short stay.'

Hope nodded. She would fight that battle once this one had been won. She put on a sober expression, although her spirits were soaring, and this feeling of release, of the shackles opening, told her she had made the right choice.

'One month,' he said. 'One month, although I wager you'll be sick of the place before then. The novelty will soon wear off.'

She opened her mouth to protest, then caught her mother's eye, and closed it again.

'You've put your poor mother through quite enough. I will have to extract your solemn promise that if we leave you here you will not disappear again.'

She nodded. 'I promise. Thank you.'

–

Her mother held her for a long time on the steps of the House of Help.

'Write to me,' she said. 'Tell me about your work here.'

'I will,' said Hope. 'And when the month is up...'

Her mother pulled away to take Hope's hands. 'Another month will follow, if that is your wish.' She smiled. 'Don't dismiss out of hand the opportunity to stay at Tylecote.'

'Mother, it's too far distant. I need to be here.'

'Then let me discuss it with your father. He needs some time.' She squeezed Hope's hands, then relinquished them and went to join him. He helped her into the carriage and followed her inside, closing the door behind him.

He had stalked from the house, had not bade her farewell and on the pavement had kept his face averted. She thought he would not acknowledge her as the carriage set off, but at the last moment he leaned forward from behind her mother, who had given in to tears, and briefly lifted a hand. She returned the gesture. It was the best she could hope for.

It was good enough.

Hope watched the carriage sway over the cobbles and onto the road, where the horses pulled it around the corner. She remained where she stood until a few moments after it was gone. In the square, small groups of gentlemen stood at the coffee and tobacco shack, conversing quietly. The butcher came out to retrieve his apprentice, who was leaning over the back of a bench, talking to the girl who sat on it. A warm breeze shook blossom from the branches of the cherry tree on the corner, carpeting the ground around its trunk. She had seen those boughs laden with snow, and would again.

She became aware of a presence by her side.

'I wondered where you'd got to, Miss Barlow.'

'I thought I'd give you some privacy.' She was holding her ledger. 'Maisie will be pleased, and Clara and all the others.'

'And you?'

'Aye.'

That was good enough too.

Miss Barlow turned to return inside. 'That report won't write itself.'

'I'll move back into the dorm tonight,' said Hope. 'Miss Barlow.' The other woman stopped and raised an enquiring eyebrow. 'I want to thank you, for your patience and for giving me a home, and a purpose.'

'Speaking of which,' said Miss Barlow, 'I could use your help with Nan Turpin.'

'The girl the constable brought in?'

'Aye. The pickpocket. She's telling tall stories and charming the birds from the trees. Thinks I'm daft as a brush. See what you can find out about her.'

'I'll do my best.'

She followed Miss Barlow inside, and closed the door behind her.

Chapter 28

A shaft of sunlight fell across the cover of the warden's book when Hetty removed it from the drawer and laid it on her desk. The plain, maroon-coloured cloth board and its green leather spine, on which *LEDGER* was imprinted in gold, held together hundreds of lightly ruled pages, a page for every girl and woman who had passed through the house.

Hetty opened the ledger to the most recent entry. Maisie Turnbull. Today, the girl was going to the address of the milliner's shop where she'd been promised a job and accommodation, but had failed to be collected as promised from the train station. Hope would accompany her. The girl's abandonment by her employer might be nothing more than a simple miscommunication. Hetty would know by the end of the day. She wasn't too concerned. There were three empty beds in the house, for a change, so plenty of room. No, this wasn't the cause of her uneasiness. Tomorrow, Mrs Calver would be paying the house a visit. A tour had been arranged by the trustees, who were inviting the former matron into the fold. Hetty would be expected to chat about her past life running a hospital. Her mouth twisted in a wry smile. She could talk until the cows came home about scrubbing floors and dodging the attentions of her lecherous landlord.

She gathered her thoughts and turned the pages of her ledger back to a morning in November. There was an entry she must update. The task felt urgent, as if setting the words down in ink might guarantee some sort of permanence, a spell being cast by the nib of her pen. She was probably as mad as old Aunt Gertie, thinking like this. Nobody could be bound by potions or prayers.

Here it was, the page she was looking for. Hope's page.

Hetty reread the entry she'd made on the morning of Hope's arrival, after the battered and bruised girl had eaten her first breakfast in the house and gone to bed to await the doctor. The words were carefully inscribed in black ink alongside the printed text.

Next to *Name, Address and Occupation of nearest relatives or friends* the warden had simply written *Unknown*.

Under *Further particulars* she had described finding the girl on the doorstep of the house in a state of distress, with complete memory loss. *The doctor is attending her today. We have given her a name for convenience, suggested by Mrs Gunson, and will call her Hope until such a time as her memory returns or she is collected by her people.*

Now she finished Hope's page, blotted it and closed the book, laying her hand upon it. The ledger now contained the girl's real name, but with a caveat. *Miss Hyde wishes to continue to be known as Hope while she undertakes her duties as honorary deputy warden, such duties to continue indefinitely.*

Hetty leaned back in her chair, her hand still curled on the ledger, and watched dust motes dance in the air. She might never discover the exact nature of the catastrophe that had landed Hope on the doorstep of the house that wintry night but the truth always rose to the surface, one way or the other. The thing that bruised Hetty's heart was Amelia's absence. The child believed she was motherless.

Might she have confided in Hetty if she had known the truth? Would a confession bond them together or would Hetty drive away her daughter forever? She recalled with a shudder the moment Gertie had screamed aloud the reality Hetty had run from nigh on twenty years ago, a reality Amelia should learn only from her mother. It was time to tell the truth.

She had her weekly report to write but restlessness drove her to the window. Amongst the people going about their business, the uniform of the train station porter caught her eye. He'd emerged from the foot of the square and was walking up towards the house, carrying a small valise and accompanied by a shawled woman who leaned on his arm. Despite the clemency of the day, she wore the shawl pulled forward so that her face could not be seen.

There was always somebody in need of a safe place in which to lay their head, and the door to the House of Help was always open. There should be no shame in seeking this haven out.

The porter caught sight of her in the window and raised a hand in salute. Hetty pulled down the cuffs of her blouse, adjusted her collar, and went to let the woman in. She would put her in Maisie's dorm, if, of course, the girl returned from the milliner's shop. Sometimes, it helped to place newcomers together. It gave strangers in a strange place something in common, creating a bond that was often the first step towards moving on with their lives.

Hetty was mulling this over when she opened the front door. The porter smiled and stepped back. 'Found our lass curled up on a bench like a cat. I reckoned I'd see her home.' The woman lifted her shawl. She wore an expression Hetty recognised – one of defiance mixed with uncertainty. And something else, a bottomless sadness in her brown eyes.

'I was that close to going back to her,' she said, 'but somehow I've wound up here instead.'

Hetty took her daughter in her arms and whispered in her ear the name she had given her.

'Amelia. Oh, Amelia. Welcome home.'

Author's Note

The House of Help for Friendless Girls was set up in 1885 at number 1 Paradise Square in Sheffield. Among the women who sought refuge at the house were those who had 'fallen from virtue', orphaned girls, new arrivals in town who had nowhere to stay, and women without a family to support them who (pre-NHS) were compelled to pawn their meagre belongings to pay for hospital treatment.

In those days, the workhouse was often the only recourse for the very poor, providing food and shelter and cheap labour. The House of Help, established by enlightened women and said to be the first of its kind in the British Isles, offered an opportunity for its residents to improve their lot. From the day it opened, the house was oversubscribed and larger premises were eventually found elsewhere in town.

All the characters in this novel are fictional – from the warden and trustees to the girls and women who were resident – although there are one or two nods to actual historical figures, such as the Master Cutler Mr Dixon.

But the House of Help was real. It remained open for over a century (with a name change or two along the way), adapting to changing times but always helping women.

Acknowledgements

A second series of Sheffield Sagas – beginning here with *The House of Hope* – could not have happened without the wonderful support of my agent, Kate Nash, and editor, Emily Bedford. I'm so grateful to both, and to Emma Clark Lam, Asha Hick, Sarah Daniels, Carly Reagon, Jess Cooke, and special mention to Ange for deciphering Victorian calligraphy and tramping around cemeteries with me. And last but absolutely not least, thank you to everybody who reads and enjoys my stories. It means the world.